Maudlin was suddenly filled with battle fury, with blood passion, with confidence. No-one could be vanquished, wearing a bandana like the one he had around his head. It protected its wearer from harm, imparting strength and vigour. It warded off blows from clubs and parried sword thrusts. It was better than wearing a suit of armour.

'Come on!' yelled Maudlin, jumping up into the rigging and waving his pole at the pirates, the tails of his red bandana flapping in the breeze. 'Think you can kill me? Not a chance.'

'Get down from there,' said a more rational and sober Bryony. 'You'll get hit by a bullet if you're not careful, Maudlin.'

'Just let 'em try, eh, Scruff? Eh? Just let 'em try.'

GARRY KILWORTH

HEASTWARD HO!

A WELKIN WEASELS ADVENTURE

CORGI

HEASTWARD HO!
A CORGI BOOK 0552 547069

Published in Great Britain by Corgi Books,
an imprint of Random House Children's Books

This edition published 2003

1 3 5 7 9 10 8 6 4 2

Set in 11/12pt Palatino by
Falcon Oast Graphic Art Ltd.

Corgi Books are published by Random House Children's Books,
61–63 Uxbridge Road, London W5 5SA,
a division of The Random House Group Ltd,
in Australia by Random House Australia (Pty) Ltd,
20 Alfred Street, Milsons Point, Sydney, NSW 2061, Australia,
in New Zealand by Random House New Zealand Ltd,
18 Poland Road, Glenfield, Auckland 10, New Zealand,
and in South Africa by Random House (Pty) Ltd,
Endulini, 5A Jubilee Road, Parktown 2193, South Africa

THE RANDOM HOUSE GROUP Limited Reg. No. 954009
www.kidsatrandomhouse.co.uk

A CIP catalogue record for this book is available from the British
Library.

Printed and bound in Great Britain by
Cox & Wyman Ltd, Reading, Berkshire.

HEASTWARD HO!

FROM THE DIARY OF CULVER THE WEASEL,
JACKSERVANT TO THE STOAT LORD HANNOVER
HAUKIN

*What a time we have had in Muggidrear City over the
last few months. We have been overrun by vampire
voles from the continent, who have been sucking the
life-blood from the population. Yet there is always one
mammal, in this case a noble weasel, who rises above
the masses and is able to thwart evil. The Right
Honourable Montegu Sylver, close friend of my
master, Lord Hannover Haukin, was that weasel.
Sylver and his friends – the vet Bryony Bludd, the
rather awful Scruff and his constant companion
Maudlin – were all instrumental in destroying the
nest of vampires, along with their creator, the terrible
Count Flistagga.*

*All is peaceful now, except for the wailing of Mayor
Poynt's sister Sybil, whose valuable collection of Mole
Dynasty vases was smashed to pieces by the above
crew of do-gooders. Unfortunately for them, at the
same time as having to deal with the vampire voles,
Montegu Sylver's cousin Spindrick was attempting to
gas all the high-born families of the city and send them
to sleep for a long, long time. Monty (if I may be so
bold) thwarted this plot too, but at the cost of those
awful vases. Priceless they may have been, but also
lacking in taste. The world is a much more refined
place without them – in my humble opinion.*

Now, what does the future hold for my brothers-in-forelegs, Montegu Sylver and his friends? Why, I have heard of a letter, on its way from the Great Pangolin, Emperor of Far Kathay. I understand from a distant cousin weasel, who is jackservant to an ambassador in those regions, that the Great Pangolin has need of Monty's services. If this is so I foresee great adventures ahead for Bryony Bludd, Scruff and Maudlin, for they go where the great detective goes. I am not envious of their opportunities to travel to exotic lands, for I am a poet, a sometime prose writer, who prefers the comfort of his small room. Their adventures are my adventures, second-hand, which I pen with great pleasure in my notebooks. I am told I have a neat paw and that my writings are the envy of literati everywhere. Being of sound mind, I am inclined to believe them.

CHAPTER ONE

Monty Sylver, private detective, was buttering a large piece of toast for his veterinary friend Bryony Bludd, when Jis McFail knocked on the door. The door was ajar and the landjill's whiskered nose was already poking round it. Monty gestured for the stoat to come inside.

'Enter, enter,' he called from the kitchenette. 'Come in, Jis McFail. You know that if the door's open, you don't need to stand on ceremony.'

'But it's the mayor,' said Jis McFail, her voice quavering with awe. 'It's Mr Poynt, Mayor of all Muggidrear.'

'What's the mayor?' asked Bryony, poring over a book on the anatomy of a toad. She looked up. 'Where is he?'

'He's on the doorstep,' replied Jis McFail, her voice still quivering with excitement. 'Standin' there, as fat and white-furred as you like.'

The mayor had actually come up the stairs behind the landjill and was catching his breath. 'Fat?' he wheezed. 'Where do you get fat from? I'm well built. I have big bones. It's the white pelt, it makes me look bigger . . .' Then he suddenly realized he was trying to justify his size to a common landjill. 'Anyway, what business is it of yours?'

Jis McFail's reverence for high office evaporated immediately. 'Don't you come it the big stoat in my house,' she snapped. 'That's my landin' your paws are on. I've entertained better stoats than you in this house, I can tell you. Why, there's Jis Bludd and Jal Sylver themselves, very respected mustelids, and they're not toffee-nosed. You just keep a civil tongue between your fangs, or you'll be out on the street quicker than a cockroach can find a crack in the wall, I can tell you.'

With that she left the mayor standing there, sucking in air, glaring at her. She stamped down the stairs, muttering under her breath.

The mayor went to the doorway and looked in, satisfying himself that these weasels lived in a hovel. See how the wallpaper was peeling! Look how badly the kitchen range was blacked! The tiles around the fireplace were cracked and worn! And the forelimbchairs were tatty and scuffed around the edges! How satisfying. How comforting. This nasty little flat was nothing like the huge grand manor in which the mayor himself lived, with its flock wallpaper and Ratgency striped upholstery. There was no comparison.

It made the mayor feel important to see how others lived: he had his big house with its big garden, both tended lovingly by his sister Sybil.

'Seen enough, Mayor?' asked Bryony. 'Do come in.'

Jeremy Poynt stepped over the threshold. 'I, er, thank you. Yes. Bludd, isn't it?'

'That's right, Mayor. Bludd by name and blood by profession.'

The mayor winced. He was squeamish. Even a mention of the red stuff and he felt a little giddy.

Monty gave the toast to Bryony on a small tea plate, then turned to Jeremy, wiping the butter from his paws on a towel. 'What can I do for you, Mayor Poynt? Piece of hot buttered toast?'

'Tempting, but no thanks. It's what *I* can do for *you*,' puffed the mayor. 'A letter!' He held up an envelope which had been sealed with green wax. 'A letter from the Great Pangolin, emperor of Far Kathay. It came in the diplomatic bag to the queen. I happened to be at the palace at the time and offered to rush it over here. It's addressed to you – the, er, Right Honourable Montegu Sylver.'

Bryony looked up, hot butter dribbling down her whiskers. Despite herself, she was impressed. No wonder the mayor had brought this missive in person. The Great Pangolin! Emperor of Far

Kathay! The Orient had always fascinated Bryony. Land of silk and porcelain. The place from whence rhubarb, which had excellent medicinal qualities, had come. Region of big-sleeved mustelid robes, junks and sampans, pointy eaves, long, drooping whiskers and plaited tails. A huge, mysterious country.

'A letter for me?' said Monty, stretching out his paw. 'How nice. I was wondering how old Pango was getting along.'

The mayor gaped. 'Old Pang—? Come off it, Sylver.'

'Yes,' said Bryony, on the mayor's side for once, 'come off it, Monty.'

Monty clicked his teeth. 'Oh, all right. I was going to kid you both that I knew him at university, but, you know, he's never been out of Kathay. I understand the only westerner he's ever met is Marko Poko, a polecat from the continent. It will be interesting to read what he has to say.'

Monty broke the seal and took out the letter, which was perfumed with a kind of musk. The page was long and yellow, embossed with dragons on the back. Monty unfolded it and then paced up and down as he read it, his lips moving with the words.

'Well?' cried the mayor, unable to contain his impatience. 'What's it say?'

Monty looked up. 'What does it say? Why, Mayor Poynt, this is a *private* letter.'

The mayor clasped his forelegs together in

disappointment. 'Aw, please, Sylver. The Great Pangolin. After all . . .'

Monty sighed. 'Well, if you must know, he wishes me to visit him in the Forbidden Palace in Far Kathay. He has some detecting work for me to do. Someone has stolen the precious jade shoes of the Green Idol of Ommm, a god fashioned in the image of a winged tree-shrew. His own mammals, pangolins among others of course, have been unable to discover the whereabouts of the precious paw-wear or the thieves.'

'Ommm's shoes?' cried Bryony. 'Why, I understand they're priceless.'

The mayor, who had never heard of Ommm, and couldn't care less about him, was deeply impressed despite himself. Fancy Sylver being asked to visit by the greatest despot in the world! Poynt might have envied the weasel detective if he had enjoyed travelling, but he hated foreign food, foreign beds, foreign languages, foreign coins and really all things foreign. The one thing he was grateful to Montegu Sylver for was smashing all his sister Sybil's priceless Mole Dynasty porcelain vases. They were huge, offensive things with lots of nasty dragons and squiggly characters on them. Sylver and his crew had shattered the lot after a masked ball at the mayor's place.

Still, here was a weasel who didn't find all foreign things offensive, and was going to travel to the Orient to meet an emperor whose word was law, who meted out justice to millions, whose vast lands stretched from pole to pole, and back again.

Envy, no. Admiration, hardly. Awe, a little.

'Well then,' he said. 'I expect you'll be wanting to pack.'

'If I go,' said Monty.

'*If* you go?' cried the mayor. 'Why, you *have* to go. After all, the request came in the diplomatic bag. The queen is involved. She might only be six years of age, but she's got a tongue on her like an asp. I myself, as the courier, am involved now. You *have* to go.'

'I'll think about it.'

'Well don't take too long,' growled the mayor, 'and when you're ready to go, let me know. I want to send the Great Pangolin a present.' And he stamped off down the stairs.

'You do have to go, you know,' Bryony said, once they were sure the mayor had finally gone, 'don't you?'

'I expect so,' replied Monty. 'But it needs some thought. I'm not going to say yes automatically, just because the mayor and the queen are over-awed by an oriental emperor.'

'Of course not.'

Later, Monty went round to see his aristocratic friend, Lord Hannover Haukin. The Sylvers and the Haukins, despite the fact they were weasels and stoats, had been very close for centuries. The original Lord Haukin had established the friendship with the weasel outlaw Sylver, back in medieval times. Hannover believed fervently in the aristocracy. Recently he had seen it whittled away for various reasons, not the least of which had been Prince Poynt renouncing his royal title so that he could stand for mayor of North Muggidrear, the animals' half of the city on the east side of the river Bronn.

Hannover Haukin lived in a very posh crescent on the other side of Gusted Manor, well away from either the Poppyvile or Docklands districts. On knocking, Monty found that his lordship was actually at his club, the Jumping Jacks. This was Monty's gentlemammals' club too, though he used it infrequently. He thanked Culver, the weasel butler, for the information, noting that the servant had blue ink all over his paws.

At Jumping Jacks Monty found that his friend was enjoying a lightly boiled sparrow's egg.

'Oh, what-ho, thingummy,' cried Hannover, who thought that pretending not to remember names was a very aristocratic thing to do. 'How are you, old weasel?'

'Fine, thank you, Hannover.'

'These soldiers,' the lord sighed, holding up a bread strip soaked in yolk. It parted in the middle and dropped with a gentle splat onto the plate. 'They don't make 'em as strong as they used to.'

'You should ask the kitchen to toast them first.'

Hannover shifted a monocle from his left to his right eye, to get the cord out of his plate. 'Why, what a good idea. What's to do then? Who told you I was here?'

'Your butler, Culver.'

Hannover's face darkened. 'Blasted butlers,' he muttered. 'D'ye know what he's doing now? Writing a blasted family history.'

'Well, I expect he wants to find some important weasel in it.'

'Eh? No, no, not *his* – mine. He's grilling me about everything. Wants the names of all my aunts and uncles, so he can interview 'em. Blasted nuisance. Digging up all sorts of peculiar characters. Did you know there was a Haukin who walked – half of it backwards – all the way from the unnamed marshes in the north to the Cape of Codliver. Y'know – that pointy bit at the bottom of Welkin? What d'you think he did that for?'

'I'm sure I don't know. Charity?'

Hannover blinked. 'No, no, I mean the backwards bit. Quite a sensible thing to do the walk itself. Bracing. Good for the legs and lungs. No, he did half backwards because he said that otherwise his front legs would wear out before his hind ones. Can you credit that? Potty as a gazunder. Don't like having potty ancestors. Can't retain one's dignity with daft antecedents. Anyway, can I get you a coffee?'

Monty accepted and then proceeded to explain why he was there. Hannover was the owner of a very comprehensive library. Monty said he would like to borrow, or at least study, some of the magnificent maps and charts on its shelves.

Hannover looked puzzled. 'What d'ye want all those dusty old things for?'

'I don't want all of them – just those showing the routes to Far Kathay.' Monty then went on to explain that he was setting out on a journey to that distant oriental land, in order to assist the Great Pangolin. Hannover switched his monocle from one eye to the other again, then shook his head and pursed his lips below his magnificent noble whiskers.

'Dangerous voyage, hazardous journey. You sure you want to do that? All that way? It must be – oh, furlongs, miles, leagues. There'll be bandits to cope with, and wild humans. Lots of humans don't like animals, y'know. According to Culver, one of my ancestors, a Lady Hannover, was a bit of an adventurer. She died of desert flea bites somewhere in Outer Mongrelia. Water can be a problem too, in those central deserts. Stinking hot during the day, freezing cold at nights. D'ye really want to walk all that way?'

'To quote a friend,' replied Monty, 'walking is healthful. Good for the legs and good for the lungs.'

'Walking, yes, but this sounds like a mad trek.'

Chapter Two

Much to anger of Thos. Tempus Fugit the mayor had organized a great steam rally, which would of course enhance the reputation of Tommy's rival Wm. Jott, the inventor of the steam engine.

'It's because Billy's a stoat and I'm a weasel, isn't it?' Tommy accused the stoat mayor. 'It's nepotism.'

The mayor had never heard of the word 'nepotism' so he quietly consulted his chief of police, Zacharias Falshed, before replying.

'It isn't nepo-whatsit, because we're not related. That's when you give your family jobs. Favouritism and all that. No, no, it's nothing to do with weasels and stoats this time. You have to admit, Jal Fugit, steam engines are much more

18

impressive than clockwork motors. All your invention does is tick and whirr and sometimes chime prettily. Well, that's no good for a day out, is it? You can't compete with great huffings and puffings, hissings and hammerings, coal being shovelled into red-hot furnaces, white plumes of hot steam billowing, and huge chugging iron monsters tearing up the turf of the local cricket pitch. No, no, I'm sorry, this rally in Hide Park is for steam engines only. Traction engines mostly, but a few other bits and pieces.'

Tommy stormed out of Jeremy Poynt's office, leaving the ermine-coated mayor alone with his chief of police.

'Blasted cheek,' sniffed the mayor. 'Thinks he can come in here and cause a fuss. Moan, moan, moan. I should have him arrested and thrown in Oldgate Prison for moaning. There is a law against moaning, isn't there? If there isn't, there jolly well should be. I'll see it gets on the statute books before next Wednesday, you see if I don't.'

'Well, Mayor,' replied the chief uncomfortably, 'he hasn't actually done anything wrong. I mean, this is the hour in your day when you say your door is open to the public, to hear their grievances.'

'Yes, but you'd think some of them would take the time to *thank* me for some of the improvements to the city, wouldn't you? What about when I restored Ringing Roger?' The mayor was alluding to the great clocktower which had been blown up by the anarchist Spindrick Sylver,

Monty's cousin. 'Did anyone come and say, "Oh, well done, Mayor, now we all know the time of day and don't need to buy pocket watches"? Did anyone come and offer their congratulations for a job well done – apart from you, of course (and you don't count because you're just sucking up)? I think that visiting antipodean – what was his name? That fat stoat from down under?'

'Ned Belly?'

'That's the one. I think he got it right. He called us a load of swingeing Pams.'

The chief coughed into his paw. 'A load of *whingeing* Pams, actually.'

'Close enough, Chief. Close enough.'

At that moment the mayor's sister, Princess Sybil, entered the office. The female side of the family had refused to renounce their royal status, so in effect she was senior to the mayor in rank, though she only ever exercised this authority at parties and when she wanted to hang some new curtains in his study. She was rather fond of her brother – perhaps the only mammal in the whole country who was – and they often worked in concert.

'Jeremy, I am exhausted,' she said, flinging herself into a forelimbchair. 'I've done so much work for charity lately . . .'

'I'll say you have, Princess,' Falshed commented. 'Why, only last week you went round the weasel orphanages giving out oranges.'

Sybil ignored the chief. 'I've decided to take a

20

holiday. I've always wanted to take a boat trip down the Nail, to see the prismids. I've booked my passage to Eggyok on the SS *Oleander*. It leaves next Tuesday.'

The mayor looked thoroughly put out. 'Oh, Sib. Who's going to tuck me up in bed with a glass of hot rabbit's blood?'

'Him,' she said, nodding at Falshed.

'Me?' cried the chief. Fond as he was of the mayor's royal sister he wasn't going to put up with this. 'Not on my duty roster.'

'No, no. In fact, the chief is going your way, Sib. He can accompany you as far as Eggyok and then go on by himself.' Poynt turned on Falshed. 'You look after my sister, Falshed. Make sure she doesn't come to any harm in those foreign climes. And don't drink the Nail water, Sib. I've heard it's full of all sorts of things – liver fluke, yellow fever, the lot. You take care of yourself. You're my only sister. I don't want to lose you just yet.'

'I don't intend to drink river water, thank you very much, Jeremy. I shall be having pink honey dews at sunset on the deck of a paddle steamer.'

The mayor's eyes went swimmy. 'Pink with rabbit's blood? I'm almost tempted to come with you. But my tummy wouldn't like that foreign food. So it'll have to be Falshed who looks after you. Then he can go on, along the Silk Road, to Far Kathay.'

'What would I want to do that for?' cried the chief.

'You have to follow that blasted weasel

detective, Sylver. He's been asked to solve a mystery there. I want *you* to solve it first, so that the mayor's office gets all the credit. Savvy? I want the Great Pangolin sending me huge pressies in the post and telling everyone what a good mammal I am for helping Far Kathay in its hour of need.'

'I don't need looking after,' protested Sybil.

'And I don't want to go,' cried Falshed.

'For once you'll both do as you're told,' growled Jeremy Poynt. 'I want my sister safe and I want to be recognized as the saviour of Muggidrear. Have you any idea what good trade relations with Far Kathay could do to improve the wealth of Welkin? Crockery and rhubarb, tea and crumpets – well, not crumpets, obviously, but certainly tea. We could be flying on a cloud of money if we got into the emperor's good books.'

'But—' began Falshed.

'No buts,' interrupted the mayor. 'Now, let's get along to Hide Park and see the chuff-chuffs.'

'I'd rather not, if you don't mind, Jeremy,' answered Sybil. 'I find these steam rallies of yours so noisy and disorganized. I think I'll go and get a book on Eggyok out of the library.'

'Noisy, yes,' grumbled the mayor, putting on his thick coat and top hat, 'but not *disorganized*.'

Jeremy Poynt shivered when they reached the street. It was a chilly, windy day in March and he felt the cold at the best of times, his forebears having opted to keep the ermine coat the whole year round. All other stoats, the chief included,

22

were brown when there was no snow on the ground, but became white-furred during the freezing mid-winter. Jeremy Poynt laboured under the delusion that the weather was always cold, be it summer or winter.

'Shall we take a pawsome cab?' asked Falshed, getting ready to hail a carriage drawn by two yellow-necked mice.

'No,' came the surprising reply. 'We'll walk for once. Do us good. And I can click my teeth and wave at the populace while we do so. Might get a few more votes if mammals see me walking like an ordinary citizen.'

One or two steam- or clockwork-driven vehicles – sedan chairs with wheels and mouse-less carriages – went by them. Most citizens tipped their hats to the mayor and the chief of police, both of whom were feared throughout the city. One or two jills with kittens allowed Mayor Poynt to chuck their darling furry babies under the chin. A weasel chimney sweep insisted on shaking paws with him – he had to wash his paw in a drinking fountain afterwards. Some scruffy weasel urchins with scraggy tails then tagged onto the pair of them and chanted some not very nice slogans. Whenever the mayor or the chief turned to chase them away, they ran like the wind yelling, 'Ercha!' over their shoulders.

'Where are the parents of those wretches?' snarled the mayor. 'I blame *them*. They ought to be in jail.'

'Most of 'em are,' replied the chief. 'That's why

23

these urchins run wild through the streets. We make no provision for the kittens after a court case—'

'Yes, yes,' snapped the mayor, 'blame it on the city.'

When the pair reached Hide Park the rally was in full steam. Great chugging monsters painted red and green, with tall brass funnels and shining brass nameplates, moved this way and that. There was the *Whistleminster Wonder*, a giant traction engine that produced the Whistleminster chimes when letting off steam. There was a tall steam engine called *Lofty Steel* that walked on stilts. Another was as large as a house and was at this moment ploughing up the flowerbeds while its owner fought with a brass wheel to get it under control. A steamroller had already flattened the bandstand – luckily after it had been vacated by the musicians. Some of them were at that moment peeling paper-thin trombones and trumpets off the roller while the owner of the machine offered his apologies.

'Heavy metal,' murmured the mayor, rubbing his paws together. 'You've got to love it.'

'Magic, colour, verve, noise. We have it all,' sighed the chief, as enamoured with the scene as his boss. 'Splendid show.'

The pair of them walked between the metal monsters. The mayor was there to judge competitions: the Most Menacing, the Best Invention, Machine of the Show, and finally and most importantly, to give a prize to the winner of the

Great Battle. This involved two traction engines moving to opposite sides of the park. They would then hurtle forwards – hurtle in a sort of lumbering, steam-driven way – and smash into each other with as much force as they could muster. The two antagonists would continue to do this until one of them no longer functioned or fell apart.

One of the combatants today – a huge traction engine with steel-reinforced bumpers, wicked pointed studs on its wheels and a thick metal rhino horn in the front – was owned by the mayor himself.

The mayor did not drive the metal giant of course. The drivers in this trial were always weasels – the mayor made sure of that. Jeremy Poynt did not want some stoat businessmammal standing up at the annual Freestoatians dinner and complaining that his son was lying in hospital with three broken legs and a set of singed whiskers because of the mayor's favourite hobby. Better to let the lower classes provide the entertainment, leaving the stoat owners to accept the awards afterwards.

'Which one is yours, Mayor?' asked Falshed.

'The one with the yellow funnel,' replied the mayor proudly, feeling quite sure he was going to award the prize to himself today. 'Isn't she a dilly?'

'She's certainly got a few weapons.'

'Yes, I designed them myself.'

At last it was time for the Great Battle. The two

traction engines went to opposite sides of the park. The spectators drew apart to leave a wide lane where the battle would take place. The mayor and the chief had a grandstand view halfway along, just where the two machines would meet with a crunch. Around each of the fighting traction engines were teams of young weasels. As was the custom, these had been taken off the street: each had an oil can in his or her paw to lubricate the wheels of the machines as they trundled towards one another. Thus the urchins had to be fast on their paws, rush in quickly, give the wheel bearings a squirt, then whip out before they got squashed under the roller. When it was all over they would be given sixpence each.

The mayor stepped out into the lane with a pawkerchief. After a dramatic pause he let it drop. 'GO!' he yelled.

The two monstrous machines thundered towards one another, with two flinty-eyed weasel drivers behind the controls. The second one had a red funnel, but its paint was peeling and it was covered in mud, dirty oil and grease. Its brass fittings were dull and unpolished, not burnished and gleaming like those on the mayor's machine. The driver looked no cleaner than his engine. He was moth-eaten and flea-ridden in appearance, though his teeth looked nice and white beneath his bent whiskers and there was a look of strong determination on his face that the mayor did not like.

It was under his disreputable-looking vehicle that an eager young weasel fell. His oil can went flying and was squashed beneath one of the huge iron wheels. It seemed likely that the youngster would suffer the same fate. The crowd gasped in horror, but at the last minute the driver managed to brake and allow the shaken little weasel to scramble out from under. The spectators cheered.

'Oh, get on with it!' cried the mayor impatiently. 'And that weasel urchin is not getting his sixpence.'

The crowd booed.

'In fact he's lucky I don't dock him for that oil can. Oil cans are expensive . . .'

The crowd booed again and the mayor suddenly remembered these were voters.

'But I won't, of course – poor fellow couldn't help it, after all.'

Red funnel got started again, and rumbled forwards. Yellow funnel had gathered quite a momentum in the meantime. With a great deal of hissing and clanging the two steel titans lumbered towards each other – fifty metres, twenty metres, ten, five . . . they smashed ringingly together to a cheer from the oil-thirsty mob. Bits of metal flew up, red-hot coals whizzed through the air like comets, steam whooshed from joints and apertures, from tubes and pipes. Whistles blew with shrill high notes.

'Go on!' yelled the mayor in a harsh, excited voice. 'Smash that red devil! Break it to bits!

Crush it to little pieces! Leave nothing but nuts and bolts . . .'

The machines backed off each other, surged forwards, crashed nose to nose. Five times they performed the same manoeuvre. Then, on the fifth collision, red funnel was pushed sideways. The mayor thought this was the end of it, but the driver was canny. Instead of trying to straighten his machine he simply drove forwards into the flank of his enemy. Having locked into the underbelly of the other machine he pushed and pushed, until yellow funnel toppled over onto its side.

Yellow funnel's weasel driver was thrown clear and landed at the mayor's feet. From the machine itself, in its death throes, came a shrill, whistling hiss. Boiling water spurted angrily from its damaged boiler. Coals sprayed onto the grass and burned holes in the lawn. Bits fell off: pistons, fenders, plates. The great monster groaned.

An incensed Jeremy Poynt resisted the urge to kick the faithful servant lying at his feet and yelled at him, 'Get back in the driver's seat, you flaming idiot! Get her back onto her wheels. Smash that red devil!'

The middle-aged weasel got up and dusted himself, then turned to the mayor and replied in a dignified tone, 'I'm not an idiot. I would be if I did what you're ordering me to do. However, I have a suggestion for *you* now . . .' And the weasel told the mayor what he could do with the remains of his traction engine, especially the piston rod – then he quietly put on his cap and walked off with his head held high. Weasels patted him on the back.

Red funnel's driver jumped down from his cab to cheers from the crowd. He held up a paw modestly to acknowledge his victory. Chief Falshed handed the mayor a large silver cup with the words FOR VALOUR inscribed on it. The mayor thrust it at the weasel driver as if it were a loathsome thing. The weasel took it, kissed it, and held it aloft to more accolades from the spectators.

'Show-off!' muttered the mayor. 'Who owns that machine, anyway?'

'I do, squire,' said the weasel.

'And who might you be?'

'Scruff's the name. Don't forget it. I'll be back again at next year's tournament.'

'I know you,' said the mayor, his eyes narrowing. 'You're that lamplighter who now works for Sylver.'

'That's me,' clicked Scruff. He turned and looked at the sorry remains of the mayor's property. 'Better get that cleared up, squire, or the park keepers will be after you. No litter, the sign says.' And with that he strolled to his huffing, puffing waiting machine, whistling a weasel tune through his two front fangs and waving to well-wishers. He climbed up into his cab and trundled off towards the park gates, leaving the mayor seething.

CHAPTER THREE

They were all gathered in Lord Haukin's library:
Scruff, Maudlin, Bryony, Monty and Hannover.
His lordship had collected together some large
yellowy maps and was spreading them over
the billiard table, which was the main feature
of the library. Lord Haukin hardly ever read a
book but he felt the room should be used, so he
had had a second billiard table installed. Culver,
his butler, who read anything, from breakfast
cereal packets to literary masterpieces, thought
this was crass and ignoble.

'So,' said Hannover, clicking his teeth, 'the
mayor was left standing amid the ruins of his
great machine? I would like to have been there,
by cracky, so I would. To see Jeremy beaten by a

lowly weasel. That must have made his blood boil.'

Scruff, who never minded being called a 'lowly weasel' by Lord Hannover Haukin, because he knew the stoat lord didn't mean anything by it, clicked his teeth along with the others. 'Oh, he was mad all right. You should've seen him. Burnin' up, he was. I heard he burst into tears once I was out of sight. Chief Falshed had to put a forelimb around his shoulder and lead him home, blubbing like a kitten. Serve 'im right. He would've had me run over that young weasel rather than stop the tournament for a moment. That mayor's an evil—'

'Yes, we understand, Scruff,' interrupted Bryony, who knew Scruff was going to come out with a rude word.

Maudlin cried, 'Why didn't you let me come, Scruff? I could've been your firemammal. I would have enjoyed that.'

'Not enough time. I only bought the machine that mornin', Maud. You was off somewhere, doin' somethin'. Couldn't get hold of you.'

Monty, intent on studying the maps before him, looked up. 'Are these charts all you've got, Hannover? I have to say, they're not very good, I'm afraid. A bit crude.'

'A bit crude?' cried Lord Haukin, sounding a little put out. 'These were drawn by my aunt Gertrude, when she crossed the Bogi.'

'The Bogi desert?' enquired Maudlin.

'Bogi *means* desert, in Outer Mongrelian,'

31

Scruff explained quietly. 'Saying the Bogi desert would be like saying the *desert desert*.'

Monty said, 'I think your aunt did very well, but they are very sketchy, you must admit. Do you have any more maps, Hannover?'

'Lots of 'em,' replied the lord, still looking somewhat put out, 'but they're all very much like this one. I'm sorry my library is so inadequate.'

Monty tried to placate the wounded stoat. 'Oh, I'm sorry, Hannover. I should be grateful for these. I am, really. I'm just a little disappointed. I'm sure in the absence of anything else these will do.'

At that moment Culver swept into the room with some rolled parchments under his fore-limbs. He tossed these onto the billiard table. 'Perhaps, sir, you will find these more to your liking?'

Monty unrolled one of the parchments and found himself looking at what appeared to be a very precisely drawn map of one of the very regions he would have to cross.

'Good heavens,' he said, impressed. 'How very efficient of you, Culver. Where did you get these from? Waterstoat's Bookshop? Ottercurs?'

'They were drawn by my late great-aunt Siddons,' replied Culver. 'She was Lady Gertrude Haukin's maid when she crossed the Bogi. While Lady Haukin was drawing charts, my great-aunt was doing likewise. She got an A for technical drawing at school, did Siddons. You will notice how beautifully blue the wiggly rivers are, and how accurately she has drawn the contours to high and low ground. See those brown swathes? They are what is scientifically known as *wadis*, or dry river beds . . .'

'Why, these are wonderful, Culver,' said Monty. 'Thank you so much – and thank you to your late great-aunt. She had a rare talent.'

'All we Culvers try our best – though it's not always appreciated,' murmured Culver. He then turned towards a rather huffy Lord Haukin. 'Oh, by the way, sir, on the family tree front, I've found another distant cousin of yours. A one Edward Bellicose, who was deported to the antipodes for highway robbery and there became an infamous bandit. I think his criminal name was Ned Belly. As I understand it, he wore armour made of old saucepans and dustbin lids to protect himself from the bullets of the law.'

'Lose him, Culver,' murmured the proud Lord Haukin.

'I'm sorry, sir?'

'Lose him. We do not want him in the family tree. This Edward Bellicose. Quietly blot him out. A large ink stain will suffice. You understand?'

'Perfectly, sir,' said the smooth Culver, before gliding from the library.

Lord Haukin put his monocle to his right eye and turned to his guests. 'That information will not leave this room.'

Monty nodded gravely. 'Of course not, Hannover. We are discretion itself. No-one will repeat what has been said here today.'

33

'Oh I say, though,' cried Maudlin, excited. '*Ned Belly!* He gave the police a run for their money, didn't he? Stole several jumbucks at the point of a blunderbuss, so I understand. Camped by a billabong with his swagmammal friend and the pair of them hid up a coolibah tree when the law came. Clever devil, that Ned Belly, I'll say . . .'

Lord Haukin was glaring at him, so Maudlin quickly changed the subject. He looked down at the maps brought by Culver. 'Oh, yes, those maps are more like it. Better than that other rubbish . . .'

Scruff quietly took his forelimb and led him from the room.

'Well,' said Hannover, now that the air had been cleared a little, 'so, you've got your maps.'

'Hannover, I'm sure your aunt did her best,' said Bryony, 'but you know, she was the leader of an expedition. She couldn't be expected to do *everything*. The details should always be left to lesser mortals, like maids and bearers and cooks. They're good at those things, because they have the time to concentrate their minds on the nitty-gritty. Your aunt was a great explorer.'

'True, true,' muttered the mollified lord. 'There are those who are born to lead, and those who are born to follow. As you say, the head of the expedition has to rely on the experts he or she has chosen to accompany him or her. My aunt successfully crossed the Bogi without losing anything but her spectacles, which now lie under some dune somewhere.'

'There,' said Bryony. 'What a successful jill she was. I expect she drew the rough maps for her own use, simply in order to give lectures to the Royal Geographical Society.'

'I'm sure you're right.' Lord Haukin was at peace with himself once more. 'You know Gertrude reached Starlingrad seven days before the human explorers, Burton and Tailor? Of course, she did not receive the proper recognition for that. These humans are so good at public relations. They came straight back here, to Muggidrear, and claimed victory. But we Haukins know that we crossed the Bogi first, and that's all that counts.'

'Thank goodness humans only live in small pockets of the world now,' said Bryony. 'I understand that the ones in Far Kathay are concentrated in the north, beyond the mountains?'

'That is my understanding too,' replied Monty. 'So, what shall we do now? How about going to Jumping Jacks, Hannover? Bryony is now a member there, since they *finally* allowed jills to join . . .'

'And what a struggle that was for Emedine Prankfirst,' muttered Bryony, still incensed by male bastions. 'You know she had to throw herself under a mousedrawn carriage to get any attention?'

'And I understand you chained your tail to the railings outside the club?' Hannover said. 'In that freezing winter we had last year.'

'It was worth it.'

'What about Scruff and Maudlin?' asked the lord. 'Shall we take 'em in as guests? We're allowed one non-member each.'

'Good idea,' replied Monty, 'and Bryony can pick some washerjill, or fishjill, off the street for her guest.'

Lord Haukin stared at Monty for a long time before saying, 'Ah, got me there, whatshisname. A joke, wasn't it? Well, come on, let's go. Toasted tea cakes all round. A sparrow's egg or two. And coffee.'

Half an hour later they all fetched up in the Whiskers Bar of Jumping Jacks, where the mayor was holding forth on the uppitiness of weasels. He was explaining to some corpulent stoat businessmammals how a weasel driver of a filthy traction engine had cheated in order to beat his wonderful shiny yellow-funnelled machine. When he saw Monty walk through the doorway accompanied by Scruff, however, he stopped in mid-sentence, then made an excuse to go to the toilet. He didn't come out for a very long time. When he did, he bumped into Bryony.

'What? What's this?' thundered Jeremy Poynt. 'A *jill*?'

'Oh, *Mayor*,' she said sweetly. 'You must have heard – the committee have voted me in. I'm the first female member of Jumping Jacks. There'll be more of us eventually, so you'd better get used to it.'

'Preposterous! Why wasn't I told?'

One of the staff said, 'Did you not read the minutes, Mayor? They were sent out to all members. You had the chance to vote.'

'I can't read every bit of paper that lands on my desk,' protested Mayor Poynt, feeling as if the whole world were conspiring against him. 'Have you seen my desk in the morning? Piled this high with bits of white paper. Most of it goes in the waste bin, I can tell you.'

'That doesn't surprise me,' said Monty.

The mayor rounded on him. 'Have you signed that guest in?' he thundered, pointing at Scruff.

'No.'

A triumphant expression came to the mayor's face. 'Then I'll have him thrown out on his ear.'

' 'Fraid you won't,' retorted Lord Haukin from the other side of the room, where he was chatting with Maudlin. 'I signed him in. Maudlin here was signed in by Montegu.'

'Oh.' The deflated mayor glared at everyone in turn. 'So you think you have got the better of Jeremy Poynt. Well, let me tell you, I can be a formidable opponent. I'm tired of being pushed around by you, Sylver, and your cronies. I don't include you in this, Hannover. You all know my ancestors were once princes – kings of all Welkin. King Redfur, my great-great-great-great-great-uncle, at one time put to death a thousand weasels, just for being what they were. Times have changed, but the hearts of the Poynts remain hard. I'll get you lot one day. Just you wait.'

With that the mayor walked from the room.

'Once a proud monarch,' sighed Lord Haukin; 'now a poor creature with nothing left but his pride.'

CHAPTER FOUR

Spindrick Sylver had a serious flaw in his nature: he was unable to physically harm other creatures. This family fault did not interfere with the work of his cousin, Montegu Sylver, since the famous detective was intent on doing good in any case. Spindrick, however, was not. He wanted to do bad. Yet he was prevented by this character flaw from carrying out his life's work of destroying present society. An anarchist, a true revolutionist, has to be able to shoot other mammals without compunction, blow up cities, destroy towns, wipe out whole villages. This kind of violence was just not in Spindrick's nature: he had this horrible angelic blemish on his soul. If only he had been born a true murderer, a creature with no conscience, he would have been able to get rid of this detested society. He would have been able to destroy the corrupt world of Mayor Poynt and build a new one from the smoke and dust.

He sighed in his sleep, crying, 'I want to be an assassin.' Yet this ugly *good* in his nature was in his way.

One bright and sunny morning he came out of a sleep and sat up quickly. The answer had come to him on the swift wings of a dream. *Why not get others to do it for him?* It was as if he had received a sudden visitation from the angel of death. Of course! Put weapons into the paws of the populace and let them wipe each other out. He would become an arms dealer. Once they all had guns they would be bound to start blasting away at each other. A little argument here, a small quarrel there – usually of little significance – and so the thing would develop. If guns were ready to paw and claw, why, flaring tempers would do the rest. It was the most simple thing.

'There will be civil war,' he told himself cheerfully, 'and chaos will follow. A red tide will sweep over the land. Then, when the last few small pockets of survivors emerge, there will be a chance to build a better world, a brave new world with brave mammals in it.'

He had a feeling someone had said this last sentence before, but things like plagiarism never bothered Spindrick.

He leapt of bed and rushed down to the paper

shop to pick up a magazine called *Guns, Guns and More Guns*. Then he strolled back to his lodgings for breakfast, finding himself first at the table. After a quiet boiled egg and a piece of toast, he studied his magazine, unfortunately finding very little to interest him between the pages.

'Catching up on our reading, are we?'

Lob Kritchit, the boring bank clerk who spoke in plurals, had entered the room. The big badger picked up his table napkin, sat down and carefully spread it across his lap. He was dressed in a dark suit with a high-collared white shirt and spats. Spindrick resisted the urge to poke him in the eye with the toasting fork.

'No, I'm trying to burn a hole through paper with my retina.'

'Ha, very funny.'

Next through the door was the retired stoat colonel. 'What ho, Spindrick. I say, *Guns*. One of my favourite magazines. Any good articles in there? Any chance of a borrow, once you've finished it?'

Spindrick lowered the magazine. 'Actually, there is an interesting piece here, Colonel. Apparently someone has invented bullets that carry their own charge in the base. You don't need a ram rod or anything. You just stick the bullet in the breech and squeeze the trigger. Very fast. You can load and fire a round every few seconds. Unfortunately, that's not fast enough for me.'

The colonel whistled. 'Sounds like some mean bullet.'

Lob Kritchit said, 'That'll mean the end of war, y'know.'

'Why?' asked the colonel.

'Well, with the ultimate weapon, no one will dare to go to war against anyone else, in case it's used on them too. If we have them and they have them, we'll both be too scared to attack. Imagine facing that kind of fire power! Well, it doesn't bear thinking about.'

'What doesn't?' asked the actress, coming into the room. Though her clothes indicated she was a female, no one was quite sure what kind of mammal she was under all her greasepaint. The three males half-stood, murmured their greetings, then sat down again. 'Is anyone going to answer me?' she continued, sitting down and helping herself to some toast. 'I did ask a question.'

The colonel said, 'We were talking about guns, m'dear. Not a suitable subject for a – a sensitive female mammal.'

'Sensitive?' snorted Lob Kritchit, whose approaches she had always rebuffed. 'She's as hard as granite, that one.'

'Only when the role requires it,' she sniffed. 'At the moment I'm playing a nun. Now, what doesn't bear thinking about? Is anyone going to tell me, or do I have to thcream and thcream until I'm thick?'

'Oh, please don't do that,' cried the colonel, 'not over the breakfast table.'

'She's joking,' replied Spindrick. 'It's a line

42

from her last role in a *Just William* play. *Violent Elizabeth Lisps Again*, wasn't it?'

'How clever you are, Spindrick. Did you come to see it?'

He nodded his head in the semblance of a bow. 'I had that honour.'

'Oh, you!' She waved a paw. 'Well, I see I'm not going to get much sense out of you lot this morning. I might as well be talking to brick walls. Oh, here are the sisters of mercy.'

Two retired schoolteachers entered the room – stoats or weasels: they were so shrivelled in old age it was difficult to tell which. Spindrick liked them – there was no malice in them and they always had a good word for everyone; they seemed to like him especially. It is difficult not to like someone who likes you so much. He clicked his teeth at them and bade them welcome to the repast.

'Oh,' cried one, 'we've got that magazine, haven't we, sister?'

'Yes, we have, sister. There's a good article in there, Jal Spindrick, about bullets that carry their own gunpowder.'

'You amaze me,' cried Spindrick, delighted. 'How did you get hold of a copy of *Guns*?'

'Oh, we subscribe to it, don't we, sister? You have to keep up with things, otherwise mammals think you're stupid,' said the shorter of the two. 'Mammals start to think just because you're old and wizened, you're dotty. A pair of spinsters like us are often seen as empty-headed.'

'We also subscribe to *Engineer's Journal*, *Bulldozer Monthly*, *Yatchsmammal*, the *Lumberjack*, *Surgeon's Quarterly*, *Hunting, Shooting 'n' Fence-cutting*, *Gallows-maker Weekly*, *Cobbler and Cordwainer*, and of course we're getting, in six supplementary weekly sections, *How to Construct a Cantilever Bridge*.'

'We don't approve of everything we read, of course. But we like to know what we're talking about.'

Spindrick's respect for the elderly sisters grew immensely on learning this side to them.

'Well,' said the bank badger, 'we know why the sisters are reading *Guns*, but what about you, Spindrick? Planning a bank robbery, are we? Going to stick us up, are we?'

'There's nothing in your bank that would interest me, Jal Kritchit.'

'Not *money*?'

Spindrick snorted. 'You don't have money in your bank. You have a lot of stocks and bonds, foreign exchange certificates, that sort of thing, but as soon as someone deposits any gold, you invest it elsewhere. The whole system of banking in this country is corrupt. Ninety per cent of what us ordinary mammals deposit in your bank is reinvested elsewhere. If there was a run on the bank tomorrow, you'd only be able to satisfy ten per cent of your customers. Deny it if you can.'

'We – we – we don't deny it,' spluttered the badger. 'But it's for the good of us all.'

'Yes, but those financial institutions you

reinvest with, they reinvest themselves, and so on, and so on, until the original money becomes a myth. Well, all that's going to stop after the revolution. Come the revolution we'll all be equal again, no-one on top, no-one on the bottom. Just ordinary mammals all, trying to help each other live in the best way we can.'

'Not that again,' groaned Lob Kritchit. 'When's this revolution going to come? Answer me that.'

Spindrick riffled through the magazine. 'Just as soon as I get my paws on a revolutionary weapon, that's when.'

'*You dirty human,*' drawled the actress, quoting from a play, '*you killed my brother.*'

'Wasn't that Jimmy Cogwheel,' cried one of the sisters, 'in that play with Humpty Boghard?'

'How clever of you to recognize it.'

'We also get *Theatregoer*,' simpered the other sister.

The colonel humphed. 'Can't understand you sometimes, Spindrick. What d'ye want with a revolutionary weapon? No good against cavalry, y'know. Mammals moving too fast, dodgin' the bullets. I once had a troop who could go out into a shower and not get wet. Fast as whippets. Ran between the raindrops.'

At that moment the salesmammal came into the dining room, looking as dapper as he always did. He had with him his suitcase full of underwear that he travelled in. He caught the colonel's last few words and clicked his teeth in amusement. 'What a load of tosh you do talk, Colonel.

Now, the only way to protect yourself is to buy some of my bullet-proof underwear. Vests and longjohns made of spider's-web thread. Toughest material known to mammal.' He took an egg from the bowl and cracked its shell. 'Stop a cannonball, they would. How about it, Spindrick? The undershorts come in all colours – purple, green, puce, magenta, you name it. Nice to wear too, silky against the fur. I can see you in purple.'

'I'd look wonderful in mauve bullet-proof drawers, I'm sure,' muttered Spindrick.

'Oooo, we are rude,' said the badger disapprovingly. 'I might remind you there are jills present.'

'Oh, we don't mind,' chorused the sisters. 'We know how crude travelling salesmammals can be. We're reading a book about it at the moment. It's called *Confessions of a Knicker Nicker* . . .'

Spindrick decided to take the train to East Cheep. Some of his revolutionary pals met in a coffee house there of a lunch time. The Teotwawki Club, they called it ('The End of the World As We Know It – but if anyone asks, it's a rare bird from down-under New Sealand, all right?'). He didn't have much time for most of them – they were nerds and geeks who enjoyed studying the business just for the sake of it. Forelimbchair revolutionaries for the most part, who collected and read anarchist literature by the wad-load. Spindrick, like his cousin Monty, was no great reader and if others could do it for him, he was quite willing to pick their brains with chat. He might be able to find out about the latest weapon on the market.

On the train, however, he overheard a conversation coming from the next carriage. Unfortunately the stream train was chuffing rather loudly and kept rattling over noisy points. But he managed to catch certain hopeful-sounding words and phrases.

'Steam-driven pistol . . . a thousand a minute . . . blasting gun . . .' came the muffled words. '. . . revolutions . . . invented by Wm. Jott . . . gone to New World.'

Spindrick was stunned by what he was hearing. His heart lifted and sang with joy. Birds in the air outside seemed to take on brighter colours. The sky turned a royal blue. The sun danced on the clouds. A new steam-driven gun that would fire a thousand bullets a minute!

'Gentlemammals,' he said, poking his head round the doorway to see two rather portly stoats in suits and bowler hats sitting opposite one another, 'did I hear right? Bill Jott's done it again? Where's he gone? The New World? Revolutions by the score out there, eh? Big market. That's the place to sell 'em, eh?'

The startled stoats nodded, their heavy pocket-watch chains bouncing on their bellies as they did so – business stoats by the look of them. Just the sort of creature Spindrick wanted to get rid of. He scowled at them, then left them to their

47

Financial Chimes, getting off at the next stop. He went into the toilets to wash the steam engine's smut from his whiskers before proceeding out of the station and catching a taxi to town. He didn't approve of taxis but there was no time to waste on waiting for more trains.

Spindrick went straight to the bank. Happily he didn't deposit his money with Lob Kritchit's firm, so there was no embarrassment there. He withdrew some money and then went to the shipping office. There he purchased a ticket for a transcobaltian crossing to the New World. With his fat wallet – the proceeds of genuine hard work digging the roads and working in factories alongside comrades who also said 'Come the revolution' twenty times a day – he intended to find the inventor of the steam-machine pistol and purchase the patent. Then it would just be a matter of setting up a factory here in Welkin, and producing firearms by the hundreds. He would release them onto the streets, along with a good quantity of ammunition, before retiring to the country to await the inevitable collapse of Muggidrear society.

How simple it all sounded! How simple it was!

CHAPTER FIVE

Bryony was packing. She was not a neat packer
by any means. Her busy life as a vet, which
included frequent unpaid visits to pauper
families at the workhouses, meant that her
natural instincts had to be suppressed. Had
her life been normal – had she been Princess
Sybil, for example – her packing would have
been ten times better. But then, of course,
Princess Sybil probably didn't fold her own
clothes anyway. Princesses had servants to do
that for them. It seemed that if you were wealthy
enough to have the time to do things, you were
wealthy enough not to have to do them yourself.
How cockeyed was the world!

When she looked up from the battered brown

suitcase on her bed, she found herself staring at an old picture. It was of a rambling old dwelling on the edge of a sprawling wood. Underneath the picture were the words THISTLE HALL. This building had once been the home of Lord Haukin's ancestor, the Thane of County Elleswhere. The wood behind the house, Bryony knew, was Halfmoon Wood, where her own ancestors had once lived and died, alongside those of Monty's.

She plucked the picture from the wall and crammed it into her suitcase along with the clothes. The journey they were all about to undertake was extremely dangerous, hazardous in all respects. It was likely that only some or indeed none of them would return. If she was going to die she wanted to have about her things that were familiar, objects that made her blood sing old songs. This painting of Thistle Hall was one such keepsake. There were others – an ancient weathered log, a stone the size of her paw, half an eggshell – which also contained some racial memories in them.

At the last minute she realized how foolish she was being and took all the keepsakes out again. 'More clothes,' she muttered. 'It will be cold.' She filled the holes with socks and scarves. Then she put the suitcase on the floor and knelt on the lid to close it, clicking the locks in place.

She left her attic flat and took the stairs down to Monty's rooms on the floor below.

'Are you ready?'

Monty was sitting in a forelimbchair staring into space and sucking on his chibouque, a long-stemmed pipe which had not seen tobacco for at least fifty years.

'What? Oh, yes. Sorry, dreaming.'

'I've been doing a bit of that,' sighed Bryony.

He gave her a look and then said, 'Well, one does, before a long journey into – into the unknown. I've just been wondering why we're doing it at all. We don't need to risk ourselves in this way. I could say no to the Great Pangolin.'

'Oh, we need a bit of risk in our lives. How boring it would be if we went for safety all the time. Certainly you and me, Monty. We're not stick-at-home mammals, are we? What's that empty box at your elbow?'

Monty glanced at the box, which said EXTRA-RARE EXTRA-RICH EXTRA-CREAMY CURDISH DELIGHT on the lid. There was a label attached which read: 100 GUINEAS – FROM FORTFOX AND MACINGS. It was open, the lid thrown back. Sherbet powder dusted the bottom of the box and was sprinkled all over the side table. Monty jumped up, a horrified look on his face. 'The mayor's present to the emperor! I've been sitting here, absently eating them.' He picked up the empty box and stared inside. 'They're all gone!'

'Oh, Monty! You did the same with those apricot parfaits I once gave you to keep for Jis McFail's Christmas gift.'

'I know. I'm sure these didn't taste like they were worth a hundred guineas. Otherwise I would have noticed I was eating them. Oh, well, I'll tell the mayor when I get back, just in case I never do get back. No sense in getting an ear-wigging for nothing.'

At that moment Jis McFail appeared in the doorway, her eyes wet with tears. 'Jal Scruff and Jal Maudlin is waiting down in the street for you, Jal Sylver and Jis Bludd.'

'Thank you, Jis McFail.'

'Oh, sir,' she finally wailed, opening her fore-limbs, 'you will come back, won't you?'

'Of course we'll come back,' he said heartily, avoiding the open invitation and allowing Bryony to cuddle the elderly landjill instead. 'Don't you fret. We'll send you a postcard from Far Kathay.'

Partly mollified, the sniffling landjill said she could hear her boiling kettle whistling and went back downstairs.

'Quick, let's get out of here before she comes back,' said Monty, grabbing a carpet bag.

Bryony said, 'You must say goodbye!'

'Haven't we done that already? I hate all this soppy stuff and you know she'll only start blubbing again.'

Reluctantly, Bryony agreed. They went down to the street, leaving the keys to their flats on the windowsill in the hallway. Scruff and Maudlin were waiting patiently on the pavement beside a less patient pawsome cab driver and his mouse-drawn vehicle. They all piled into the coach and set off towards Docklands.

'You 'aven't left nothin' behind?' asked Scruff. 'Compass, maps, firearms, torch, alarm clock . . .'

'I think I have everything in paw, Scruff,' replied Monty.

'I brought some fruit cake,' Maudlin said. 'It's got honey dew in it.'

'Ho, well done,' said Scruff. 'You think of everythin', Maud.'

Maudlin beamed.

'Heastward Ho, it is then,' cried Scruff. 'Hoff we go!'

'Eastward Ho!' chorused the others.

By the time they reached Muggidrear's great port, situated on the river Bronn, they were in a state of high excitement. They jumped down from the cab and Monty paid the driver. Then they picked up their cases and stared up at the great steamship that was to carry them on the first leg of their voyage, to the land of Eggyok on the shores of the Sapphire Sea. It was a magnificent vessel, with four tall funnels belching smoke and steam.

'Not like that boat we took to Slattland,' Maudlin said. 'That was big, but not this big.'

They went up the gangway and were greeted by the purser, a polecat with a squint, who welcomed them aboard. They were then shown to their cabins. Bryony had to share with another jill, a dowager stoat who felt it was an imposition to have a weasel in her cabin.

'Are there no other stoats on board?' asked the

dowager. 'I have nothing against weasels, of course – some of my best friends are weasels – but one likes to have something in common with one's cabin-mates, and I'm afraid I would have nothing to talk to a weasel about.'

The cabin-mammal told her that all the cabins had been allocated and that none of the other passengers wanted to change. When the dowager learned that Bryony was a qualified vet it simply meant that she went through a long list of her medical complaints, including a sore throat, which Bryony privately felt came from talking too much.

Scruff, Monty and Maudlin had a three-berth cabin just below the waterline, so they could see fish through the porthole.

'Bit like havin' a built-in aquarium,' said Scruff.

Before they sailed, they all met in the passengers' lounge.

'Well, it's going to be a longish voyage,' said Monty, 'so we'd better get used to this room – at least until we reach warmer weather. Then I expect we can spend more time on deck. Hello, here's a surprise!'

He pointed with his claw: on the other side of the lounge sat Princess Sybil Poynt and Police Chief Zacharias Falshed.

Bryony, being more curious than her fellows, got up and crossed over to them. 'You two running away with each other?' she enquired, more in fun than anything else.

'Certainly not!' retorted Sybil.

A dreamy look crossed Falshed's face for an instant, before he too replied, 'No, of course not. How dare you suggest such an improper thing. I am escorting Princess Sybil to Eggyok.'

'Oh? And you won't be together after that?'

'Not unless – no, no, I am simply her protector for this stage of her journey,' continued the chief, his tail getting tangled with his legs as he tried to stand up. 'I am at the princess's disposal for as long as she requires me – which I understand is as far as the destination of this ship.'

'Oh, sit down,' snapped Sybil irritably. 'You don't have to explain anything to anyone.' She turned her furry face towards Bryony. 'Aren't you one of those weasels who destroyed my priceless collection of Mole Dynasty vases?'

'Well, we were trying to save mammalkind from destruction.'

'That was no excuse then, and it's no excuse now. What are you doing on board, young jill? Where are you going? Eggyok?'

'Initially – then on to Far Kathay, as I'm sure the chief knows.'

'Far Kathay? Perhaps you'll be able to replace my vases then? They came from that part of the world, of course.'

'I'm afraid I wouldn't have that kind of money.'

'Oh, money's no object. Ship them to the mayor's address, cash on delivery. I would die to get my collection back again, or replace it. Now, off you go.'

Bryony went back to the others. 'She wants us to buy her some more Mole Dynasty vases. You remember we smashed all the others when Spindrick filled them with soil that let out poisonous fumes? She doesn't forget easily, that jill.'

'It's a possibility, but I'm not going to make it a priority,' replied Monty. 'Hey, we're on the move!'

The ship's horn sounded and they could see masts and funnels of other ships going past. The four of them rushed out on deck. Other passengers were lined up against the rail, waving pawkerchiefs at well-wishers standing on the dockside. It was an emotional scene. The four weasels joined in, though there was no-one there whom they knew. The ship steamed towards the river mouth. As it did so they realized there was another great vessel also heading for the open sea. When both ships reached the wide blue waters of the Cobalt they turned in different directions. Monty stared at the stern of the other vessel and was astonished to see his cousin Spindrick at the rail. They stared at each other without speaking, until they were too far apart to communicate. On impulse Monty went up to a crew member.

'Where's that other vessel bound?' he asked.

'Than 'un?' muttered the marten. 'New World, I thinks. Yep, that'll be the *Ammericy*, headed for the New World.'

Hmmm, thought Monty, what's Spindrick up to now? It's certain he's not emigrating. He's not the emigrating sort. That weasel cousin of mine is up to something. I hope he's not after some way of blowing up Welkin while I'm in Far Kathay. I wouldn't put it past him.

'A penny for your thoughts,' said Bryony, coming to stand next to him.

'Spindrick,' he replied, 'and you can have them for nothing.'

'What about him?'

'On that boat, heading west.'

'While we're heading east? How fortunate.'

'Perhaps.'

They said no more for the moment. Scruff and Maudlin went back into the lounge to play a game of hollyhockers. Bryony and Monty stayed on deck to watch the sun go down. It was a beautiful sunset, even though there was a cold wind blowing and the sea was kicking in its traces. White wavetops chased each other across the surface. The land slipped away slowly behind them. For a while they could see the lights of cities glowing in the lower stretches of the evening sky, but after a time this too became darkness. Both were still reluctant to enter the bright lounge with its false gaiety.

'Funny thing, being away from land,' said Bryony after a while. 'I feel sort of detached from reality.'

'So we are in a way. We're someone else's responsibility for the time we're on board.

We just have to go with the flow, so to speak.'

They stayed for a while longer, then the wind became even stronger and began flicking spray over the deck, so they joined Scruff and Maudlin in the lounge.

CHAPTER SIX

Life on board ship tended to drift into a dream-
like existence. There were games, of course –
deck quoits, deck tennis, strolling the deck – and
once the ship entered warmer weather there
would be deck lounging in a deck chair.
(Everything that was not associated with the
lounge-cum-dining room was connected with
the deck.) Mammals became bored and could be
found staring out at the horizon as if there were
something to look at – which there wasn't, apart
from waves and the odd cloud. Some mammals
claimed to have seen big creatures in the water –
sharks, dolphins, whales or porpoises – but
since such glimpses were fleeting, they couldn't
share their sightings and often ended up

wondering whether they'd really seen anything.

Maudlin and Scruff invented new games, like spitting over the windward side to see if they could hit an open porthole. Or pointing silently into the distant greyness and waiting until they had a crowd around them, only to walk off without a word, leaving the curious spectators wondering. Or sounding the dinner gong some time before the meal was due and watching the milling passengers thronging at the doorways to the dining room. But even exciting new games can pall after a while and they too slipped into a lethargic longing for meal times to move closer together – eating was the only activity that stirred mammals from the deck and cabins.

Sometimes they would pass an island and the whole ship would be afire with gossip for an hour or two, even though all that could be seen was a thin dark line – or, at night, twinkling lights. Sometimes another ship would pass magically by, also encrusted with lights, and mammals would speak of wondrous things, things fantastical, well into the night. The words 'leviathan' and 'kraken' would be on every tongue, but by morning the magic would all have dried up and blown away, and breakfast would be a dull affair of clattering cutlery and china.

There was a ball, of course, which livened things up. And a daily competition to guess how many nautical miles they had travelled the previous day. And a band which played incessantly.

One part of the voyage would never be forgotten: as they crossed the Bay of Biscuit a terrible storm had them all hanging over the side or cuddling buckets in their berths. Many wished for death during that white-water gale, with the bows crashing down into tempestuous seas and the stern disappearing under the ship's own wake. When the storm was past they were all still alive – pale and delicate, but definitely within this world. Several had repented of their sins and promised to lead better lives, an oath which was forgotten before noon of the first calm day. Many had vowed never to go to sea again.

'Land!' cried Maudlin one day. 'Over there!'

'Yeah, I know, just out of sight,' replied a morose Scruff.

'No, really – look.'

And Scruff did look and saw an island which was not much more than a huge, pointed rock, jutting from the sea. Then the mainland appeared behind the rocky island, and when they looked to starboard they saw the distant coast of a southern continent, lean as a rasher of mouse-bacon.

'It *is* land,' sighed Scruff, thoroughly fed up with watery wastes. 'We've reached the Gibarbary Straits. That there's Spangle, on the left, and that great continent to the south is Afrormosia, or the Heart of Palm as some call it.'

'What's the little island, Scruff?'

'That there's Gibarbary itself, where the apes live.'

'No humans?'

'Oh, one or two, but they tend to live up on the top of the rock. Look, you can see one now . . .'

They continued to sail through the Sapphire Sea, past several islands. Princess Sybil emerged from her cabin for the first time since the voyage had begun. She looked a little pasty about the whiskers. Falshed, who had also been absent most of the time, fussed around her, finding her a deck chair, fetching her drinks. By the time the ship arrived at Eggyok, most on board had recovered from the horrible storm, and were milling about the deck, pointing out wondrous sights, such as the giant statue of a cat which stood at the entrance to the harbour to this, the land of felines.

'My mother died here,' said Falshed, looking across at the sandy regions of Eggyok. 'She left a clause in her will—'

'Claws?' cried Maudlin. 'Her actual claws?'

'No, no.' Falshed was irritated. '*Clause* – paragraph. In it she ordered that if she died abroad I was to ship the body home and bury her in her own Muggidrear garden.'

'And did you?' asked Bryony, as they walked down the gangway to step onto the dockside.

'Couldn't afford it,' he replied miserably. 'She'd spent all her money on the holiday in the first place, and I didn't have any.'

'Oh dear,' said Maudlin. 'Mother's wishes ignored. Terrible thing, that. Wouldn't want to be in your shoes, when you die. She'll be waiting for you, you know, ready with the rebukes and a clip round the ear.'

The group of weasels booked into a plush, if a little dusty, hotel near the souk. Bryony was free to go and look at the fabrics and jewellery on sale and Scruff and Maudlin went with her. Monty went off to find a guide. They needed a mammal who knew the Silk Road like the back of his paw. There were treacherous deserts out there, passes which favoured ambushing bandits, and mountain ranges the like of which a weasel had never seen before. Even Monty felt a little out of his depth.

In a dark coffee house, with brass-topped tables and little stools to sit on, a local cat in a red turban served Monty with a thick syrupy-looking substance.

'Coffeeeee,' said the cat, extending his 'e's as all cats did. 'No milk here, I'm afraid.'

If the waiter had wanted an argument he wasn't going to get it from Monty. Several other local cats had half-inclined their heads in the gloom, watching with a cat's eye for any unfavourable reaction.

'That's fine,' replied Monty. 'Just as I like it.'

The waiter nodded in satisfaction. 'Anything else I can bring you? We make a nice honeeeey cockroach here, in a parcel of filo pastreeey.'

'Yes, I'll take one of those. Also, I'm looking for a guide to take me along the Silk Road to Far Kathay. Any ideas?'

The cat's eyes widened. 'The Silk Road?

Dangerous journeeeey, that. But there's plenteeey who'll take you along it, for the right fee . . .'

Before the waiter had even finished his sentence a creature appeared as if by magic out of the folds of the tapestries which lined the walls. It was not a cat. It was not any mammal Monty had ever seen before: it resembled a gerbil but with long hind legs like a kangaroo. It leaned over Monty, revealing a scarred and patchy face, one eye half-closed, and whispered, 'I'm your mammal.'

'Who are you?'

The waiter drifted away as the stranger sat down at Monty's table and returned with a saucer of flat, crisp cockroaches toasted to a turn. He put them in front of the stranger, along with a glass of murky-looking melon dew. This mammal was obviously a regular customer at the coffee house. He looked up and nodded at the waiter before crunching a brown cockroach crisp and swallowing some of the drink.

He replied to Monty's question. 'Calabash Brown, at your most positive service, sir.'

The stranger had a red bandana tied around his head, a long shirt of something that resembled hessian covering his hairy body, and a tail without its tip. He looked as ravaged as a chunk of sandstone left out in a barren place to be battered by the elements. There was a mixture of grit, shiftiness and plain eagerness in his expression. He looked just the sort of creature who would lead an expedition into hell – and leave it there.

'What is the profit, sir? You will pay in coinage, yes? If they have your queen's head, I shall not defer them. I have not the prejudice when it comes to money.'

'Perhaps,' said Monty on reflection, 'I should have said *what* are you? I'm not being impolite, you understand, Jal Brown. I simply have no idea of your species. Are you of the rat family?'

'If you want me to be.'

'Just tell me what you are.'

'Jerboa. We have been termed the "desert rat", being, as you speak, of the rodent family. Twenty-five species altogether,' he added proudly, 'all as magnificent as the mammal you perceive before you with this sandy-coloured fur – please to excuse the dust – and these large soft eyes. We are humble rodents, and my own species the humblest of them all. Also very poor,' he added quickly, 'and the best guides in all the empire.'

'Which empire?' asked Monty.

'Why, the empire of – of – is it Welkin you aspire from, sir?'

'Yes, but we have no empire, not any more, thank goodness.'

The jerboa tried to look sad. 'For myself, I like empires. They bring rich foo— rich mammals to my land.' He clicked his teeth and resumed his former merry but cunning expression. 'So, my fine weasel sir, from the distant Welkin, what do you say to me? Am I your guide?'

Cats and other mammals within the establishment, including the waiter, shook their heads slowly behind the jerboa's back.

But there was something about Calabash Brown and Monty was reluctant to send the jerboa away. He wanted to talk to him further.

'You don't even know where we're going yet.'

'I think I do,' cried the jerboa indignantly. 'You are going to Far Kathay, along the Silk Road, which I am comprehending as well as my own front teeth. Many times have I led such famous explorers as Magenta along the Silk Road, past the human castles which line the route, over barren wastes, through tall-reeded marshes—'

'Ferdinant Magenta was a sailor.'

'Before that he was discovering the great continents of the earth, with me as his guide.'

'Look, let's get one thing straight,' said Monty. 'If I *were* to hire you, I would demand honesty from you. That would be a basic requirement of the job. I can't hire a guide who tells lies and makes up stories.'

'Of course,' cried the jerboa. 'Honesty is the best politic. All right, all right, my dear sir, I did not take the great Magenta along the Silk Road, but I did take the Welkin explorer, Bruton.'

'Didn't he disappear in some foreign desert?'

'Not on Calabash's expedition,' cried the jerboa, looking affronted. 'Some other mammal lost him.'

'Is that the truth?'

'Cut off my tail and hope to die.'

The waiter brought Monty's cockroach in filo

pastry, soaked in honey, placed it before him, and winked knowingly.

Monty sighed, wondering if he would regret what he was about to do. 'Jal Brown, I like you. I don't know why I like you, because you strike me, on first meeting, as a rodent who is trying too hard. I'll tell you what I'll do. If you can prove to me that you actually do know the way along the Silk Road, then I'll hire you. We can agree terms later, but I'm reasonably generous, so you need have no fear of being underpaid. But I do want this proof, you understand. There are other lives at stake besides mine, and I must be sure we are being led by a competent and knowledgeable creature.'

Tears came to the eyes of the jerboa. He reached forward with his claw and gripped Monty's paw. 'You, sir, will not be regrettable. I thank you for this gesturing. Tonight I shall come to your hotel with my proofs. Your courage, sir, will be rewarded with great servitude and very fine tracking. Tracking such as you have never witnessed in all your living nights. I shall lead, oh, how I shall lead you and your companions, safely to the ends of the earth.'

The Eggyok cats shook their heads and pursed their lips behind his back, indicating to Monty that he was making a terrible mistake in hiring this vagabond, this ruffian of the desert, this mercenary adventurer.

CHAPTER SEVEN

The jerboa was hired, much against Bryony's better judgement, but she was up against Scruff, who always liked to give a mammal a chance. Maudlin naturally voted with Scruff, which left the deciding vote to Monty himself. Having interviewed several other guides, Monty was inclined to the view that while the character of the jerboa left a lot to be desired, he knew his stuff. Discreet enquiries revealed that the jerboa had indeed made a journey with the great Welkin stoat explorer Bruton, and had returned to Eggyok with him by his side. Also Calabash showed Monty the gifts he had brought back for his family and friends (such as they were), which proved beyond doubt that the jerboa had been to regions uncharted.

'So, Calabash Brown, you are to be our guide.'

'Thank you, sirs, thank you, madams,' said that long-hind-legged creature. 'These will not be regretting times. I shall prove the worth you require of me. I am come out of the desert myself, so I know the ways of living there. My tribe of desert rats (*click, click*) still remain in the great dunes of the Saltana Desert, their bodies coloured red from the dye of the cloaks they are wearing. A warrior tribe. I too am a fierce warrior and will protect my sirs and madams from the savage bloodthirsty bandits who descend on caravans such as we like wildcats.'

'They do?' whispered Maudlin, his eyes bulging.

Bryony said rather stiffly, 'You will notice there is only one madam here – I mean, jis. Stop speaking of me in the plural.'

'Sorry, sorry, sir,' Calabash said to her, bowing as he did so, 'my Welkin speech is not so good with its aim. If you speak Eggyok we may converse at a swifter speed.'

This, as Calabash knew it would, put Bryony in her place.

'So you,' said Monty, 'are from the Red Devils of the Saltana? Why didn't you say so before? I much admire that particular tribe.'

Bryony said archly, 'You believe in pillage?'

Monty turned to her. 'They no longer live by raiding and plunder. That is consigned to history. They have their own farms now and do very well

– very well indeed, considering the infertility of the soil.'

'So,' said Calabash, 'we leave at dawn. If you are giving me the monies I shall purchase supplies. We shall be walking on footlings of course. No mouse could survive the desert. We shall carry our water in vole-skin bags, one for each of us. Anyone is wanting a walking stick with lots of badges on it?'

'Me, me,' said Maudlin, a little too eagerly.

'That too, then, I shall purchase. Please to give me the monies?' He held out his dusty paw.

Bryony looked at Monty, who shrugged, as if to say, *If we can't trust him now, we need to know it anyway*. He passed a purse full of coins over to the jerboa, who counted them carefully, wrote out a receipt using an alphabet that no-one could make tail or head of, and then left by the side door.

The group then made for the dining room, where they found Falshed eating alone. He nodded to them, then finally came over to their table.

'I suppose you know,' said the stoat, 'that I was told to follow you along the Silk Road and try to thwart your expedition.'

'I did guess as much,' replied Monty.

'Well,' confessed the other, 'I shan't be doing that. Princess Sybil – well, she's sick. Sminx tummy, I'm afraid. We took a visit to the prismids and our water ran out. She became desperate for a drink and the only water available was from the Sourwater Nail.'

70

'You gave her Nail water to drink?' cried Bryony. 'Don't you know there are dead camels floating in it? There are diseases in there nameless to mustelids! I'll be surprised if her kidneys survive.'

'I gave her nothing,' replied the chief haughtily. 'It was – it was our guide. He said he'd been drinking it all his life and was perfectly healthy. I actually didn't touch mine. It was swimming with mosquito larvae and that put me off for a start. But the princess was terribly thirsty. Now she's got the – well, I think I've said all I need to say.' He turned to Bryony. 'I wondered, vet, if you might just pop upstairs and have a look at her, see if there's any more to be done. I shall of course stay here now and nurse her to health. I feel it's my duty.'

'Of course you do,' said Maudlin, 'you being besotted with her.'

'I beg your pardon?'

Bryony left the group and returned a little later. The chief was still standing by the table. 'She'll live,' said Bryony. 'She's in a bad way but I've given her some powders which may help. I've left some more on the bedside table, Chief. Give her one three times a day. Also, you'll have to worm her once she's better.'

'Worm the princess?' cried the horrified Falshed.

'Worms aren't fussy about whose abdomen they enter,' replied the vet. 'I expect they're royal worms. Don't worry, they're only the long, thin,

71

round variety. I don't think she has a tape worm.'

'I should say not!'

'Well, she did put herself at great risk of it, drinking Nail water like that, and it wasn't much fun finding out, I can tell you. Finally, she's going to be pretty run down afterwards. You may find it necessary to de-flea her.'

'De-flea the princess?'

'I can't say it plainer.'

The chief spun round in a daze and staggered off to the bar, where he bought himself a large melon dew.

'That was a bit cruel, Bryony,' said Monty.

'Cruel, but necessary. Look, he's coming back, a little more fortified.'

'You know,' said Falshed, 'all along that river—'

'The Nail,' Scruff said.

'Yes, all along the Nail there are stoat fisherfolk, stoats tilling the soil. There's an underclass of stoats here, would you believe.'

'Histories do not run in parallel,' said Bryony. 'Just because stoats got the upper paw early in Welkin does not mean they did here. The cats would not have put up with it – they were once worshipped by the humans.'

'Where are the humans, by the way?' asked Maudlin.

'South, as always, and along the coast. They do love the sea. Few of them come up here.'

'Thing is,' continued Falshed quietly, as if he'd never been interrupted at all. 'Thing is, these foreign stoats, they were looking at us. I mean, I know – strangers and tourists and all that – but they were looking quite hard at us. I don't know what it was. The strangest thing. Made my fur stand on end all over ...' The chief would have gone on, but there was a call from one of the hotel staff that Zacharias Falshed was required in the Blue Suite, which was where Sybil was lying, drained and strained. 'Got to go. Got to go. Good luck on the expedition. No, I really mean that. I don't think we'll see you again. Not ever, I'm afraid.' With that he hurried off in the direction of the stairway.

'Well, that was a nice vote of confidence, I must say,' said Scruff. 'Personally I think we'll come back with our tails in the air. That's my personal opinion, for what it's worth.'

They had their meal then retired to their rooms.

At five o'clock they were roused from sleep by Calabash, who had all the equipment – backpacks, shovels, food, water – standing in the lobby. He had proved his honesty.

Bryony pulled on her backpack. It felt as if it were full of rocks. 'It's still dark outside,' she complained. 'Why so early? Surely this isn't necessary.'

'Necessary for me,' murmured Calabash Brown, peering out of the doorway into the gloom. 'Many mammals are owed money.'

'You're in debt?' said Monty. 'Why didn't you

say? I'll advance you some of your pay to settle up before we leave.'

The jerboa looked horrified and actually jumped a few centimetres on his kangaroo legs. 'Pay before I *have* to? It is against all principles. Mammals may have moved to Icingland when I return. They may be dead. I would be paying them for nothings. Only when they drag me from my house!'

'Suit yourself. It seems a very precarious life.'

'I spit in the face of danger,' said the jerboa, checking the dawn one last time before they left the shelter of the lobby. 'I am known for my aggressive nature.'

They walked through the sleeping houses, along the bank of the Nail, where indeed there were many stoats sleeping, or just rising to light their charcoal fires. They glanced curiously at the group, but certainly they did not stare. Monty decided they had looked hard at Falshed and Sybil because they were rich stoats in a land where stoats were generally poor.

The group crossed the bridge, heading east (or 'heast', as Scruff would have it), the low, bright rising sun in their eyes. They wore no shoes, which were an encumbrance in the desert, since they filled with sand. All of them wore the white cotton shifts that Calabash had bought for them, and headscarves wrapped around in the local style. Maudlin had left a flap to cover the back of his neck, knowing it looked naff, but more concerned with avoiding heat stroke.

'You are seeing the ridge of hills?' said Calabash, as they walked.

'Yes,' replied Monty. 'They must be the Scarab Hills.'

'Well, we must seek their shade by noon or we shall be toast. It comes very hot in the desert. Halfway over there is a well, with fresh water, but we must steal it, for it belongs to a tribe of skinks who would bury us up to our ankles and leave us in the hot sun to die.'

'Ankles?' cried Maudlin. 'Head, surely.'

'No, they bury us upside down.'

Monty asked, 'Who is the leader of these skinks?'

'He is known as the Shamelion.'

'Ah, yes, I've heard of him. A formidable creature, so I'm told. But why steal the water? Can we not come to some agreement with the tribe?'

'No, they kill us first, then they make agreements.'

Maudlin added the last words: 'I knew I wasn't going to like this trip.'

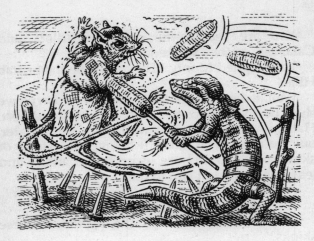

CHAPTER EIGHT

During the morning they passed a wondrous sight. In a rocky valley between some limestone cliffs in a corner of the Naffrude Desert stood the magnificent ancient city of Petal, carved from stony cliffs by desert mammals long since disappeared from the face of the earth. Behind paw-worked facades 'there were hollowed-out caves and mammal-built tunnels, forming a vast community of dwellings. The ancient ones had taken roughly hewn efforts of wind, sun, frost and rain, and turned them into great works of art. Moreover, they had done it with claw and a simple adze.

Flower-topped pillars adorned the entrances, shaped animals, centripetals, likenesses of ivy and laurel leaves, all kinds of embellishments and adornments had been lovingly cut into the limestone. There were steps cut in the rock, to high places with stone altars and porches which overhung the portals of crumbling temples. Some of the carvings had never been finished. It was like a three-dimensional sketchbook – as if the sculptors had been working away on one section, only to abandon it halfway through for another more promising area.

'*A cream-hued city, twice as old as hope,*' murmured Scruff, as they all stared at the fabled city.

'Why, Scruff!' said Bryony. 'I didn't know you read poetry.'

'Ho, there's lots you don't know about me. I picks up bits and pieces, 'ere and there. It's a wonder, though, ain't it? Makes you think – where've all the mammals disappeared to who built this place? Must 'ave bin thousands of 'em living here at one time, in them dwellin's. Gone, all gone. Left it to the scorpions and snakes.'

Maudlin shivered and looked around. 'I wish you wouldn't mention such things. I keep managing to forget about scorpions and snakes, then you go and remind me.'

They walked past this beautiful testament to mammals' ingenuity, leaving the dust devils to sweep through its silent paths and upper walkways, trying to reclaim for nature what mammals had borrowed for a time.

Next they passed the Salt Sea, which held no

living thing in its viscous waters. Scruff and Maudlin had a dip in it and found they could not sink, even if they tried. The water was so buoyant it held them up as if in the palm of its hand. Afterwards they had to scrape the salt from their fur and were forced to put up with itching and scratching for the next hour.

Closer and closer they came to the forbidden well. For several hours now they had been marching across the rippled sands and over the scattered grit and stones, their heads bowed with the heat. Everyone was feeling the need for more liquid, having drunk all they carried. Scruff was even sucking a pebble, which he had heard helped when one was desperately thirsty. Scorpions scurried out of their way. Snakes wriggled under rocks. Maudlin was happy to see that such creatures preferred to avoid him.

All the while Calabash Brown, that intrepid jerboa, looked about him with unease. By the time they reached the hole in the rock with its natural spring beneath, Maudlin was a bag of nerves.

'You sure this is all right?' he said. 'You sure we won't be attacked by skinks?'

'Calabash is not certain of any such thing,' replied the jerboa, clearly almost as nervous as Maudlin was himself. 'See—' he held up a flaccid vole-skin – 'our water bags prefer to remain flat, even though we chastise them with bitter tongue. We must drink at the well, fill our water bags, and be quickly away from this dreaded place.' Once more his eyes scoured the surrounding rocky outcrops for any sign of reptiles.

Once they had filled their bellies and their vole-skins, they were ready to move on.

'What is a *skink* anyway?' asked Maudlin. 'It sounds like some sort of slimy, slinky creature.'

'More slinky than slimy!' said a voice from above Maudlin's head.

Maudlin turned, like the others, to see who had spoken. There on a rock overhang stood a lizard-like creature, up on its hind legs. In its right foreclaw it held a wicked-looking spear. There was a brave yellow bandana around its head and burnished copper hoops about its waist. More copper amulets decorated the upper parts of its four limbs. Its tail, though, was tipped with a silver cone, which fitted it exactly. Here indeed was a tribesmammal of the desert; a creature of the sand.

Calabash cried, 'The Shamelion!' He immediately looked around and saw the moving lumps in the sand.

'Yes, we are all about you,' cried the Shamelion. 'You have drunk from our well at your peril!'

At that moment a hundred or more skinks, much like the one standing on the rock, appeared from under the surface of the desert. They were creatures who could burrow, having smooth, pointed bodies which moved through sand like a shoal of fish through water. They surrounded the five travellers, waving their spears and muttering foul oaths.

The Shamelion said, 'Tell me why I should not kill you all where you stand.'

'Because,' said Monty, stepping forward, 'we have done nothing wrong.' The weasel detective had a peculiar feeling about this ambush. There was something in the attitude of the skinks that didn't feel quite right. Nothing he could put his claw on – just a feeling that there was acting, rather than natural emotions at work here.

'Nothing wrong?' thundered the Shamelion in a highly elaborate gesture of rage. 'Is it not wrong to be a thief in your country?'

'In my country the water from streams and rivers, and indeed springs, is free. The right of any traveller to drink from such places is a given thing. Also, we do not execute thieves, not any longer. We used to. We even deported them. But not these days. We imprison them.'

'I would rather die than be imprisoned!' cried the skink.

'I would rather be imprisoned than die,' replied Maudlin, 'if it's all the same to you.'

Monty ignored this interruption and continued, 'Of course, were you to execute us for drinking the water from this well – without which we would have died anyway, I might add – you could then steal all our goods. Is that the idea? That with the owners out of the way, your tribe can plunder this small caravan? Now that is the worst kind of theft, to rob the corpses of the slain.'

A low muttering came from the skink warriors.

'How dare you suggest we would commit such a ghastly crime,' cried the Shamelion. 'I suppose *he* told you that?' The spear was pointed at Calabash Brown. 'That scallywag, that scurrilous knave of a sand rat. High time we slow-roasted him over a very hot fire. He shall walk the Rope of the Dead, while my warriors beat him with loofahs. And you –' he pointed at Monty – 'you will dine with the Shamelion at Wadi Drumm!'

This was quite unexpected. A death threat, the sentence of execution, had suddenly turned into an invitation to dine. Yet it was not an invitation. It was a demand. They were hobbled by the ankles and had to hop most of the way to the skink tribe's village in Wadi Drumm. There they were given food – roasted sparrow drumsticks and unleavened bread – and told to rest in the shade. Maudlin was suspicious of this change of behaviour.

'They're fattening us up,' he moaned, 'for the kill.'

'Whatever else they are,' Bryony told him, 'they're not cannibals. They won't eat another intelligent creature.'

'The bone-cracker is correct,' said Calabash, referring to Bryony by her profession as a vet, 'we will not be eaten. But still I do not trust these slithery tribesmammals. I think for two copper brooch pins they will nail us upside down to palm trees and drain us of blood.'

Shortly after this prophecy, Calabash was untied and made to walk blindfold along a rope which followed a shallow ridge of sand. On either side of the rope sharp knives had been stuck into the ground, handle first. If the jerboa overbalanced and fell from the rope, he would be impaled on the points of the knives. But he was not allowed to simply tightrope-walk to freedom. All the while he stood, sweating and swaying, on the rope the skinks hit him with soggy loofahs to make him overbalance and fall to his death.

'Do not worry,' he called to the other prisoners in trembling accents, 'I have been in many tight places and lived. Once, I remember, I was in this cave with a huge stone ball rolling after me—'

'SILENCE!' roared the Shamelion. 'You will walk the rope of death without speaking to your friends. You may whimper and moan, if you wish, and cry for mercy, but no chit-chat.'

Calabash did as he was bid, his trembling claws gripping the rope tightly, while his fore-limbs and tail were stiffly outstretched, in an effort to balance himself on the wobbly rope. Eventually he reached the end and fell in a trembling heap onto the sand, where they continued to thump him with the loofahs. Maudlin booed. Scruff hissed. Monty demanded they stop their beating. Bryony demanded that she be allowed to administer aid to the victim. When she was finally allowed to do so, she found Calabash clicking his teeth, trying to contain his merriment.

'Why – why, you're – you're not hurt at all,' she cried.

Calabash sat up and regarded the weasels. It was obvious he was overcome with mirth. Some of the tribesmen could not contain themselves either, and had dropped their spears and sat on the ground clicking their teeth. The Shamelion too was clacking away like mad, obviously overcome by his part in the joke.

'Oh, we had you there,' he cried, in his lizardy voice. 'Calabash does this every time.'

Monty shook his head. 'It was a set piece,' he said. 'I was beginning to suspect as much.'

'Oh,' cried Calabash, the tears streaming from his eyes, 'it is all for the entertainment of *you*, my fine friends. You are the guests and you must enjoy the joke – all done in aid of you. Of course we shall encounter *real* dangers out there on our trekking along the Silk Road, but I was thinking you would appreciate this funny thing. Why are you not clicking your teeth? Why do I not hear the clack of fangs? This is very funny. Very funny indeed.'

'I'm glad you think so,' said Bryony.

Maudlin was furious. 'You frightened the fur off my neck,' he cried. 'I was so scared I nearly shed my pelt. I thought we were going to die. I thought—'

'Yeah,' said Scruff, clicking himself now, 'but you got to admit, Maud, it *was* funny. They had us there, all right. I thought we was roasted for sure, and in a way, we was.'

CHAPTER NINE

When they had calmed down, Monty and the
others saw the funny side of things. They had
been taken in, good and proper. Around the
camp fire later, with the smell of roast vole in
their nostrils, they talked about their journey to
Far Kathay with the Shamelion.

'I do not envy you your task,' he said. 'The
next part of your long and hazardous trek is over
the watery marshlands to our east. Wild humans
inhabit the reed beds. They live on fish and grass
seeds, but will not hesitate to attack any group of
animals who appear to be carrying supplies.
If I were you I would hurry on through, or
you may find your skulls decorating wooden
spikes.'

Maudlin's whiskers twitched. 'Joke, right?'

'No joke,' Calabash told him gravely. 'I have viewed these humans. They are wearing the skins of intelligent creatures, as well as dumb ones. A weasel-skin hat displays their heads as well as a vole-skin one. We must gird our loins, my friends. Stay close on the trail. Keep a pointed eye.'

Maudlin stared at the cave walls in the fire-light, at the shadows which danced there. For the first time he felt he was in a really alien landscape. Back in Muggidrear he had known one or two humans. But this was the first time he would be likely to encounter wild humans. They had wild humans in Welkin, but on the islands in the far north, beyond the unnamed marshes where the rats had their homes. Humans with shaggy beards and savage eyes. One part of him wished he were back in Muggidrear – dear old Muggidrear with its foggy cobbled streets and dark, dank alleys – and the other half of him thrilled to the fact that he was living an adventure. Here he was making a legend. Historians would speak of this journey. His name would undoubtedly be carved in the da-da rail of the Royal Geographical Society, along with those of other great mustelid explorers.

Yet – yet – oh, how cosy was the fire in his little basement flat in East Cheep . . .

'Maud?'

'What? Oh, sorry, Scruff. Were you speaking to me?'

'I was sayin' we'd better get some sleep. Long day tomorrow.'

'Yes, all right. Scruff, do you miss Muggidrear?'

'Miss old Muggs? Draughty place. Wet, dreary, full o' yellow smog half the time. Beggars in the streets. 'Orrible gloomy prisons with grey walls on every corner. Rotten peelers ready to nab you for nothin'. Pawpads lurkin' in dark corners, waiting to clobber you and take your purse. Dead bodies in the river every mornin'.' He sighed. 'Yeah, course I miss it. Don't you?'

'Yes. 'Night, Scruff.'

''Night, Maud.'

The next morning they were up with the dawn, ready to be on the move before the heat of the day really set in. The night had been bitterly cold. Water had frozen in the vole-skins. Monty had awoken with icicles on his whiskers, unable to feel his feet. Sleep had been difficult because the extremes of heat and cold, day and night, made the rocks expand and contract. During the dark hours they cracked apart with sounds like gunshots. That's what made deserts what they were: inhospitable places where little would grow and not many creatures wanted to live.

Monty pounded some feeling back into the blocks of ice that were his hind paws, while Bryony did some doctoring on the skinks, who did not see a vet from one year to the next. They were already up and had started the breakfast fires. Monty knew that reptiles were cold-blooded creatures. All their warmth came from the sun and they had to lie in it to revive themselves after the freezing night. One of them came up to the weasels now, rubbing its forefeet together.

'Porridge all right? It's all we've got. We put salt in it here.'

'Yes, of course.' Salt was easily lost through sweat in the heat of the day. 'Porridge is fine.'

'I don't like porridge,' said Maudlin. 'Haven't you got any eggs?'

'Yes, I've got some eggs,' answered the skink, sounding surprised.

'Well then, I'd like a couple of those, lightly boiled.'

The skink's eyes narrowed and she went away. Scruff pursed his lips.

'What?' cried Maudlin. 'What did I say?'

'You asked her to cook you her eggs.'

'*Her* eggs – I – oh, I see.' Of course, reptiles laid eggs themselves. Maudlin had meant sparrows' eggs; she had been speaking of her own young. There she was now, lying on them, glaring at Maudlin. He went across to her. 'I – I'm sorry, I didn't mean *your* eggs.'

'Whose did you mean then, those over there?'

'No, I didn't mean any of yours. I – I meant birds' eggs. We often eat birds' eggs. Never lizards'.'

The female skink was not impressed and Maudlin left her to her brood. It was just like him, he thought, to get it all wrong. 'What's the porridge like?' he asked the others when he got back to them. 'Salty?'

Scruff sucked in his cheeks as if he'd just taken a bite out of a fresh lemon.

'Yes, well then,' Maudlin said, 'no need to answer, is there?'

After breakfast they said their goodbyes and were on their way again, Calabash out front, setting a brisk pace with those long, jumpy legs of his.

Halfway through the morning they came across the giant statue of a dog. It had toppled at some time and lay in several large pieces on the lone and level sands.

'Look at the size of that!' said Scruff. 'Who was it?'

'Some ancient ruler of this land,' replied Calabash Brown. 'Some mighty king of all he surveyed.'

'He was a surveyor then?' said Maudlin.

'Not a surveyor – a great monarch,' Calabash repeated. 'See there his hulkless legs. And on the head, that tall crown. No-one knows who he really was, but by the curling lip and grizzling sneer you could see he was used to giving orders that had to be obeyed.'

'I think you're right,' murmured Bryony. 'Look – what's that written on his brow? It's very weathered, very faint, but you can still make out the words – *My name is Bozzicanine, top dog of top dogs: look on my marvellous buildings, you lesser mammals, and fall into utter dejection.'*

They looked for his works, but there was nothing there except the ruins of the huge statue.

'Some builder!' snorted Scruff.

'Oh,' babbled Maudlin quietly to himself, because no-one was listening, 'not a surveyor – a proper qualified architect.'

Monty said, 'I think the lesson here is humility. No-one can withstand the ravages of passing time. No-one is immortal or stands above his fellows for very long. In the end . . .'

'Dust,' finished Bryony, not without some satisfaction.

They left the sad ruins of Bozzicanine to his empty kingdom.

At noon they reached a watercourse, a wadi, where Calabash dug down to find some water. It was while they were filling their bags that the storm came. A real blaster. They hunched down below the banks of the wadi, their blankets up around them, to keep the sand from getting up their noses, in their eyes, down their throats.

When the sandstorm had blown itself out they emerged from their hot blankets, and found themselves staring at yet another ancient city. Unlike Petal, which was visible all the time, these ruins had emerged from under the desert. It seemed that this sandstone wonder appeared and disappeared at the whim of the desert. Sometimes it would be visible; at other times it lay under the surface. What was even more amazing was the speed at which the city was occupied, once the veil of dust had been removed and it was exposed to view.

Insects of all kinds marched in straight away, and mammals came out of the east, with carpet bags full of their possessions. They took over the red stone houses without any argument as to who should go where. Bed linen was unpacked, little stoves appeared, furniture was dusted off. Soon there was a thriving community going. As Monty said, 'You would think they'd been living there without a break for the last thousand years.'

He spoke to a family of rats, who had come with a mousedrawn cart laden with their family goods. 'How did you know that the city had been exposed?'

'Oh, we watch for it, you know. We've been living in camps for the past three years. My youngest has never seen his real home until now.'

'What will you do here?'

'Me? I'm a carpenter by trade. Mammals will want tables and chairs, cupboards and things. My eldest, Hannina, she's a cobbler. And that one over there, with the bit out of his ear, is the middle one.' The paternal rat sighed. 'We're not sure what to do with him. My Mabel says he might make a good unblocker of pipes – you know, sewage and water pipes – very necessary in a place that gets buried every five minutes. He's always messing about with drains, so she could be right. But then again, I had hoped *one* of them would be artistic . . .' He went on at length, until Calabash told Monty they ought to be on their way.

They left the city of the sands to its devices, and came to the marshlands. These were definitely spooky – there was no other word for it. The reeds were tall and, weasels and jerboas being close to the ground, they had to hack their way through with big knives. Snakes there were aplenty. And marshes tend to be soggy places. There was always the danger of quicksand – or rather quickmud – which would suck a mammal down and leave only bubbles on the top. It was a treacherous place, with the added danger of running into wild humans.

This they did before very long. Two humans appeared on a shallow lake between the island marshes. They were in a long punt with pointed bows and stern. Sitting right on the bow was a gun, a fowling piece with a huge calibre – a long cannon really. Having seen the weasels and the jerboa the humans let out an inhuman cry. They waved their arms and shook their shaggy heads. Then one of them reached down and, with a triumphant yell, pulled the trigger of the gun. It went off with the most tremendous crash, echoing across the surface of the glades. The ball struck the water ahead, bounced three times like a skipping stone, then clipped through the reeds close to Calabash's head.

'A close tell,' cried the jerboa. 'Swiftly, my friends, it is time for disappearing into those yellow flags over there.'

They quickly ducked down and waded to hide among the flowers. A second shot, preceded by the same excited yell, followed. This took off the bloom of a flag, went zinging over the surface of the water, and hit a duck. The duck died instantly with a last squawk. It rolled over and lay still, its webbed feet standing stiffly in the air like banners.

The humans shouted out again and paddled their punt furiously towards the duck. Having apparently forgotten about the weasels and jerboa, they threw the dead bird into the bottom of their boat and headed south. Every so often they let out a whoop which made Maudlin jump.

'Wild, I suppose, but they seemed very happy,' said Maudlin, once he was sure they'd gone. 'All that yelling and stuff.'

'Maniacally happy,' Monty agreed. 'Happy as a crazy loon.'

CHAPTER TEN

Spindrick went down the gangway to put his foot on the soil of the New World for the first time. What a vast land! What a fantastic place! Mammals of all kinds were busy on the docks, loading and unloading. Ships crowded New Lankaster harbour. Busy, busy, busy. Such a place. Beyond the dock gates, in the great city itself, were beautiful wooden houses: white-planked, red-roofed and with picket fences. Some had columns at the portals, like houses in Welkin. Others were built in the classic style of a Slattland dwelling. Clearly there were many immigrants in this wide, soaring, rushing land.

The vast majority were indigenous though. One of them, a mammal about the size of a housecat with grey-blackish fur, black eyes, black ears and a pointed nose, confronted Spindrick. The creature wore a tall, black stovepipe hat which he doffed in a polite manner.

'Can I help you, sir? Are you looking for work here in this glorious land of ours?'

'Not work, no,' said Spindrick with a little shudder. 'You may be able to help though. I'm looking for a gunsmith.'

'Particular, or any?'

'Oh, any gunsmith will do. By the way, *what* are you?'

The creature puffed out its chest beneath its waistcoat. 'I? I, sir, am an opossum, and proud of it. We are the top creatures around here, just as you stoats are back in your old country.' He showed Spindrick a mouthful of formidable-looking teeth, but the gesture was one of friendliness, rather than hostility.

'I'm not a stoat,' replied Spindrick, a remark the opossum gave no indication of hearing.

'If you will allow me, sir, I shall lead you to the workshops of our city's most famous gunsmith, Jal Samuel Bolt. Jal Bolt has invented the seven-shooter, sir, a most prestigious pawgun which will fire seven bullets without reloading. It has a cylindrical magazine which revolves, thus placing the next bullet in line with the breech. It has revolutionized the art of duelling. Two very short-sighted mammals may now stand three metres apart and happily blast away at each other until one eventually falls. No more of your prissy single-shot pistols, both myopic mammals missing their target, then coffee–' his voice was now loaded with contempt – 'for two afterwards.'

'Why seven?'

'Seven what, sir?'

'Seven shots.'

The opossum showed his teeth again. 'Why, surely, sir, that must be obvious to a stoat of your intelligence. One for every day of the week. What if you are of good eyesight? A hawk amongst mammals. What then if you had seven opponents to fight? Sunday, Monday, Tuesday, Wednesday, Thursday, Friday, Saturday. Not an unusual occurrence out West, where mammals take offence at the slightest little thing. Jal Bolt's revolver will allow you to kill all seven without reloading. Down south even the humans have taken this weapon to their hearts, though they have modified it somewhat.'

By this time Spindrick had his suitcase in his paw and was walking alongside the tall opossum, who led him through the dock gates into the vast sprawling city.

'Modified it?'

'Yes, they made it the *six*-shooter. They don't fight on Sundays for some strange reason.'

'Oh.' All this sounded very promising to Spindrick who, though horrified at the thought of mammals going round challenging each other to duels all the time, was here in this land to find a devastating weapon whose introduction to

Welkin would ensure revolution and an eventual decline into the beloved chaos he wanted.

'These incessant duels – haven't they resulted in chaos?' he asked the opossum, whose name he still did not know. 'I mean, mammals fighting all the time must mean little work is done.'

'Oh, it only takes ten minutes to shoot someone,' replied the opossum, sticking a thin black cigar into his mouth and lighting the end. 'You can do it during coffee break. To be quite honest, sir, duels are not performed so much this side of the continent any more. They have gone a little out of fashion. The practice, the art, has moved West with the gradual colonization of the interior and the Specific Coast by stoats. "Go West, young mustelids," said one Horface Grinder, and they took him at his word.'

'So that's where most of the duelling is done now?'

'They don't call it *duelling*. That's too fancy a word for those roughs in the West. They call them shoot-outs or gunfights. You mentioned the need to keep these gunfights out of working hours. Well, sir, that's just what they do in the West. Most duels are carried out at sundown, in the main street of the town, for everyone's benefit. You can see one any evening of the week, from your own porch, while partaking of a local cactus dew. But for those who are impatient to see their adversary lying dead in the dust, high noon is an option, it being lunch time. Two such noonday gunfights have taken place recently, one at a corral the name of which escapes me, but I seem to recall it began with O; the other in a town where the sheriff had to fight four opponents and killed them all on the stroke of twelve, just as lunch was starting.'

'Amazing.'

'This is an amazing country, sir, even though I say so myself. Big, expansive, and growing more prosperous by the year. I am a native, sir, but many of your kind have come here and been swallowed up by the vast outdoors, and no mistake. Opossums, skunks and – out West – the gophers have been here since time began. We get on fine with the stoats who come over from your old country, and those lemming creatures.'

He lowered his voice. 'Now, with the humans it has been a different history, sir. Recently they have not been at peace with each other, the settlers and the natives. They have great differences which they are at pains to resolve, but find themselves at war with one another. A sad state.' He shook his head. 'A very sad state of affairs. Ah, here were are . . .' Spindrick looked up to the sign of a gunsmith above his head.

The opossum doffed his hat again, before saying, 'Glad to be of service, sir. My card. Colonel W. W. Trappit. Should you require further assistance, you will find me at the offices of my newssheet, the *New Lankaster Chimes*. Do not hesitate. Pleased to make your acquaintance and hope we meet again.' With that the colonel strolled off down the street in a cloud of cigar smoke, nodding to gentlejacks and doffing his hat to gentlejills, murmuring, 'How do, sir? Good morning, ma'am. What a pleasant day it is, and that's a certain fact in the almanac . . .'

'What a nice jack,' said Spindrick to himself. 'Now, if that had been Muggidrear docks, and I a visitor to Welkin, I should have stood until doomsday before someone came and helped me.'

He entered the gun shop and found, this time, a hairy monochrome creature standing in front of racks filled with firearms.

'Good day to you, sir. Can I assist you?'

Such politeness. So refreshing after the rudeness of Muggidrear.

'Most certainly, er, sir. Are you Jal Samuel Bolt?'

'I am that most humble skunk.'

'You're a skunk? How interesting,' Spindrick said, genuinely excited at meeting creatures he had never seen before. 'You're the ones that cause all the stink!'

The skunk looked a little offended. 'Only in times of grave danger, sir. And you are a stoat by your pelt. Welcome to New Lankaster, sir, but please be a little more careful with your words while in our country. There are mammals here far more sensitive than I am. If a prairie dog even gets the hint of an insult, he'll gun you down soon as look at you.'

'Forgive me, I meant nothing by it. To business. I understand you have invented a marvellous seven-shooting pistol. You're not also the inventor of a steam machine-gun, I suppose? I'm looking for the mammal who owns the patent to that particular weapon.'

'Not I, sir, not I. I'm sorry to disappoint you. Are you a stoat from Welkin by any chance? Another of your kind recently got off the boat – a one Wm. Jott, an inventor like myself. An interesting talker.'

'I'm from Welkin, but I'm not a stoat, I'm a weasel.'

The skunk appeared not to have heard this and Spindrick did not pursue the point. He continued, 'So, Jal Jott has emigrated.'

'Immigrated, from our point of view.'

'Just so. But he's here. Why?'

'It seems, sir, he was disaffected with one of your city mayors, who seemed to favour the inventor of clockwork machines, one Thos. Tempus Fugit.'

'I've come halfway across the world to find someone who was reared in my own back yard. But I'm told you New World mammals don't appreciate irony. You don't happen to know where he's staying, do you? I should like to get hold of him straight away. I'm anxious to catch the next boat home.'

Samuel Bolt frowned. 'You don't like our fair city?'

'It's adorable, absolutely, but I'm eager to start my work. Once I get things going in Welkin, I'll be back here like a shot.' Spindrick looked out of the window at the amazing city, where buildings seemed to be going up by the minute. In Muggidrear a new building only went up half a century after an old one fell down. Here they were chucking them together in an hour or two. And an hour after the last nail had been hammered home a business would be thriving in that self-same building. It seemed they could not construct the city fast enough. Mammals with fat wallets were queuing on street corners to open new premises. The whole thing smacked of commercialism and money-making, two of the things Spindrick hated the most. 'Yes, sir,' he murmured, 'I can't wait to return and get something moving here too: you do have *poor* mammals, I suppose, as well as rich?'

'They get off the boat every day.'

'Excellent. A little chaos would not go amiss in this city, I can see.'

The skunk looked startled. 'Eh?'

'Oh, nothing. Now, what about Wm. Jott?'

Jal Bolt looked a little smug. 'That might be a problem, Jal Stoat. Wm. Jott left just ten minutes before you entered my shop, for Kaliphornya, on the West Coast. He called in here to consult me on one or two things to do with my art and craft, that of gun-making, and then set out for the West, where they love guns more than they love life.' The skunk stared at Spindrick for a second from under his monochrome eyebrows and added, 'And if that isn't a brilliant example of irony I don't know what is.'

Spindrick let out a cry of anguish. 'He must have been on my boat!'

'If you have just disembarked, yes, that would be the case.'

'How was he getting to this Kaliphornya?'

'By train, of course. The first cross-continental railroad has just opened up communications between the East and West coasts. The final rail was laid just yesterday.' The skunk consulted a pocket watch. 'If I'm not mistaken his locomotive left just two minutes ago.' He looked up again. 'Two days ago, he would have gone by wagon train, across the Midwest, taking six months or more to reach the New Mountains which divide fruitful Kaliphornya from the dusty interior of this vast country. You would have caught up with him on a fast horse within the hour. Now you will need the speed of a comet to catch him. You are a most unfortunate stoat.'

Spindrick let out a second cry of anguish.

Chapter Eleven

Spindrick caught the next train west. It was a long, long journey across mountains, rivers, but most of all plains. Spindrick thought the plains had been aptly named. They were plain. There was not a lot to do while crossing these grassy, sometimes dusty flatlands except lean out of the window and blow raspberries at the wagon trains, moving at snail's pace. It was a big country, though. No doubt about it.

'You want to come and shoot mozzies from the roof?'

The offer to pick mosquitoes out of the air had come from another weasel, one who had been in the New World for some time. He owned two silver seven-shooters with mother-of-pearl handles which he could draw from their holsters before you could spit in a sparrow's eye. The guard had told Spindrick that the weasel was a dead-shot and could take the feeler off a cockroach at twenty paces. He called himself Welkin Bob and said he was a lord and had estates back in the old country. Spindrick wondered what he was doing in the New World, playing with guns, if he was rich and titled as he made out.

'No thank you.'

'Suit yourself.'

Spindrick was left to himself again. He sighed. He had to admit that train journeys, wherever you were, tended to become boring after the third day. Some excitement had entered the carriages on the second day, when it was held up by robbers, but Welkin Bob had shot them all within the space of five minutes, so that was short lived. Then some renegade gophers had tried to derail the train on a bridge, but a cunning device like a pointed shovel fixed to the front of the locomotive had scooped away the barrier and cast it down into a raging torrent below.

Spindrick met another passenger on the train who was to change the whole vision of his scheme to lead the world into anarchy. It was a civet cat who had travelled from Far Kathay, by the name of Jinrummee. Jinrummee had once worked for the Great Pangolin as a palace guard, but had been sacked by the emperor, who thought he had something to do with the theft of the jade shoes of the Green Idol of Ommm. The

Great Pangolin had promised to sack one guard a month until the shoes were found.

'You could not do better than start your world revolution in Far Kathay,' suggested the bitter civet cat. 'There are vast millions of creatures just waiting to rise up against the Great Pangolin. He is a despot, of course, and a tyrant. Give your repeating guns to the population of Far Kathay and sit back and watch the explosion!'

'What a grand idea,' replied Spindrick. 'Monty's on his way there at the moment. It would be nice to catch him in situ, as it were. Let's see whether that famous cousin of mine can deal with a massive civil war. Thanks for that. Now, will you have some more custard tart, Jinrummee? My treat, of course.'

That night, however, they pulled into a one-mouse town called Applelane and the guard announced that they would be staying over until the next day. 'I suggest, sir,' he said to Spindrick, 'that you get yourself a bed in the local hotel and stay in your room. This is a rough town. Three days ago our sheriff and his deputy, a pair of badgers, were shot dead in the street.'

Spindrick took his battered suitcase and walked down the dusty main street to the only hotel in town. This also happened to serve as a saloon, a trading post, a schoolroom and the town's seat of justice. The ground floor was crowded, but there were several rooms available on the first floor (which the local gophers called the second floor for some reason), and it was to one of these that Spindrick was shown. He sat in a room overlooking some tennis courts trying to concentrate on a map.

Some time after six the first ruckus developed below, but Spindrick was too immersed in his maps to investigate.

When he finally emerged and went downstairs for a meal, everyone kept saying to him, 'Howdy, stranger,' or 'What are you doing in this one-mouse town?' At eight o'clock, just after the soup, there was a tremendous pawfight in which mirrors were smashed and bottles broken. It seemed to happen for no reason whatsoever. Gophers, skunks, prairie dogs, weasels, stoats and opossums were all in on it, breaking furniture, windows, even the door.

'No work for me out here,' muttered the weasel anarchist with a sigh. 'This place is already in chaos.'

On further investigation the fight appeared to have been started by a big gopher called Duke from the state of Plexus. He explained, 'I have a creed I live by. I won't be spoke down to, I won't be laid a paw on, and I won't be poked in the eye with a sharp stick. I don't do these things to others and I don't expect 'em to do it to me.'

This all seemed very reasonable to Spindrick, though he guessed it must have been one of the first two which had upset the gopher, who already wore a black patch over one eye.

At midnight there was a more serious occurrence.

Spindrick had heard a conversation coming up from the street, which went something like this:

'Stop! I am the sheriff and this is my deputy.'

'If you're the law, where are your badgers?'

'Badgers? We don't need no stinkin' badgers!'

'Well, this town don't need no damn marmots.'

And then a gunfight started.

Someone shot the new sheriff – a prairie dog called Chuck Woody who had apparently cleaned up Deadwood – and the deputy too. 'Someone called the sheriff a "marmot" and that was that,' explained a spectator. 'The shootin' started. O' course, all prairie dogs *is* marmots, but they don't know it. They's so dumb you call 'em by their proper name an' they take it for an insult.'

Both bodies were carried away on the door, which had been ripped off its hinges in the earlier pawfighting, up to a hill which had something to do with cobblers. Who had drilled the local constable and his assistant was not evident, though some believed it to be a gopher called Liberty Bodice.

'This place is *really* wild,' Spindrick said to the owner of the hotel, a skunk with a dubious taste in waistcoats. 'I could live here, if I hadn't things to do at the far ends of the earth, in Kathay.'

'Don't get no wilder,' answered the skunk. ''Cept on Saturday nights – this bein' only Wednesday, o' course.'

'What happens on Saturdays?'

'This is a mousejack town. Mousejacks come in

from the ranches every Saturday. Shoot the place up a mite. Bullets flying everywhere. Games of hollyhockers in every room. Cheats getting shot to pieces. Murderers getting lynched. Marshals going without their suppers. Terrible place on a Saturday. Sunday, though, peaceful as the grave.'

'That would seem to follow, after so much violence and bloodshed.'

The skunk's eyes narrowed. 'You criticizin' our way of life, stranger?'

'Who, me?' cried Spindrick. 'Wouldn't dream of it.'

Early the next morning the hoot of the locomotive whistle woke Spindrick. He packed his case, breakfasted on something called grits, which certainly had grit in it, and then walked along the main street back to the wooden train station. On the way he clicked his teeth, thinking of the experiences he had to tell when he returned home.

In the West they bred a cross between a vole and a mouse: a pack animal they called a vule. A mousejack rode into town on one of these stolid, stubborn-looking creatures. He was wearing a blanket with a hole for his head. When Spindrick glanced at him riding by, the rider asked with narrowed eyes if Spindrick was making fun of his vule. He seemed disappointed when Spindrick said he wouldn't dream of it.

One last stop at the barber's, where he got his whiskers trimmed and his tail-end cropped, and he was on the train again, heading for Kaliphornya.

Spindrick arrived to find the place in an uproar. Someone had apparently discovered gold in them there hills. For at least two seconds yellow-dust fever swept through him. Then he remembered who and what he was: Spindrick Sylver, anarchist, about to start a civil war in Far Kathay. Let others go chasing after nuggets; he was here to find one Billy Jott.

'Gone to San Ferryanne,' said someone. 'Left on the boat from Bo Jangeles.'

Spindrick followed suit, sailing to San Ferryanne. The port had a large harbour. Behind the harbour was a town of wooden shacks and one or two more substantial public buildings. The place was full of polecats carrying harpoons. San Ferryanne was a fishing town. Here they hunted the dangerous barracuda. One captain, a polecat with a wooden leg and a missing ear, was gathering a crew to go out in search of one particular barracuda. He explained that his prey was an albino fish they called Dhobi Mick. This pink-eyed, white-scaled creature, once the proud owner of the world's only undersea laundry, had robbed Captain Apeg of his rear left leg, bitten off his ear and generally left him a scarred and broken polecat.

'I will have my revenge,' said Apeg savagely to anyone who looked in the least bit interested. 'I will send him to Tom Jones's locker. Are you with me or not, stoat? There's a silver coin in it for you.'

'Call me a coward,' replied Spindrick, 'but I've got better things to do than go chasing predatory fish all over the seven seas. By the way, you *can* also call me a weasel, which is what I am.'

Spindrick wandered the town in search of Wm. Jott.

'Gone up north,' said a landjill, who told him that Jott had stayed at her establishment for one night. 'Gone to bear country, ay. Gone to the land of maple dew and beaver, ay.'

'Keep missing him,' muttered Spindrick fiercely. 'If I didn't know better I'd say he was doing this on purpose.'

A weary Spindrick stayed the night at the same lodgings. With his eyes almost closing he went down to a supper of clams, lobster and steaming crabs with the rest of the lodgers. They were a crusty lot of tars, who had more salt in their fur than nits. There he met Quikquik, a very tall polecat with strange designs cut into his fur. Quikquik came from a tribe of hunters in the far north, on the edge of the polar regions.

'I just finish voyage with Cap'n Apeg,' said Quikquik. 'I take you to land of beaver tomorrow.'

'Thank you,' replied Spindrick, trying to get some crab meat out of a claw. 'I would appreciate some company. Look, can you do this? I can't seem to hook it out. It's driving me crazy.'

'I just finish terrible voyage,' said Quikquik,

managing to scrape a few more strands of crab meat from Spindrick's claw. 'Just terrible. Storms, bad fish, wild seas. We lose one sailor.'

'Just one?' murmured an uninterested Spindrick.

'They call him Fishpail. He fall overboard when Cap'n Apeg startle him with crying out, "There she streaks." '

'But everyone else made it back safely?'

'No, many die.'

'And you failed to catch the rogue barracuda?'

'This is true.'

'Not much of a story, is it? Now if the ship went down with all paws and the white barracuda ate all those who didn't drown, leaving just one survivor to tell the tale – but of course, it didn't. And if you'll take my advice, always begin an anecdote like that with the words: *It was a dark and stormy night. Suddenly . . .* Then continue as you will. Ah, well, you can't win 'em all. Wake me at seven, will you, with a cup of tea?'

With that Spindrick's chin dropped onto his bib and he went into a deep sleep. The rest of the lodgers continued their conversation around him, sometimes nudging him for an answer to a question, but Spindrick remained asleep throughout the meal, and on through the night.

He awoke next morning to find he had been robbed of all his clothes, except for his shoes – and those were only on his feet because he had tied his laces too tight and the thief had been no good at undoing knots.

'Never mind,' said Quikquik. 'We find you sailor's clothes in wardrobe. Plenty there from harpooners who not come back after voyage. Mostly drowned. Some fall from rigging and killed when they hit deck. Vicious barracuda take many lives.' He looked Spindrick up and down. 'Mostly polecat, though, and martens. Bigger than you. Still, we roll up trouser leg and woolly jumper sleeve to make fit.'

'I can't understand it. How did they get my clothes off without me waking?'

'You very deep sleep. Deeper than the Marianas Trench. Nobody wake you last night, that's sure.'

'I shall be glad to leave this town. It reeks of nothing but fish. I've never known anywhere so fishy. What's for breakfast? Clam chowder? You can keep it. I'll get a bun and a coffee somewhere on the way. Come on, Quikquik! For someone with your name you're very slow. I need to catch up with a stoat by the name of Wm. Jott. You know him? No. Well, never mind, we'll find him somehow. Come on, get your socks on, and you'd better tie up those laces or you'll trip over them in the street . . .'

CHAPTER TWELVE

The five weary travellers came to a temple on one of the high mountain passes. It was a low, rambling wooden building, built on a jagged ledge, which followed the contours of the bare rock face. Seen from afar the structure appeared quite extraordinary. The region was known as Mgrz in the Ksdtzynk range, where no-one believed in using vowels. Vowels were the letters of the unspeakable and vile Aeiou, an evil god, while consonants belonged to the good and all wise Bcdfghjklmnpqrstvwxyz. Followers of the latter never sullied their mouths with the Five Unmentionable Letters of the alphabet. Only bad mammals, lurking in dark holes in the ground ready to pounce on unwary travellers, owed any allegiance to Aeiou.

This peculiarity made it very difficult for mammals passing through the region. Fortunately for the weasels Calabash Brown could just about get his tongue around the language, though not without suffering mouth cramp. The priests who lived in this temple that dangled from forbidding crags listened to Calabash's efforts at their language with infinite patience in their eyes, while drumming their claws on the woodwork.

When the jerboa had finished his tangled conversation it appeared that it would be fine for the five of them to bed down for the night.

'It's cold in here,' whispered Maudlin. 'Even with all those candles lit.'

There were indeed many candles. The place was a forest of small flickering flames. Incense burned in every room, mingling with the scent of pine and mahogany. Every so often a gong or cymbal sounded from somewhere in the many-roomed temple.

'Colder out there,' murmured Scruff, pointing to an open window, 'on the mountainside.'

This was true. Flurries of snow were falling, finding cracks in the rock. Every so often there was a dull thud on the temple roof as a high-flying sparrow's wings iced over and it dropped from the sky. It was a lonely and remote place, though shelter it was and they were glad of it.

'Don't the priests find this place bleak?' asked Monty of Calabash.

'Bleak isn't a word they use,' replied the jerboa. 'Bleak has two vowels in it.'

'I know that, but they must have an equivalent word. Something that means stark or brumal. Something that describes cold desolation?'

'They would not know it. Born here, die here. In between there is a sort of living, though they have only bean curds to eat. Tofu fried in bat's lard, which they scrape from the rafters. Not what mammals call living, really. They pray to mountain gods, sew their robes, clean under their claws and meditate. The last they are good at – meditating.'

'What a life!' cried Scruff. 'Why bother?'

Bryony said, 'Don't judge the lifestyle of others by your own, Scruff. To them it may be very exciting – all that . . . bean curd and meditation.' She did not sound too convinced herself.

All night the wind howled through the hollows of the mountains and round the eaves of the temple. It was cold lying on the bare floorboards and though he had become used to hardship, finally Maudlin could stand it no longer and got up. The others were asleep. Scruff was snoring loudly. In various corners, as he walked about, Maudlin discovered dreaming priests.

He went out onto the balcony. There he looked over, down into the dizzying depths. A hollow blackness of several thousand metres lay below. Above him the stars were swimming silently through the night. He felt suspended from a thread, just as a mountain spider must feel, over a pit of nothingness. Giddiness overcame him. He tried to step back from the rail, but trod on a wet patch in the poor light. He fell forwards, slipping between the struts of the balustrade and out into the darkness. The terrified yell that escaped from his mouth was cut short as he hit a lower ledge, and lodged there.

'Oh, gawd!' he cried, when he had recovered his wits. 'Scruff? Monty? Bryony?'

But he knew in his heart of hearts that he could not be heard. The wind was howling too loudly, carrying away words with full-blown vowels to keep them buoyant – each O as round as a fat, gas-filled balloon; a large U like a boat, floating on the back of the night. He realized at once that he might anger the good god who lived in these craggy regions, but he could hardly yell out 'Scrff' or 'Mnty' or 'Bryny'.

No-one came. In the end, assisted by the courage that comes with sheer terror, he managed to gain a better grip and scramble into the branches of a small gnarled tree that was clinging to the ledge. There amongst its foliage he drew breath, gulping down the night humours in full draughts. How he bit his knuckles in anguish now, and cursed himself for being so stupid as to walk on a balcony in a strange temple. Oaths he uttered which had more vowels hanging like overripe fruit from the branches of spiky consonants, until finally these awful profanities aroused the interest of the terrible, evil god who skulked in the foul fissures of the rocks.

Aeiou appeared before Maudlin in his ugliest form, that of a frog with bat's wings and the tail of a scorpion.

'Ah, a weasel caught in the throat of the night,' said Aeiou, hovering before the terrified Maudlin. 'What would you give to be released from your predicament and returned to your bed?'

'Anything. Anything.'

'Your soul?' cried the evil god. 'Would you trade your soul?'

Now Maudlin was – well, some would say he was – a coward. However, there was also a great deal of the shrewd bargainer in his character. This trait now rose to the fore, overshadowing his fear of falling. He did not like to be cheated in any way. To be taken advantage of galled him. He had heard stories of mammals who had sold their souls and they had got a lot more for it than their lives. Usually the seller of a soul was rewarded with untold riches, or great power – thrones, cities, dynasties, kingdoms. A soul was a pretty precious commodity, when it came down to it.

'And what else?' he asked.

Aeiou's jaw fell as he hovered there like a humming bird. 'What else *what*?'

'What else do I get for my soul? I'd like a kingdom or something. Surely you've got more to offer than just my safety.'

'Well, how about the *whole world*?'

'That's more like it.'

'I was being sarcastic,' growled Aeiou. 'It may have escaped your notice but there's not a lot to be had in this region. I'm only a regional god, after all. Nobody else prays to me in any other parts of the world.' He paused before muttering, 'And precious few here, actually. What I'm trying to say is, the mountain crags is *it*. There's not a lot else that comes within my scope.'

Maudlin was beginning to feel peeved, despite his anxiety to get off the ledge and back into the temple. 'You don't have much bargaining power, do you?'

Aeiou became truculent. 'Are you trying to dent my self esteem? I'll have you know there was a time when I ruled half the world's nefarious creatures. Then it was taken away from me – by Time, by other gods with larger portfolios. I don't have to prove anything, you know. I've done it.'

'Well, I had the feeling that souls were quite valuable. I once saw a play called *Fowst* in which Mefistofeles—'

'Oh, not *him* again,' snarled Aeiou. 'Pleeeease. If you're going to tell me something, please make it original. If I hear that name just once more, I'll spit. Look, I've made the offer. Your soul for your safety. I can't say fairer than that. Take it or leave it.'

The sun was now coming up behind the mountains, flooding the crags with light. The flying frog with the scorpion's tail was beginning to look a little ridiculous in the dawn's rays. Hope mingled with Maudlin's absolute determination not to be conned into giving up his soul cheaply. A certain courage entered his bones.

'I think I'll just stick here until my friends get me down.'

'Well, good luck,' hissed Aeiou, not meaning it. 'I'll just wait down there until you fall, then I'll get it for nothing.'

He flew off, spiralling downwards, forcing Maudlin to look below at the horrible gap between his flimsy branch and the jagged rocks of the far distant valley floor.

For the next hour or so Maudlin yelled. He grew hoarse with calling. It was no use. No-one could hear him. Birds, flying by, were beginning to taunt him by mimicking his cries. 'Scruff,' shrieked a passing buzzard in delight. 'Scruff, Scruff, Scruff.'

'You shut up, you,' yelled Maudlin.

'Careful,' said the buzzard, wheeling round. 'I'm bigger than you, with bigger beak and bigger claw. I usually eat voles, but don't tempt me.'

Maudlin didn't tempt him. Eventually he began to climb up the mountain face. Here and there were small cracks he could get his claws into and little tufts of grass he could cling to for a rest. Slowly, gradually, he inched his way up. He had to keep reminding himself not to look down. A claw in a crevice here, a grip on a rock with his fangs there, his tail outstretched for balance. Little by little he crawled his way up until at last he could touch the edge of the balcony. But this formed a projecting ceiling above his head and he had to hang onto one of the planks, dangling there, his heart racing, as he went paw over paw to reach the point where he could heave himself up and over, to safety.

'Done it!' he yelled throatily in triumph. 'I've done it.'

He wept hot tears of victory. There were bits of twig and leaf stuck to his fur with tree sap, gathered from the little shrub that had saved his life. He began picking them off, then gave up when the job became too tedious. Finally he went looking for his friends, who must – he thought – be frantic by now, searching every nook and cranny of the temple for him. How they would greet him with joyous relief, Scruff falling on his neck and thanking the gods – the good ones – that his friend was safe and well. And Bryony seeking to find out if he was hurt in any way. And Monty being stern with him, telling him never to frighten them like that again.

He found them looking at a chanting stone.

'See here, look at these symbols,' Monty was saying. 'How elegant they are. Carved with sacred tools. Such craftsmanship, such art.'

'Hello,' said Maudlin.

Scruff turned. 'Oh, hello, Maud. Hey, you seen this? Brilliant, ain't it? You couldn't see nothin' like this, back in Muggidrear.'

Maudlin was speechless. They hadn't even missed him. He could be lying at the bottom of a chasm, every bone in his body broken, for all they cared. He was about to have a tantrum, remonstrate with them, call them heartless, fickle weasels, when something deep inside stopped him.

He had a secret now. A very honourable secret. It was something to cherish, not to throw away in a flash of temper. If he yelled at the others, made them feel bad about not missing him, this strong feeling of accomplishment – the refusal to sell his soul cheaply, the arduous climb back to safety – would be diluted. Of course, he knew he should not contemplate selling his soul *at all*, but perhaps he never would have done? Even if he had been offered the world, he doubted whether he would have accepted the trade. That was something that should remain unspoiled.

Thus he kept his adventure to himself. It felt good. It felt very, very good. Especially when Scruff put his forelimb around his shoulder and said, 'Hey, Maud, ain't it a beautiful day? Have you seen outside? Sun shining, everythin'. Come on, buddy, let's get some breakfast and then get out there. I can't wait to get back on the trail.'

'Maudlin,' said Bryony, walking behind him as they went in to breakfast, 'what a mess you're in. How did you get all these bits of vegetation in your fur?' She began picking them out for him but soon, like Maudlin himself, gave up.

'Ah, as to that . . .' cried Maudlin, then

remembered it was an honourable secret. 'Oh, somewhere, I don't know. Been for a walk in the forest.'

'What forest, you old fibber?' cried Scruff. 'There ain't no forest, less it's straight down a mile below in the valley. He's a card, ain't 'e, this one.' And they all clicked their teeth in glee.

CHAPTER THIRTEEN

Although the five travellers were not attacked by
bandits when descending the other side of the
mountain range, they did run into a grave
problem. Bryony fell sick. In fact she was so ill
she lost consciousness and since she was the vet
amongst them they were at a loss to know how to
treat her. Calabash Brown knew a little about
herbs, but it was all he could do to stop her
temperature soaring.

'At the foot of these hills is a low, wide valley,'
he said. 'Here there is lush vegetables—'

'Vegetation,' corrected Monty automatically.

'Yes, vegetation. A village, almost a town,
has blossom there. The mammals are simple,
but they have an apothecary in their number.

122

We must seek his advice.'

'Not a veterinary surgeon?'

'No, someone who has studied the *old* ways.'

Monty knew it was the best they were going to get. 'We'll make a litter for her,' he said, 'and take turns to carry her.'

They cut poles from trees and used two of their coats, slipping the poles through the sleeve holes. Gently Bryony was lifted and placed in the litter. Scruff and Monty carried her first. It was an arduous task – not that Bryony was especially heavy, but the path was rugged and awkward, and it took all their efforts to keep their feet.

Calabash and Maudlin took over when the other two grew so tired there was a danger of tipping Bryony out.

For two days and two nights they took turns to carry the sick weasel, until at last they sighted the valley. Late in the day they entered the village, which appeared to be populated by a furry creature, a rodent of some kind. The locals wore vole-skin coats, dyed red and yellow, and thick hats which fitted close to their heads. The head-mammal of the village met them at the entrance. There was a discussion between her and Calabash and eventually the jerboa said, 'She says we can stay, but we must keep the sick one separate. They want no plague in the village.'

'Plague? Bryony hasn't got the plague,' Monty said.

'These are deeply superstitious mammals, Monty. Whenever anyone gets sick they always

123

suspect it might be the plague. You must not blame them. Many times they have been devastated by unnamed sicknesses sweeping through the valley. Outsiders bring in germs that have not been known here. I think it is good they let us stay, Monty. I think we should be grateful for little tiny mercies.'

'You're right,' Monty replied, sighing. 'I'm too quick to judge these days. Will the apothecary see her?'

'Oh yes, it is his job. He might make us pay him many gold coins, but he will see her, certainly.'

Monty had luckily had the foresight to bring with him a money belt full of gold coins. It was heavy but he had guessed there would be times like this when international coinage would be needed. Gold was acceptable anywhere, even in the meanest and remotest of villages. Everyone took gold, from a peasant to an emperor.

They were shown to a hut on the outskirts of the village, just beyond fields full of wild flowers where the vole herds grazed. It was simply furnished with wooden tables, chairs and bunk beds. They put Bryony on one of the lower bunks, forced some water down her, and then waited for the apothecary to arrive. In the meantime they washed and prepared a meal. Maudlin went out and picked a waxy but beautiful cream blossom from a magnolia tree and put it on Bryony's pillow, where she would see it when she regained consciousness.

Monty now looked the part of the explorer and traveller, as did all the weasels from the city of Muggidrear. His shift was dusty and caked with mud; he wore a ragged turban on his head to protect it from the sun and rain; his backpack looked battered, worn and frayed. Around his hind legs he had wound more rags, to prevent his ankles being scraped on rocks or prickled by thorny plants.

If Monty had walked into his club, Jumping Jacks, at that moment it was doubtful he would have been recognized. Newspapers would crackle as their readers lowered them. Emerging heads would turn and faces would register disapproval. Mutterings would be heard in the corridors of power and in the reading rooms of the club's intellectuals.

Monty recalled the stoat whom meerkats called Al Offence. He was actually a Welkin army officer, Lieutenant Lowfence, who had been sent by the queen to the Khalifrat Desert. Under the queen's orders he had been helping the meerkats fight a merciless army of mixed predators. Yet when he returned to Welkin he made the mistake of wearing his desert clobber to the club. Gentlestoats had turned their backs and called him names. They said he had 'gone meerkat' and scorned him. Eventually Lowfence left the army and returned to the desert, never to be seen or heard of again. Such was the narrow-mindedness and bigotry of some city gentlemammals.

'When's this mammal coming?' complained

Monty, as Bryony tossed and turned, soaked in sweat. 'Doesn't he know how serious it is?'

It was at that moment that a local stoat appeared on the porch. He was dressed in a long white robe with designs round the neck and hem. In his paws he carried a case full of potion bottles. The bottles were all of different colours, some ridged, which meant they were poison. The tall, willowy creature entered the hut and immediately said, 'Weasels!'

'Yes,' replied Monty. 'Weasels.'

The apothecary shrugged. 'So be it. I take it you are honest weasels? Where are you bound?'

'For Far Kathay,' replied Calabash. 'I am their guide.'

'A long and difficult journey. So, where is the patient? You must understand that I am not a vet. I merely know about potions and powders. If I recognize the symptoms I shall treat her. If not, we must discuss what it is best to do next. The village is worried about the mange, mammal flu or ringworm or any of those flash-flood diseases that sweep through a valley. If your friend's condition is highly infectious, then we must kill her and burn her body, before hundreds of others catch the disease.'

Scruff stepped forward crying, 'You're not killin' anyone! I don't care who you are or what yer name is. No-one lays a claw on our Bryony.'

'Quiet, Scruff,' said Monty gently. 'No-one will harm Bryony.'

'Oh, but they will,' replied Calabash. 'You do

not understand. If they decide an epidemic will rage, then they will burn down this hut with great vigour and speed.'

'This is true,' confirmed the apothecary. 'I myself will be exempt from the fire, due to my immunity to disease. Never have I caught any of my patients' illnesses, not one day of sickness in my whole life. This is because I ate charcoal as a small kitten, in lumps, crunching them to bits then swallowing.'

Monty snorted. 'I may not know much about vet practice, but I do know that charcoal dust protects no-one from disease.'

'Ah,' nodded the apothecary. 'You know, but the villagers do not. They believe it implicitly.'

'I see what you mean.'

The apothecary, who was not even a mere physician, went to the bedside of the sick patient. He used his claw to open her eyelids and look inside. He used a spatula to open her mouth and do likewise. He felt her toes and noted the dryness of her fur. Finally, after inspecting her for about ten minutes, he stood up and shook his head.

'We shall have to consign her to the flames – she is incurable.' He began to open a folded square of paper which appeared to contain some red powder. 'I shall give her this. Her death will be painless. It will take but a moment for her to slip peacefully away.'

'You quack!' yelled Maudlin. 'We'll singe your hide first, you can be sure of that. You give her that deadly poison and I'll make you eat and drink everything you're carrying.'

The apothecary carefully refolded the piece of paper and put it in his carrying case. He began to move towards the door, but Monty now stood in his way, a pistol in his paw. Scruff had moved to the window and blocked it with his formidable presence. Maudlin had picked up a log of wood and was holding it like a club. Calabash Brown was simply standing there, looking nervous and worried. Monty spoke to the apothecary.

'What have you got in those bottles and boxes? Out with it, stoat. Something to bring down a fever?'

'You would not shoot me.'

'I would certainly shoot you. That's my life-long friend lying there, needing help, and I aim to make sure she gets it. If you don't attempt to treat her, you will regret it, I assure you. Now, do as I say. Give her something to relieve the fever. Also something which will help keep down any liquids we give her. Something to control her bowels too, which—'

'Yes, yes, you don't have to paint pictures,' grumbled the apothecary. 'I am aware of her problems in that area.'

'Do it then. You've got all those kinds of potions, I'm sure. They're common enough.' He stared at Bryony. 'If we can't cure the disease, we'll try to control the symptoms. It's not the best method of treating a sick mammal, but in the absence of deeper knowledge ... Hurry up, stoat, my paw is shaking and my claw tightens on the trigger. I might get a spasm if you don't hurry and we shall all be upset – you because you have a bullet in your brain and we because we have no apothecary to help us save our friend.'

The apothecary began to administer potions and powders to his patient. At one point he took some drops from a blue bottle with ridges on it and Scruff yelled, 'He's givin' her poison!'

The apothecary gave Scruff a withering look of contempt. 'Yes, it's a poison if taken in large quantities, but not in small doses. Two drops of this will excite the body's nerves and bring them to a state of high expectancy. It will strengthen her general condition and regulate her heartbeat while the other potions do their work. Do you know nothing of the science? Then be quiet and allow a qualified apothecary to do his job.'

Scruff glanced at Monty, who nodded and indicated they should trust the stoat.

The apothecary plied his medicines for some time. Then he wrapped Bryony in a blanket and put a hard pillow under her head. After which he sat down and waited, as did the others, for something to happen. For three hours they all sat there, staring at the inert body of the jill weasel, until, sometime after the clock had struck eight, she began to twitch. First came the fluttering eyelids and the trembling mouth. Then more violent movement. She started to jerk spasmodically. Finally, she suddenly sat bolt upright (scaring the living daylights out of Maudlin) and stared around. The whites of her eyes were still yellow with illness. Her nostrils looked dry and crusted. Her normally pink mouth was pallid. Her breath smelled of old drains.

'Monty?' she said hoarsely. 'I'm sick.'

CHAPTER FOURTEEN

With Montegu Sylver and Princess Sybil out of
the way – not to mention Falshed, the chief
of police, and Spindrick Sylver – the mayor
expected to run riot. With no restraints on him he
planned to launch various schemes he had
thought up over the years.

One of these schemes was a height tax. He
intended to charge adult males a tax for being
'too small' for the Granite Arch at the beginning
of Moxy Street. Mayor Poynt had set a standard
of 200mm. Weasels, stoats and all other mustelids
would pay a penny for every millimetre they
measured under this height. Thus a jack weasel
198mm tall would pay two pence every time he
passed under the Granite Arch, which he would

have to do to enter Moxy Street, where all the shopping bargains were to be had.

'The effect,' said the proud mayor to his new crony, a weasel called Pontifract Pilote, who had suggested the scheme in the first place, 'is two-fold. Those weasels who are under the height will have to cough up plenty of pennies. Of course, this means that a lot of them will stay away, but that will allow stoats to snap up the best bargains from the stalls.'

Stoat jacks were, on average, 400mm tall, and therefore passed the mark on the upright pillars of the Granite Arch with a great many centi-metres to spare.

The mayor rubbed his paws together. 'My policemammals have already collected quite a substantial sum. You know, a lot of the market traders in Moxy Street are bent and crumpled weasels. Not enough milk when they were young. Lack of cal–cal—'

'Calcium?' suggested Pontifract Pilote.

'Yes, that's the word. Couldn't get my tongue round it. Anyway, it makes their bones grow bent, so they can't stand up straight. And the market traders have to reach their stalls in order to trade, don't they?' The mayor nodded at Pontifract. 'Easy money, my friend. Easy money.'

Pontifract Pilote was in fact from the other side of Welkin, and not from the city at all. He had grown up in a spiritual retreat, the son of a mill owner. Since coming to the city he had been, variously, a lawyer, a vet, a university lecturer, the owner of a newspaper and a floor cleaner in a museum. It was during his first week as a pelt comber in a fur salon that he met the mayor. Like most pelt combers he chattered while he worked, combing the knots from the mayor's ermine coat. The mayor had been impressed by the length and breadth of Pontifract's knowledge, and invited him to be his personal assistant.

The mayor's secretary, a timid jill weasel, crept into his office and announced that Lord Haukin was on his way up.

'Oh, dash it, I know what he's come for,' snapped the mayor, in a panic. 'Sylver probably asked Hannover to keep an eye on me while he was away. Blast and blast him.' A certain tremor had entered his voice. Hannover Haukin was a stoat Jeremy Poynt admired and wished to keep as an acquaintance. He hadn't got that many acquaintances. Hannover was a powerful mustelid in a quiet sort of way. He was chair-mammal on an awful lot of boards and was regarded by the business world as steadfast and true. Moreover, stoats all over the city looked to him for guidance in matters of manners and morals. 'What am I going to tell him?' whined the mayor.

'You will tell him,' said Pontifract, after a moment's consideration, 'that you're making this charge because small creatures are holding up to ridicule the exquisite space provided by the architect of the Granite Arch. That great stoat Mikelambulo deliberately created a beautiful sweep of air between the ground and the top of the arch, so that mammals could show it to its best advantage. The *way* mammals enhance the space under the arch is to walk through, their heads neither touching the top, but also not being so low down as to make the space look absurdly oversized. Those who do *not* show it in its best light deserve to be fined.'

The mayor looked at his elderly new friend in awe. 'Brilliant,' he breathed. 'I might have to ask you to repeat that in a minute.'

Lord Haukin had indeed come to ask what in thunder the mayor was playing at charging undersized mammals for the privilege of using the arch. On hearing the explanation he stamped his paw.

'Poppycock!' he said, his monocle flashing dangerously. 'Absolute drivel.'

'Yes, I was afraid you'd say that,' muttered the mayor, 'but this creature here persuaded me to raise the tax. He's my new chancellor.'

'Well, he needs his head seeing to.' Hannover sniffed loudly and moved further away from the new chancellor. 'And what's he wearing on his fur? Daffodil soup?'

'Here, I say,' said the pomaded Pontifract, affronted. 'That's a bit rude.'

'It was intended to be. Now look here, Poynt, it would have made more sense if you charged creatures for being too tall, but even that would be ludicrous. You can't go charging mammals for using the space under an arch. Space is free.' He

134

waved his paws around to emphasize this free-ness. 'It would be like taxing air. Now if I hear any more of this nonsense, I'm going to have to mention it at the next meeting of the city bank managers. They might find your methods of financing the city coffers a little unorthodox.'

'No, don't do that,' groaned Poynt, who relied on the goodwill of the bank managers to see him through the financial year. 'I'll cancel the tax, Hannover.'

'A very sensible move on your part,' growled Lord Haukin. 'Now, I'm off to Jumping Jacks. Are you coming?'

'No, no, I think I'll stay here. I do have to raise a tidy sum in order to get the city back on its paws by April, you know. If I can't charge for things like this, I'll have to find some other way.'

'Suit yourself.' And Lord Haukin left.

'Well, what next?' the mayor asked his new assistant. 'Come on, I didn't employ you to stand around sniffing. By the way, what *is* that smell?'

'Pomade,' replied the other stoat, becoming animated. 'Isn't it amazing how you can make your fur do anything with pomade? You can slick it down or you can stand it on end. I like to spike it. The *hedgehog* look. See how it shines in the early morning light too! It's all the rage, you know. Everyone's wearing it.'

'Everyone's not. I'm not. Lord Haukin wasn't. I happen to know he despises the stuff. I saw him once box the ears of a bell jack in a hotel lift because he stank the place out with the stuff.

Didn't you hear his contemptuous snort when he smelled you?'

'Well, anyone who's anyone. Of course, if mammals want to be fashion rejects, well then, there's nothing to be done with them, is there? But for those who want to show their pelts to the best advantage—'

'I'm not messing up my beautiful ermine with that greasy stuff. Anyway, it stinks.'

Pontifract was affronted. 'It has the scent of musk in spring.'

'Stinks.'

'It's a fragrance, not a stench. Hey!' Pontifract clicked his claws and his eyes widened. 'I've got another scheme for making money. Look, see, we buy the factory that makes this stuff – it's called "Dapper Dude" by the way – we purchase the factory and all the stock, and then issue an edict or law or something – you can do that, can't you? – to say that all stoats and weasels – and any other mammal for that matter – living in Poppyvile and the Docklands areas – that cuts you out, Mayor, because you live in the posh area – they all have to wear Dapper Dude pomade.'

'Why?'

Pontifract gave the equivalent of a stoat smile, which was actually a grinding of the teeth. 'Because they stink.'

The mayor frowned. 'It's true that it's mostly weasels who live in those districts – there's only down-and-out stoats who would buy or rent a house in Poppyvile, and no stoat would live in Docklands.'

'Exactly!' Pontifract was triumphant.

Jeremy Poynt shook his furry head. 'It doesn't make a lot of sense to me. You tell mammals they've got to put this smelly stuff on their fur in order to cover their stink?'

'Trust me. Not everyone has your aversion to pomade. Most mammals like the scent of pomade. Most mammals, however, dislike the stink of sweaty creatures coming out of Poppyvile and Docklands. Even Lord Haukin would approve of making them more acceptable.'

'You say everyone's wearing it?'

'All fashionable creatures.'

'You get good ideas, Pilote, but you get them the wrong way round. It was you who suggested a tallness tax, while I saw the benefits of a small-ness tax, in order to catch weasels rather than stoats. I keep having to stand your ideas on their heads to make them work. So, right then, rather than make creatures wear pomade, I'll slap a tax on it – so those who are slicking their coats down will have to pay through the nose.' He paused before adding, 'That's a joke by the way. Paying through the *nose*.'

'Eh?' cried Pontifract, looking upset. 'I wear it myself.'

'I know. Cough up! Half a crown.' The mayor held out his paw. 'Yes, wonderful, a *pomade* tax! Come on, two and six. Either that or go and wash the stuff off now.'

Pontifract grudgingly paid his half-crown. 'Why didn't you like *my* idea? This way you'll catch stoats as well as weasels.'

'Because,' said the mayor sweetly, 'you have to nobble those who've got the ackers, the dripping, if you catch my meaning. If my tax penalizes some of the stoats, so be it, I can't be protecting them all the time. A tax on them *not* wearing it wouldn't work. It'd make things worse. Poppyvilers or Docklanders haven't got any money. I'd have to throw them in jail, which would fill up the prisons and put more of a burden on the city's coffers than before. Those who can afford it – your fashion slaves, Pilote – live in Gusted Manor and are as rich as Creases. Ha!' He rubbed his white paws together. 'This is good. This is very good. A pomade tax.'

When Jeremy Poynt met Hannover Haukin at Jumping Jacks later that day, and told him of the scheme, Hannover seemed to approve.

'If you've got to tax something, pomade is as good as anything else. After all, the humans on the other side of the river have a window tax. That's the same as taxing sunlight, ain't it? Almost as bad as taxing air. Listen, Poynt, are you sure the city's finances are in such bad shape? I thought your sister Sybil kept the books for you? She's away, ain't she?'

'Yes, she's away, and yes, the city is in terrible difficulties,' lied the mayor. 'The whole fabric of society is crumbling. We have no money for roads, pavements and – and all that sort of thing. If we're not careful it'll all be worn out before my sister comes home from Eggyok.'

'I wonder if you're exaggerating things,' grumbled the young lord, 'but we'll let it pass for now. Just spend the cash wisely.'

'Oh, I will,' said the saintly looking mayor. 'I surely will.'

CHAPTER FIFTEEN

'But I never get sick,' said Bryony.

'Well, you are for once,' Monty assured her, 'and we need you awake so that you can tell us what to do. This apothecary here says you are incurable, but what does he know?'

Bryony, whose head was splitting open with pain, whose vision was so impaired that she saw several images of everything, and whose heart was so slow it had almost come to a halt in her chest, agreed with the apothecary. 'I'm done for,' she groaned, falling back on the pillow. 'You go on, Monty. Leave me here to die.'

'What kind of talk's that?' cried Scruff, frightened in spite of himself. 'Look, this 'ere's only a 'pothecary. You, you're a fully-fledged vet.

You're as good as any yuman physician, you are. You gotta be able to think better than he can.'

The apothecary did his best to look offended, but in his secret self he agreed with the dirty flea-ridden weasel who had spoken: he *was* only a dispenser of powders and pills, of potions and lotions, and she, the one with the terrible illness that ate a mammal away in less than a fortnight, she was a real vet, trained, experienced, qualified and everything.

'Scruff's right,' said Monty, no pity or sentiment in his strong voice. 'Veterinary surgeon, cure thyself, as it says in the book. You have to tell us what to do, and we'll do it. But I don't want to hear any more of this whining and sweating about your condition. You have to dig deep, Bryony, and use those reserves of strength to help yourself. Now, what is it that you believe you have?'

'Tropical stinkwater disease,' she groaned. 'In two days all my fur will drop out. A day after that my bare skin will begin to rot – I can smell it now, can't you? A horrible stench—'

'I can give you some pomade to cover that,' murmured the apothecary. 'Made from the boiled-down gum of a tamarind tree.'

'Shut ups,' snarled Calabash Brown, standing high on his long kangaroo legs. 'You make the matters worse with your suggestive offerings.'

'Yes, we're grateful you got Bryony's eyes open and her brain half-working, stoat, but you're not helping with remarks like that.'

'. . . then my toes will drop off, claws and all, in ones or in bunches . . .' continued Bryony.

Maudlin gave a loud sob and ran from the room, not wishing to hear any more. He was the wisest one in the place.

'. . . finally my eyes will swell to huge proportions and burst, squirting pus and brains all over the bedclothes,' finished Bryony, 'at the same time as my liver shrivels to the size of a dead leech drying in the hot sun and my spleen explodes up into what's left of my toothless, rotting mouth.'

'I think we get the picture, Bryony,' said Monty, through gritted teeth. 'Now, there must be something we can do, something we can give you to prevent all this rather upsetting destruction of your bodily organs? What if we were to carry you back up the mountain, to the priests? Would they have any cure? I have heard that faith and medicine—'

'Hopeless,' she moaned. 'Utterly hopeless.'

'Do not talk to me in that fashion!' snapped Monty sternly. 'I will *not* have it, do you hear!'

The tone of his voice shocked Bryony into a more alert state of mind. Monty had *never* spoken to her like that before. It was unthinkable for the kind and generous weasel who was her best friend to shout at her.

'There – there's one chance,' she whispered hoarsely.

'Yes. Out with it.'

'Possibly – oh, I don't know – possibly the bark

and dried leaves of a *Firmiana simplex* Wight. I have heard of one case – yes, now I remember—' the pupils of her dry yellowed eyes were spiralling with the effort of thinking so hard – 'I read of it in the *Veterinary Journal* – April issue, I think it was—'

'Never mind what issue.'

'No, no, of course not.' Her voice was getting fainter. 'Issue not important. Number twenty-three, volume six though. Page seven, paragraph three—'

'Bryony!' snapped Monty. 'Stay with it!'

'Yes, yes, of course. Patient survived. Have to – have to boil the bark and leaves to a soup and administer.' She fell back on the pillow, crushing the magnolia blossom left there for her by Maudlin. Her eyes glazed, her teeth chattering wildly. Her breath was indeed rank, but not as rank as the stench of her skin. A pawful of fur came away when Monty touched her. He gave a strangled little sob.

'What on earth is a *Firmiana simplex*?' he cried. 'Wake her up again.'

'No need,' murmured the silky apothecary from behind, making everyone jump. 'I know what it is. The common name for it is the oriental parasol tree.' The stoat described the tree in detail, the texture and colour of the bark, the shape and quality of the leaves and the fruit it bore. 'It grows in mountain crevices, usually halfway up an unclimbable cliff face. You could get a trained bird to take you to one, if we had a trained bird, which we don't, of course. They take exception to being trained, most birds do. Peck your eyes out first.'

'Thank you for that, apothecary,' grated Monty. 'You've been extremely helpful with your knowledge and skill, but now I think you can leave the job to us.' He hesitated, then said, 'I take it you have no boxes or bottles of oriental parasol tree leaves and bark?'

'Never keep the stuff. Didn't know it had healing properties, or I would've. Very difficult to find, though. Usually guarded by mountain gods and such. Gods who eat mustelids for breakfast. Good luck. If you do find a tree, and manage to climb up to it, some god will probably knock you off the face of the cliff just for the hell of it. Or a local bird will peck your eyes out and you'll have to climb down again blind. But don't say I didn't warn you. I always like to warn mammals. Then afterwards I can say I told you so.'

The stoat apothecary left the dwelling. Monty gathered some things in a pack with determined efficiency. Putting it on his back he turned to Calabash Brown, that faithful jerboa. 'Would you look after Bryony for us, please? Someone has to stay with her while Scruff, Maudlin and I search for this elusive tree.'

Brown looked a little apprehensive so Monty added, 'Of course, if you are concerned that you will catch the illness, I would quite understand a refusal.'

'No, no. It is not this that concerns me. In any

cases, I think this terrible disease come from being bitten by a bugs or something, not from catching the germ. No, it is you who is the worrying factor, Monty. What will happen if you all die? It is very easy to fall down from a mountain.'

'If we die, then Bryony will die. I trust you will see that her remains are taken care of in a respectful way. You don't need to perform any ceremony.'

Calabash nodded. 'I shall do as you say.'

Monty thanked him, aware that time was passing. Time was something very precious now. Every second had immense value. The two weasels left the hut. Maudlin was sitting on the porch, his head in his paws.

'Up!' ordered Monty, striding forth. 'We need to go back up into the mountains to find a parasol tree.'

'What's one of those?' asked Maudlin, jumping to his feet and trotting after his friends. 'Do you know what they look like?'

Monty repeated the apothecary's description of the parasol tree. 'We have to find one before noon,' he muttered, 'or I fear Bryony will be too far gone to bring back.'

The three of them went back up into the mountain passes, their heads continually swivelled upwards, searching the natural shelves above them for small, elegant trees with a spread of branches resembling the cowl of a green umbrella. All they saw were fir trees, clinging to cracks in the rock which sparse soil had filled over the years. Once or twice these firs had taken on a shape which had the spotter crying, 'There's one!' the tension, the anticipation, the desperate wish for a swift find priming their tongues.

'There!' shrieked Maudlin, sure he was at last correct, as he saw the silhouette of a parasol shape moving in the wind above them. 'Up there on the track above.'

It seemed too easy: to find one on the very path they were treading. Monty whipped out his spy glass and peered at the object, which now seemed to be moving towards them. It was indeed what it appeared to be: a parasol made of woven vegetation, probably rattan. It was carried by an oriental rodent who was leading a herd of voles down the mountain path. The rodent stared at them as he approached, probably concerned about bandits. Monty held his paws high, to show he was not carrying weapons. The other two did the same. The rat remained wary. Monty spoke to him.

'Sir,' he said, 'you are obviously a creature of the mountains. Perhaps you could help us . . .'

But the rodent drifted on by without responding, his eyes flicking nervously over the three weasels. Soon he was gone round the next bend, his gentle herd clattering amongst the stones, following his lead.

Scruff said angrily, 'I could go and get him,' but Monty said no, the creature obviously didn't understand and they would only succeed in frightening him half to death.

'We'll go on,' he murmured. 'We'll find one, don't you fret.'

Thus they continued their search, first in the hanging valleys, then higher up amongst the crests. They sweated and toiled the whole morning long, with Monty looking at his pocket watch every half-hour, the concern within him growing. 'Perhaps we should have roused the village?' he said as the sun rose high in the sky. 'I've done this all wrong. These creatures know the mountains. They could have—' His words were cut short as a brown snake, large enough to swallow a weasel whole, reared up in front of them.

Monty's reactions were swift. He threw his pack into the face of the striking serpent. It was enough to put the creature off its aim. The next instant Scruff had gathered up a pawful of dust and thrown it into the snake's eyes, while Maudlin, standing his ground for once, gave it a blow with his walking staff. The snake hissed its fury and slithered away into the rocks, leaving the three weasels limp with aftershock.

'That was close,' muttered Monty, retrieving his pack. 'We must keep our wits about us. We must stay alert.' Something caused him to start forwards. He stared at the ground where his pack had been. Littering the area were crispy brown dead leaves. Surely the leaves of the parasol tree? His head jerked upwards. There! There, high above them, on a narrow ledge, was a tree shaped like a delicate green umbrella!

'We've found one,' he cried, unable to maintain his usual calm. 'We've found an oriental parasol tree!'

CHAPTER SIXTEEN

Monty studied the situation. The rock face was indeed as sheer as the apothecary had warned it might be. It seemed as smooth as glass. Perhaps it was indeed made of obsidian. The ledge itself, some two hundred metres above, was occupied not only by the parasol tree, but also by a nest. It appeared, from what Monty knew of nests, to be the home of a buzzard, kite or eagle. Eagles, kites and buzzards were not fussy about what they ate, be they scavenging from a carcass or consuming a live, wriggling prey. Certainly a weasel might be regarded as a tasty dish to set before a mate with chicks, or even as a takeaway snack for oneself.

'This don't look good, does it, guv'nor?' said Scruff.

Monty shook his head. 'No, it doesn't. But we owe it to Bryony to try to get what we came here for.' He tried to add some cheer. 'The hard part is over, though. We've actually found a parasol tree. Now all we've got to do is get some bark and leaves. Not a lot. Just a little. Maudlin?'

'What?' cried Maudlin, in a panic. 'Why me?'

Monty turned to him and said gravely, 'I was going to ask you to remain here with the pack, while Scruff and I attempt to climb up to that shelf. I want you to be our eyes, yell up to us and tell us if there are any clawholds nearby. It'll be easier for you to see a likely route from down here, than for us when we're actually on the face.'

Maudlin blinked. 'Oh, yes, of course, Monty. Anything you say.'

'Thank you. Scruff? How about it?'

'After me, guv'nor,' said Scruff, tying a rope around his middle with a bowline knot. 'I'll take the lead. I'm good at rock climbing. Never fallen yet.'

'I suspect you've never tried it, Scruff, but I'm pleased you offered. I shall go first. When I was a kitten I used to climb a two-metre brick wall to get at some plums which grew from a tree on the far side. I became quite good at it. Of course, the wall was crumbling in places, and there were quite a few clawholds, but the experience has stood me in good stead. Watch where I put my claws and use the same holds. We shan't rope ourselves together. If I fall don't attempt to grab me. Let me go. It's more important that one of us reaches that tree up there. I don't want to tear you from the rock.'

'Likewise,' said Scruff, undoing the rope. 'If I drop, then you go on, Monty.'

'Nobody's going to fall,' cried Maudlin, pacing up and down. 'It's going to be all right.'

'That's the ticket,' said Scruff, slapping his friend on the shoulder. 'Positive thinkin'.' He wiped his paw on his bottom. 'Yuck! You still got all them sticky bits of twig and stuff in your fur, Maud.'

'It's the resin, or sap or something. It's matting my fur. I can't get it out.'

'We'll give you a bath later. That 'pothecary said there was hot springs somewhere outside the village. I'll make sure you get a dip.'

'Thanks.'

Monty glanced nervously at the sky. He didn't need to look at his watch. The sun had reached its fierce noon. It seemed to glare down on him with malevolent satisfaction, saying, 'It's too late, weasel. You'll never make it in time now.' He began climbing, slowly but carefully, up the smooth face. It was true he was a good climber, but he had never before attempted something as difficult as this cliff. Scruff followed behind, not too closely, in case his leader fell and took him down too.

Maudlin remained on the ground, yelling instructions to the two climbers, who worked tirelessly up and up the face. The hot sun beat down. Progress was made. Within an hour

Monty and Scruff were halfway to their goal. Maudlin, his mouth dry with fear and excitement, felt flickerings of hope course through his body. Surely they were going to make it! Then the worst but inevitable happened. One of Monty's paws slipped. His body slithered down the sheer face of the rock, missing Scruff by centimetres. He didn't actually fall out into space, which saved his life, but he did slide all the way to the bottom in a jerky fashion as his claws dug in at various points in an attempt to stop his progress earthwards. He landed with a thump on the hard earth at the base of the cliff. Maudlin rushed to him.

'I'm – I'm all right. Just – just winded. No bones broken. Leave me be for a minute, please, Maudlin.'

Monty was actually more disappointed than injured. There would be bumps and bruises but it was the bitterness of failure that swept through him, not the agony of physical pain. He was in despair. They had to get those leaves, that bark, or Bryony would die a horrible death. Surely they could do this small thing for their friend, who would have sacrificed just as much, perhaps more, if they were in her position?

'Where's the next hold?' shouted Scruff from above.

Attention immediately focused on the remaining climber.

'Up to your right,' yelled Maudlin. 'That's it, about eleven o'clock . . .' His voice trailed away.

A huge shadow was sweeping up the face of the rock. It passed over Scruff, who turned his head but was unable to see what was casting the shade. Icewater gushed through Maudlin's veins. At the same time a harsh, rasping cry echoed through the mountains. A giant feathered predator was returning to its nest.

'Eagle!' he yelled. 'Eagle, Scruff!'

What Scruff was supposed to do about the raptor was not clear. It was all he could do to cling to the cliff. However, as always in dangerous circumstances, the wild creature inside Scruff came to the fore. He did what his ancestors would have done. He made himself as small as possible, curling up in a tight spiral, flattening his ears and pulling in legs and tail. What dangled from the cliff looked very much like a ball of fluff. The eagle swooped down on it twice, skimming by Scruff and letting out a loud 'CAAARRRRRK', which made his head ring.

However, though the creature was obviously agile in the air, it could not get close enough to the cliff face to snatch Scruff from his perch. Its wings got in the way, and there were dangerous updraughts. It clearly *wanted* to grab the weasel-thing dangling under its nest, but soon realized it was an impossible task. It finally flew up and settled on its nest, looking over and down on Scruff, as if to say, 'Come on then, I'm waiting for you.'

Scruff had no option but to climb slowly down again. When he reached the ground he saw how wretched Monty was feeling. 'Never mind, guv'nor. We'll go an' look for another tree. There's bound to be one hereabouts. You don't ever just get one of sumthin'. There's always another near by.'

'No, no.' Monty shook his head and let out an enormous sigh, 'I fear it's already too late. By the time we find another parasol tree, climb up to it – well, even now she may have slipped away from us . . .' He took out his spy glass and studied the shrub that was so close, and yet so far away from them. 'Such distinctive leaves,' he murmured. He snapped the spy glass shut and sighed again. 'We ought to be getting back. I don't want Bryony to – to leave without us being there. To die alone is a terrible thing.'

The dispirited group trudged off down the mountain paths again, passing the same vole-herd they'd met that morning. He seemed just as shy and they did not bother him. Soon the hut was in sight. Monty hurried along, anxious to be there to hold Bryony's paw when the worst was happening to her. He knew she would be afraid – anyone would – and he wanted to offer such comfort as he could.

Monty turned to Maudlin, who was trying to keep up with his pace. 'I'll run ahead,' he said. 'All right?'

Suddenly, Monty stared at Maudlin's coat. Reaching out he picked out one of the bits of the foliage that clung to his fur. He stared at it closely, then snatched another bit. 'Where did you get this?' he cried at Maudlin. 'Did you fall in a bush?'

'I didn't tell anyone, but I fell from that monastery place – off the balcony. I was going to but no-one seemed interested . . .'

'You fell into a tree?'

'It saved my life,' said Maudlin.

Monty yelped loudly. 'You fell into a *parasol* tree, Maudlin. You've got bits of it all meshed in with your fur. Quickly, Scruff, help me pick them out. Don't drop any. The twigs too, because they've got the bark attached. Leaves, twigs, everything. Oh, heavens, I hope we're not too late.'

They managed to fill a tin mug with the twigs and leaves taken from Maudlin's pelt. Then Monty ran ahead to boil it on their little primus stove. When the other two arrived he was busy blowing on the concoction, trying to cool it down so that they could administer it to Bryony. Calabash Brown was sitting her up, but she was so droopy she kept sliding back down again. Finally they had her in a reasonable position and Monty began spooning the liquid between her jaws. She was just about able to swallow.

Maudlin went out onto the porch. Some mountain stoats had gathered outside. They were lean, rangy-looking creatures with open faces and wide eyes. One of them enquired of Maudlin how the 'foreign weasel jill' was doing. The enquiry was meant kindly and Maudlin explained what had happened and what they

155

were doing. The stoat who had spoken said he lived in the first house in the village and that they were always looking for a cure for the dread disease.

'You will please to let us know if it will be working?'

'You'll soon know for yourselves,' said Maudlin, pointing back at the door with his claw. 'They're giving her the medicine now. I can't watch, in case it doesn't work.' A tear trickled down the fur on his cheek and dripped off the end of his nose. 'She's my friend, you see. I don't want her to die.'

The villagers all hung their heads in sympathy. The sun began to descend behind the distant peaks. The fragrance of mimosa cloyed the evening air, mingling with the scent of nettles. A bell was tolling somewhere in the mountain fastness to the west. Lowing herds of voles were winding over the lea. A ploughmammal plodded his weary way homeward from the terraced fields, leaving the world to darkness and to Maudlin. One by one the villagers began to drift back to their pretty mountain houses. Maudlin remained, sitting on the porch, until the stars were lit from behind the sky, to brighten the far darkness of space with their tiny candle-flames.

CHAPTER SEVENTEEN

At three o'clock in the morning Maudlin was awoken by a sharp cry.

He leapt to his feet and immediately fell over. His legs, jammed against the wooden steps, had gone to sleep. He realized he had dropped off where he sat on the porch. The stars were still clustered above, boating around the dark sea of heaven. He rubbed life into his hind legs, wondering what the loud cry had been. Once he could walk again he went into the hut.

Scruff was sound asleep on a wooden cot. It was he who had given the troubled shout in his sleep. They still felt a great deal of concern about Bryony and Scruff was no different from the others. Maudlin's eyes went to Bryony's bed. She was there, poor dear, a wraith of a creature. Monty was awake, sitting in a chair by the bed, his fur matted with the sweat of worry. A candle burned by his head, one of many that had been lit that night, judging by the pool of wax that had gathered on the shelf: it hung like a white curtain of frozen lava over the edge. There was an unopened book by the candle, with the remains of some dusty dead moths on its cover. Clearly Monty had intended to read to take his mind off his friend's plight, but had been unable to open the pages.

'Ah, Maudlin,' said Monty softly. 'Glad of a bit of company.'

Maudlin approached the sickbed. He could smell Bryony's musty breath. She looked shrunken and dreadfully old. Her eyes were like tiny pits in her skull. Thin claws gripped the edge of the blanket, the knuckles prominent and bony.

'How – how is she?'

'A lot better, thanks to you, Maudlin. If you hadn't fallen in that tree . . .'

'It was an accident.' For once Maudlin did not want to claim undeserved credit.

'Nevertheless, a happy one. Serendipity, Maudlin. I am so grateful to you. And so will Bryony be, once she pulls through.'

'She will get better then?'

'We hope so. We hope so.'

Bryony stirred, her teeth clicked and she muttered something.

'Was that her clicking?' said Maudlin wonderingly.

'I think something amused her, in her delirious state of mind,' agreed Monty. 'How strange is the mammal psyche! Even so close to death something humorous must have flickered through her brain and her teeth and face muscles responded to it. Look, she did it again. Now that's not like Bryony at all. She's probably a kitten again, being chased through the park by a brother or sister. See how her whiskers twitch? How singular.'

The pair of jacks watched her, lost in these antics. It was not that Monty had shed any of his anxiety, but fatigue had overcome him and he was in that state of mind where life is more a dream than a reality. If you touched him, he might have burst into tears, so close to the surface were his emotions.

While Bryony stirred the cobwebs of her memories, her body sometimes registering her thoughts, the other two talked softly of old times, about the selflessness and generosity of this jill they watched over. Finally, in the very early hours, before the grim grey dawn got its teeth into the edge of the world, Bryony opened her eyes and said, 'Oh, you two? What time is it? Did I hear you say I was a near-perfect mustelid? I can't believe it.'

'Are you awake?' asked Maudlin.

'Would I be speaking if I were not?'

'Why yes,' replied Monty, relieved and happy to have her with him again, instead of off somewhere in a far distant land where fevered mammals gathered, 'you've been talking all night. What secrets we've heard.'

She looked a little shocked, given her private feelings towards Monty. 'Tosh,' she said. 'I haven't got any secrets.'

'Oh no?' Maudlin cried. 'Well then, you've got nothing to worry about, have you?'

At that moment Scruff woke up. He quickly assessed the situation and then said, 'I'll go and get water. You can help me, Maud.'

'Not me. I've been awake all night.'

'On yer feet, matey,' ordered Scruff. 'This morning I listen to no nays or nixes. You're comin' and that's that.'

Maudlin could see his friend was serious and so he climbed wearily to his feet and picked up another bucket. The pair of them went through the doorway, out into the greying light.

When they had gone, Bryony managed to pull herself up on her pillow a little bit, and was again shocked, this time by her own skeletal frame. 'Oh, I've lost weight.'

'I should say,' clicked Monty. 'How do you feel?'

'Like death.'

Monty's expression hardened. 'Don't use that word.'

'Oh. I'm sorry, yes. Have you been sitting there all night? What did you give me?'

'Some juice – Maudlin had parasol leaves and bark in his fur. It came in very useful. You seemed to rally a little almost immediately after we gave it to you. Then you sank into what appeared to be a deep sleep. At about one o'clock this morning your fever left you. It left almost visibly – I swear I saw it flee, like some ghost departing your poor racked body. You failed to respond to my questions, however, and seemed locked in a distant world. There you stayed, breathing very lightly, all night. Maudlin came in the middle of the watch and kept me company. We caught you making merry in your dreams once or twice.'

'Oh, I don't think so,' said Bryony quickly.

'Yes, I'm very much afraid so.'

Bryony argued no further. She felt very weak and light-headed. There was no question of getting up yet. She had not the strength to hold her eyes open for more than a few seconds at a time before the lids got heavy. It was going to be a while before she stepped on the boards again. What worried her was that she stank – horribly; partly of dried sweat and other bodily fluids, and partly her skin seemed to have shed a layer under her fur and was filling the bed with white flakes. It was not very nice. Not very nice at all. She really didn't want Monty to see her like this.

'Could you – could you let me have some warm water, for a wash?' she asked. 'Then could you go away for a little while? I wish to give myself a blanket bath.'

'But you're too weak to wash yourself. I'll do it.'

'No.'

At that moment Calabash Brown came out of a dark corner. 'I shall be giving the jill her blanket washes,' he said. 'You, sir – Monty – will go out. This is not for the sightings of someone who has no experience of tropical diseases. It will make you puke to take back the bedclothes and breathe the fetid fumes. Go. Go. Outsides please. She has the feelings that she is not palatable to the nose and this distresses the female mind. Out now, sir. Begone for a few minutes.'

For once, Monty did not argue. He had no desire to see Bryony in the worst state of any mammal and, yes, it was distressing her that he was present. He didn't really under-stand why, but then he understood very little about how jills felt and thought. They seemed to be a different species of weasel altogether from jacks. Clearly Bryony would rather a stranger helped her with her ablutions than a close friend. It was most peculiar, but he was in no state to question it. Within five minutes he was asleep on the porch, curled up in almost the same spot as Maudlin, while the sun-warmed breeze of the morning ran its claws through his fur.

Bryony recovered gradually over the next few weeks. Hot finch soup and dry toast was her diet and it seemed to suit her very well. At the end of three weeks she was almost back to her old self. The morning came when they were ready to march forth again along the Silk Road. All the mountain-dwelling villagers turned out in their thick vole-skin coats to see them off. They even gave them a pack-mouse to assist with their provisions. Monty had never wanted to use any kind of pack animal; later he could tell the Royal Geographical Society that they had done the journey unaided, with just the packs on their backs – but how could he refuse the stoats' generosity? And Bryony needed someone to carry her pack for some time yet, despite her miraculous recovery.

'Well, we're on our way again,' said Maudlin, as he trotted alongside Scruff. 'What's the next stop?'

'Sumerkand,' breathed Scruff in rapturous tones.

'Why did you do that?'

'What, breathe "Sumerkand" in rapturous tones?'

'Yes.'

'Because, me old mate Maud, I've wanted to go there ever since I was a kitten. Sumerkand is a fabled city, the halfway house. At one end of the line, Welkin – at the other end, Far Kathay. In the middle, Sumerkand, with its blue-stone mouseleum containin' the remains of that mighty conqueror and proper rat barbarian, Timberbrain. Cor, he was a godless roof rat, he was. Bashed his way across half the world, and back again. Everyone was scared of Timberbrain, even the emperor of Far Kathay. Scared the livin' daylights out of anyone, he would. They built a wall to keep 'im out. Him and Gangly Kan, another scallywag rat warrior. Right pair of marauders, them two. Villains from nest to the grave.'

Maudlin couldn't help catching a little note of admiration in Scruff's voice. 'So this is where east meets west?' he said.

'No, that's a bit earlier on – there's only a little bit of west and quite a sizeable hunk of east makin' up the world.'

'Why's that?'

'Just the way things is, mate. Most of what we've got is made of H two O. Water, me old biscuit-nibbler. Cobalt Sea an' all that. Most of what lies to the east of the Welkin Channel – which them folks on the other side call the Gallbladder Channel – is hard rock.' He stamped his foot to emphasize the point. 'Dunno which is best. Both got their fors and againsts.'

Up front, Bryony was still trying to thank Monty for saving her life, but he would have none of it.

'Serendipity, my dear Bryony, serendipity. If Maudlin had not had pieces of leaf and twig in his fur, you would not be here today. He's the one you should thank, not me.'

But she knew who had been the driving force behind the search for her cure, and she knew who had sat up all night over her sickbed, and she knew whose face it was she saw on first opening her eyes. Bryony was not going to be fobbed off by Monty's casual refusal to accept her gratitude gracefully. Someday she would repay him. That much she vowed.

CHAPTER EIGHTEEN

Now that Sybil had got over her sminx tummy,
Zacharias Falshed was beginning to regret that
he had not followed the weasels along the Silk
Road to Far Kathay. Here in Eggyok Sybil was
ordering him about as if he were a servant. She
was one of those tourists who want to see everything in one day – and then some more. Then
there were the stoats along the banks of the Nail.
They would stare so! It was getting on both their
nerves.

'Today we shall visit the prismids,' announced
Sybil, up early and clattering around on the
tiles of her hotel room, annoying the very devil
out of the mammals in the room below. 'I shall
need a sun hat, and a parasol – definitely a

parasol – and also a shawl in case it turns chilly.'

'Turns chilly?' expostulated Falshed down the telephone – his room was on the other side of the hotel overlooking a cess pool, while Sybil's had a view of the river Nail. 'It's over thirty-five degrees Centigrade out there.'

'You never know, Chief. I once thought it was safe to go out without one to the annual Muggidrear regatta and caught a dreadful cold.'

'But that's back in Welkin.'

'Better safe than sorry. By the way, I haven't got a parasol with me, so would you be a dear and dash down to the souk and get me one. Don't forget to bargain for it. They like to haggle, you know. It's part of the game.'

He dashed. The souk was barely awake. Hardly anyone was about. One or two cats sipped coffee in their tents. Luckily a stoat with gummed eyes and a drooping tail was just opening his shop. Falshed approached him.

'Ten whatchamaflips for that pink parasol and not a sou more,' he snapped.

'Done,' yawned the stoat. 'I was going to charge you five. I hate all this haggling business.'

'Blast!' Falshed kicked himself mentally. 'Why can't I keep my trap shut? If you see a jill stoat carrying this –' he blew dust and sand off the item – 'tell her I only paid you three.'

'It'll cost you an extra two to tell fibs.'

'Blast!'

Falshed paid up and was about to walk away, when the stoat called him back again. The creature tucked in the tail end of his turban, looked about furtively, then spoke.

'That jill – the one of which you just spoke. Where – where does she come from?'

'Why, Welkin, the same as me. We live in Muggidrear city. I'm Chief of Police there, actually.' Falshed puffed out his chest.

'She has never been to Eggyok before?'

'Not to my knowledge. Us Welkonians are not great travellers.'

'Not passing through to Xanadoo?'

'No – I just said.'

'Nor on the way to Mandelay?'

'Look . . .'

The stoat seemed nervous and pulled him inside the shop. The creature's breath was rank with garlic. He breathed all over Falshed, who had trouble finding fresh air.

'It's like this. She's the dead spit. In fact the stoats along the Nail, my cousins, brothers, uncles and sisters, my kin-mammals, so to speak, believe she is the reincarnated one.'

'One what?'

'Queen Neferhapen. An ancient Eggyok queen who led her mustelids to freedom from oppression, to a land flowing with soup and syrup. The stoats along the Nail think she's returned to lead them to freedom again.'

'But,' cried Falshed a little testily, 'aren't they already free?'

'Well, technically yes,' agreed the stoat, 'but they haven't got a land flowing with soup and syrup. They have to ply their wares up and down the Nail in their feluccas, and plough the fields and scatter the good seed on the land. They have to *work* for a living. In the old days they didn't have to *work*. They got it all for free. Given to them by Queen Neferhapen.'

'You're potty. What makes you think Sybil is able to give you a land where you don't have to work any more? Surely that's just a legendary region? Mythical. There's no such place really.'

'Ssssybil,' murmured the stoat. 'So that's our queen's new name. A very sibilant name, worthy of ancient royalty. How apt. How very apt. Isn't *apt* a nice word? A bit like *apse* – you know, a semicircular or polygonal recess? Or *asp*, the snake that Queen Neferhapen clasped – you see how I managed to get *asp* into the middle of that word *clasped*? – to her bosom.'

'What are you talking about, you mad-mammal?' cried Falshed. 'I have to get out of here. It's too early in the morning for all this.'

Falshed got away, but out of an alley staggered an old stoat with grey fur and glittering eye. He held him with his skinny paw.

'There was a ship,' croaked he.

'Hold off, unpaw me, grey-furred loon!' cried Falshed.

He hurried off down the narrow alleys which made the souk a warren of shops and stalls. The day was beginning to get hotter and Falshed had always had a thick pelt. Here in Eggyok it was his tail that suffered the most, since it rarely saw the shade. He himself might duck under awnings and covers, but his tail seemed always to be outside, under the searing sun. By the time he reached the hotel, with its cool marble walls and tiled floors, he was already intensely bothered. He hurried upstairs to Sybil's room with the treasure that had cost him so dear.

'Oh, Zacharias!' she exclaimed. 'Is that the best you can do?'

'What do you mean?' This through gritted fangs.

'I mean to say, *pink*. That's for kitten jills, not for grown-up weasels. Pink? Whatever were you thinking of? You couldn't go back and exchange it for another colour, could you?'

'No, I couldn't,' he said firmly, 'and I think you ought to be thankful you've got this one, frankly.'

She was immediately upset. 'Oh, dear – you're being sharp with me. And I told my brother on the phone just a moment ago what an angel you were being . . .'

Falshed went pale beneath his fur. 'Your – brother – the – mayor – phoned?'

'Yes, he was wondering why you weren't following the weasels to the four corners of the earth. I told him it was because I'd been unwell and you were gentlestoatly enough to stay and care for me. I think his answer to that was, "I'll kill that constable with my bare claws." Yes, in fact I'm sure that's what he said.'

'Constable?' quailed Falshed. 'You mean chief of police.'

'No, he definitely said *constable*.'

'Oh, my – well, you told him it was necessary to stay and watch over you, a friendless female in a foreign land. He saw that, didn't he? He saw that I was doing you, and therefore him, a great service?'

'I could make him see.'

'Yes?'

'If I had the right colour parasol.'

Falshed ran all the way back to the same shop, found the same stoat. There was some awkwardness over more money before a green parasol was in Falshed's paws. Then he ran back to the hotel again. This time Sybil was pleased. 'It matches my eyes, don't you think?' she said, blinking.

'Er, yes.'

'You should have said that, not me.'

'You didn't give me time. I wanted to.'

'Well, never mind. Hail a water taxi, will you? Let's go to the Great Prismid of Chops.'

Falshed wearily did as he was told.

When they arrived at the great glass tomb of an ancient king there were dozens of stoat guides, all vying for business.

'Please, I will show you magnificent sights,' said one, shouldering three others out of the way. 'I am the best guide. Look not on these others, who are paltry stoats with no understanding of culture. Our great heritage is locked within my lips. Several large coins will be enough to release this knowledge. Come, my friends, let me enlighten you.'

They found themselves being shoved towards the entrance to the tomb, where they had to pay for the guide's ticket as well as their own. In truth he was very good. He knew his stuff. When it came to the wall paintings he became a little coy. One of them was of the ancient queen, Neferhapen. Falshed put it to Sybil that they could be twin sisters, she and this monarch.

'I can't see the likeness,' she insisted.

'But Sybil, you're the dead spit of this beautiful queen.'

She shrugged. 'If you say so, Zacharias. I still can't see it.'

The guide moved closer to her ear and anxiously whispered, 'Please, you must lead us to freedom. We are all ready. The word has travelled along the banks of the Nail. Our kittens are ready. Our kittens' kittens are ready. Three thousand years we have been waiting for your return. Now is the hour of the mustelid. Now comes our saviour. We are ready. Give the word. If we have any trouble from the local cat authorities I'm sure you can visit the land with a few f-plagues – fleas, flatulence, fur balls. Give me a sign, o Queen, that I may tell all stoats to rise up and march with you to the land flowing with soup and syrup.'

'What is he on about?' Sybil asked Falshed, brushing the guide away. 'He's not right in the head, is he?'

'This is about you, Sybil. They think you're a reincarnated queen, a stoat back from the dead, come to set your mammals free.'

'I thought they were already free.'

'So did I, but apparently not.'

As Sybil moved through the passageway of the glass prismid, which sparkled in the bright sunlight, murmuring stoats flocked to her entourage. When she finally came out the other end there must have been close to a thousand of them trailing behind her, all muttering about freedom. Falshed tried to shield his princess. It was becoming quite dangerous. Someone only had to say the wrong thing and there would be a riot. In fact the local cats saw the situation developing and called in reinforcements. There was an army of them waiting at the exit.

'Come with me,' ordered a cat, placing a paw on Sybil's person. 'You're charged with fomenting mutiny and discontent amongst the masses.'

'If you take her, you'll have to take me too!' cried Falshed.

'We were going to anyway,' they told him in a rather nasty tone. 'You're just as bad as she is. You ought to know better, being a policemammal.'

'How do you know I'm a policemammal?'

'The hind paws – they always give it away – flat as pancakes, yours.'

Indignantly, 'They are not.'

'Are so.'

Falshed and a protesting Sybil were marched

off to the jail – not the prettiest building in Eggyok: grey, windowless and with a barred door. Inside they were manacled and chained to the wall. Falshed was beside himself, but Sybil took it all in her stride, yelling that her brother would see to it that they all lost their jobs, if not their heads. Falshed demanded to see a lawyer and one was duly sent for. She arrived at three o'clock in the morning. Falshed was surprised to see that she was a foreigner, like them, a female lemming from Slattland.

'My name is Sveltlana,' she told the pair. 'I am here on holiday and heard that two stoats had been arrested. We have met before, but I doubt you would remember. I can have you released immediately, but of course there is the matter of my fee.'

'I shall wire my brother . . .' began Sybil, but Sveltlana shook her furry head.

'No. I do not require money. I desire information.'

Falshed said, 'What kind of information?'

'I – I am an old acquaintance of your Welkin weasels – the intrepid Montegu Sylver and Bryony Bludd. I happened to catch a glimpse of them in the souk some time ago. You could tell me what they're doing here.'

Sybil said, 'They're on their way to Far Kathay, so far as I'm aware. They stopped here to pick up a guide. Why?'

'Why are they going to Far Kathay?'

'I'm not sure we should tell you that,' broke

in Falshed pompously. 'That's classified information.'

'Then you rot in jail,' said Sveltlana simply. 'The judge is a friend of mine. He will not be lenient, believe me.'

Sybil said, 'They're going at the request of the Great Pangolin. The jade shoes have been stolen from the Green Idol of Ommmm.'

'I think there's one too many "m"s in there,' replied Sveltlana, her eyes narrowing, 'but I get the gist. Monty is going out there to solve the mystery? Is that correct? He has been sent for to do detective work?'

'That's classified information,' said Falshed, but Sybil trod on his paw.

'That's correct,' she replied. 'Now, will you get us out of this hell-hole? If I get one more cockroach crawling through my fur, I'll start screaming and never stop.'

The pair were released on promise of not 'inciting the stoatish mobs to violence' and they went back the hotel.

There a second terrible thing happened to Zacharias Falshed, which would remain in his memory for the rest of his life.

CHAPTER NINETEEN

He was awakened in the early hours of the morning. His bed sheet was wrapped and twisted around his body, so that he had to fight to release himself. Once he was free, he looked around his moonlit room, wondering what had woken him.

'Must have been the crickets,' he told himself. 'They get pretty noisy out there in the foliage.'

In the garden there was a small oasis with a fountain, which attracted all manner of birds and insects. He went to the glassless window and looked out, studying the white statues scattered about the hotel grounds. All seemed perfectly still and proper. Nothing really sinister going on. Yet the chief felt uneasy for some reason.

'*White fonts falling in the courts of the sun,*' he

quoted, '*and the sultan of Byzimian is clicking as they run.*' He was pleased with himself. It was not often he remembered poetry, especially at three in the morning.

A shadow passed over the moon. He shivered. There was a cool breeze coming off the desert. Was that all? Was that why he had shivered?

'Zacharias?'

'Yes, Mother?' he said automatically, reacting to her voice.

Then he remembered. His mother was dead. She had died here – had been mummified, as was the custom, by the local cats. Her body had been incarcerated somewhere in the region, in a cheap timber sarcophagus painted with pitch. It was all he could afford at the time.

'Zacharias.'

His nerves jangled. That *was* his mother's voice. He slowly turned to see a figure wrapped in what looked like dirty white bandages, standing in the middle of the room. A scream escaped him. It pierced through the walls and woke Sybil, and just about everyone else in the hotel. He could see two cold eyes looking at him through a slit in the bandages. They were accusing, sorrowful eyes that cut right through him to his very soul.

'Mother?' he whimpered.

The mummy moved two awkward, plodding steps forward. In life his mother had been very agile. Now she was like – well – a walking mummy.

'You left me here,' she accused in a monotone. 'You left me in a foreign tomb with foreign corpses and foreign ghosts.'

'I – ah – I – what's wrong with – er – foreign? They're nice mammals, the same as us. I admit the food's not what I hoped, but—'

'Stop babbling, you idiot. Let me tell you what I wanted – what I still want. I want my hollyhocks, my roses, my geraniums. You left me here with oleander and bindweed. O faithless son. To abandon a mother. Shame on you. Shame on your head, o false offspring.'

'It wasn't *my* fault,' he told her. 'You spent all the money.'

'You're well enough off now.'

'Yes, *now*, but I don't know where you are. I mean, you're here, obviously, but I didn't know where you were before you went hiking, did I?' He began to feel misunderstood. 'The blame lies elsewhere.'

'It always did, didn't it, son?'

'Look, when I go home, I'll have you shipped back with us. I'll bury you in the garden. It's not quite the same as when you left it, of course. I'm not the horticultural mammal you were. There's a few weeds here and there, and the apple tree hasn't been pruned for several seasons, but if you want it, you can have it.'

His mother's mummy went and lay on the bed. 'I'll stay here until we're ready. They put me in a stone-cold tomb. It gets into your bones. I don't want to go back there ever again.'

'How can you feel the cold? You're dead.'

'Believe me, you do.'

At that moment Sybil opened the door and came into the room. 'What on earth are you yelling about?' she hissed. 'It was loud enough to waken the dead. Hey –' her voice took on a hurt, accusing tone – 'who's that on your bed? You didn't tell me you had company, Zacharias.'

'The dead,' he explained. 'It's my mummy's mummy. She's left her stone-cold tomb to come and haunt me. I've got to take her home when we go.'

'Yech!' cried Sybil, pointing to a pool of liquid on the floor by the bed. 'She's leaking.'

Falshed felt he ought to defend his mother. 'She can't help it. She's been dead for seven years. It's probably the embalming fluid or something.'

'So. A mummy-mummy. Well, that's something new. I'll leave you to it then.'

'Thanks for nothing,' muttered Falshed bitterly.

'While I'm here, have you any ointment for my wrists? Those manacles cut into them and left them feeling sore. Some sort of balm?'

'Try the bathroom,' replied Falshed despondently.

Sybil disappeared into his bathroom and came out with a small jar. 'She's been in there too,' she said. 'It's all over the floor. Smells awful.'

'Thanks again.'

'Don't mention it. And don't bring her to

breakfast in the morning. Don't forget, ten o'clock sharp. We're going down the Nail in a river barge – a copy of the one Neferhapen used when she travelled between palaces. I'm looking forward to it. Get a good night's sleep. I want you fresh.'

Once Sybil had gone Falshed lay down on the other side of the bed. His mother was hogging the sheet, but he wasn't going to argue with her. The stench of her putrid flesh was enough to make his head swim. But what else was he to do? Sybil wouldn't let him use her couch, of that he was sure, and there was nowhere else in the hotel to sleep. The laundry room? That might be an idea. If he could find it. Perhaps the best way would be to go down one of the chutes into a linen basket below. Yes, that's what he would do.

'Sleep well, Mother,' he murmured to the now stiff corpse on the bed. 'I intend to see to your needs.'

He took the laundry chute, but there was no linen basket at the bottom. He hit the floor with a thump. However, there were plenty of dirty sheets and towels to sleep on. It was a most comfortable night. The following morning, when they unlocked the door to the laundry room, he dashed by some startled maids. He went straight to reception.

'Can I send a telegram from here?' he asked.

'Certainly, sir.'

He was given a form and he filled it in. 'To Messrs Herk and Bare, Lowgate Cemetery,

Muggidrear, Welkin. It would be to your advantage to come to Eggyok stop Fares and all expenses will be paid on arrival stop Signed Zacharias Falshed.'

When he returned to his room, his mummy's mummy was still on the bed. She seemed to have lost her powers of movement and speech with the coming of daylight. Falshed was pleased about that. He had no desire to be harangued by his mother while he showered and cleaned his teeth. After clipping his whiskers he went down to breakfast.

'Good rest of the night?' enquired Sybil.

'Good as could be expected.' Falshed realized that mentioning his mummy's mummy would not go down well.

'Well then, let's not waste any more of the day. Our barge awaits.'

Once he had taken two mouthfuls of toast Sybil dragged him from the dining room, out into the street and down towards the river, where the tourist barge was waiting. She went on board and Falshed followed her. The bargemammal pushed off from the landing stage and then they were making their way down the lovely river Nail.

All along the banks there were stoat farmers and fishermammals. They dropped their tools and nets on seeing the barge and bowed low as it went past. Most of the tourists assumed it was a quaint old custom to genuflect before the ancient royal barge.

'It comes from way back,' said a badger from Welkin. 'Habits are hard to break, even after generations have passed.'

But Falshed knew that the local stoats were bowing because Sybil was on board – their messiah who would lead them forth. Sybil herself was both annoyed and a little frightened. What did these creatures want of her? She was really not very good at leading mammals forth, fifth – or anywhere else for that matter. She knew where her strengths lay. Organizing parties, balls, picnics, literary gatherings – that's what she was good at. But rallying a downtrodden nation, perking its inhabitants up and pointing their nose in the direction of a promised land of their own was not her forte at all.

'Zacharias,' she whispered, 'what am I to do?'

'I don't know.'

'Well, think of something! This is spoiling my holiday.'

A shout came from the bank. 'Three cheers for Queen Neferhapen. Hip-hip.'

A loud hooray and two more followed.

'Well, I say,' said the puffed-up badger from Welkin, 'how jolly gratifying. It's probably because they don't see many foreigners. I didn't know our barge was called *Queen Neferhapen*—' he tried to look over the bows and almost fell in the river – 'but I must say the civility shown by the locals is extraordinary. I was in Slattland last year and the locals there couldn't have cared less. Never mind we were boosting their economy with our custom, they kept shaking their paws at us and telling us to go back where we came from.'

'I know, I was there,' replied a mammal of unknown origin, clearly a female under all her make-up. 'They were most rude.'

'Lemmings, you know. Terrible manners, lemmings.'

'Not like these Eggyok stoats. Look, they're bowing again. You'd think they worshipped tourists, wouldn't you?'

'Most gratifying. Most polite.'

'Shut up, you silly old fools,' cried Falshed, who had had enough of them. 'You have straw for brains. It's my companion who's the object of their affections. Not this barge. Not blasted tourists. Not *you*.'

The badger stiffened visibly; the unknown mammal likewise. They moved away from the rail, to the far side of the barge.

'Some creatures,' muttered the badger, 'are so egotistical. They can't bear others to share in the passion. He *must* come from Slattland.'

'Oh, without doubt,' replied the unknown mammal. 'I've never seen a worse case of jealousy in my life.'

Later, when the police rushed onto the barge to arrest someone for fomenting rebellion and general unrest amongst the masses, the badger and the unknown female were the first to point at Falshed and Sybil.

'There they are,' they cried, 'the guilty-looking ones.'

CHAPTER TWENTY

After resting in Sumerkand, the four weasels and the desert rat continued across the rugged terrain of the interior towards the borders of Far Kathay. They were still in the cold regions, the roof of the world, where the mountains only dipped to shallow valleys, rather than running down sharply towards sea-level. Up here there was the possibility of encountering not only such ferocious creatures as tigers and snow leopards; huge footprints in the snow indicated the possible presence of a yeti. Maudlin had no desire to meet a yeti and was forever looking over his shoulder.

One night, after the sun went down, the group saw the light of a fire in the distance.

'It is of great imperativeness that we hasten towards that fire,' said Calabash Brown from under the broad brim of his hat. 'I have employed the last match and we have no means of warming ourselves now the sun has gone to bed. If we do not ask to share in the enjoyment of those flames we will freeze tonight.'

'What if it's a yeti?' asked Maudlin anxiously, swishing the snow with his tail.

The jerboa shook his head. 'Yeti do not make the fire. They are of an impervious hairy nature to resist the cold mountain airs. Yeti *like* the cold.'

True enough, as they approached the fire, they could see it was a small mammal enjoying its flames – a creature which Monty identified as a mole-rat, a burrowing rodent. He was dressed in thick robes and remained hunched over the fire as the weasels and jerboa approached. He only looked up when they stood over him and Calabash Brown addressed him in several languages until he came upon one that caught the listener's fancy.

'Then good evening to you, local rodent! Do you mind if my companions and I share your fire?'

The mole-rat shrugged, which they took to be a yes.

They sat down and warmed their paws, Monty saying, 'Tomorrow we should be out of the mountains and down on the Great Plain, where it'll be warmer.'

'Ah,' said the mole-rat, his head coming up

at last, 'you speak Welkin, another of my languages. Are you from Welkin?'

'Do you know it?' asked Bryony. 'Have you been there?'

'A long time ago, with my grandfather, who was a great seafarer. He took me along as a cabin-kitten when I was knee-high to a shrew-mouse. I was shown many kindnesses in Welkin.'

Bryony and Monty and the others were glad of that. If some stoat or weasel had given offence, they might be thrust out into the dark and cold of the unforgiving mountains. As it was they could sit comfortably and feel no pang of conscience for their country.

'What was your grandfather doing – in Welkin, I mean?' asked Monty. 'If you don't mind answering the question, that is.'

'Not at all. He was trading in silks and brocades, purchased in Far Kathay for next to nothing and sold for considerable sums on the Welkin market. There was the danger of the voyage and other hazards, so the high prices of his goods were justified. With the money he purchased cheap tin trays to trade with the apes and peacocks of the island of Walk – known to you as the Spice Island – for nutmeg.'

'And what did he do with the nutmeg?'

'Took it to his home in the land of Uz, where he made a fortune: it is prized there as an ingredient in pomades, its scent being so wholesome and refreshing.'

'I see,' said Monty, 'but forgive my ignorance:

why would the islanders on Walk want cheap tin trays?'

'Roofs, for their huts. They were fed up with the sound of palm leaves, which rustle noisily in the wind, especially when they grow brown and crispy. Of course, they later found out that when it rained the drumming on the tin roofs was deafening, but by the time the monsoon season came my grandfather was back in the land of Uz and safe from harm. Otherwise he might have been the contents of a casserole.'

The flames of the fire leapt up to lick the hem of the night as the mole-rat threw more faggots on. The mountains, which seemed to be creeping in towards them, jumped back again to their rightful places. Somewhere out in the passes a wolf howled and was answered by the grunt of a lone yeti. Maudlin suddenly felt the need to keep the conversation going.

'Er, might I ask what you do now – now that you don't sail the nine seas with your grandfather any more?'

'Certainly,' replied the mole-rat, looking on Maudlin with hollow eyes. 'I'm a ghost catcher.' He nodded to a rock overhang and for the first time the weasels and jerboa saw a large, full sack. It seemed to be struggling from within. 'This is the region of hungry ghosts. I offer myself as bait. When I have trapped enough of them and my sack is full, I descend to the valleys to trade them, usually with their relatives who want to put them to rest.' He shrugged again. 'It's a business.'

Scruff queried, '*Hungry* ghosts?'

'They are never satisfied. They eat and eat, yet never ease their starvation. They have no stomachs, you see. Only a voracious appetite, a longing for living flesh, possibly to replace that which they have lost.'

Maudlin looked at the sack again. 'It – it is secure?'

'Oh, tied at the neck with my famous Gordonian knot. Gordon is my name.'

Curious, Monty got up and went to look at the sack. He could see it moving, as if it contained an animal of some kind. Then he heard a low growl that made the hairs all the way down his spine stand on end.

'These ghosts . . .' he said to the mole-rat. 'Who or what were they in real life? Weasels? Stoats? Mole-rats?'

'Keep guessing.'

Bryony, the most knowledgeable of the weasels on natural history, took over from Monty. 'Oh, how about something exotic – an animal of these regions? How about a ferret badger? *Melogale moschata?*'

'How about,' said the mole-rat, 'a wolverine – *Gulo gulo*? Plus a few stone martens.'

'A wolverine?'

Maudlin did not like the way Monty said this word. It came out with a sinister ring to it. He looked from one face to the next, before asking nervously, 'What's a wolverine?'

'They calls 'em *gluttons*,' replied Scruff. 'I've

heard of them. Vicious devils, so I understand. Always walk alone. Get two wolverines in one room and they'd kill each other, 'less one was a jack and the other a jill o' course. Their jaws is so strong they can crush bones. Good job that's just a ghost of one in there. A real one would've et his way out by now.'

'Yes,' squeaked Maudlin. 'Good job.'

'Would you like to see it? My wolverine ghost?'

'No.'

'Yes, I wouldn't mind,' Scruff said, and Monty, Bryony and Calabash said they would also like to see it.

The mole-rat rose from the fire and went to his sack. 'I'm the only one who can untie this knot,' he said. 'That's why I invented it. It's one of the most complicated knots in the world, the Gordonian knot.' He struggled with it in vain for at least twenty minutes, using both teeth and nails, before taking out a pocket knife and cutting the cord. 'Sometimes I myself am too good at tying things.'

He opened the sack just a little, while Calabash stood over him with a brand to light the interior.

'Oh, my,' said the mole-rat, looking in, 'just as I thought.'

'What?' cried Maudlin.

'The wolverine's eaten all the martens. I thought that might happen. I only had one sack, though, and he's the most valuable. I wasn't going to sell him back to his relatives – I wouldn't be able to find them and if I could they'd

189

probably kill me rather than pay me – they wouldn't want him anyway, being solitary creatures all their lives – they probably don't know their own relatives—'

'Get to the point,' Bryony said.

'I'm going to sell him on to one of the mountain villages. To stoats, or perhaps weasels like yourselves. Even human villages need ghosts to patrol their perimeters, to keep out evil spirits, especially in the mountains. A wolverine's ghost is very good at such work, highly prized. Would you go near a village with a wolverine's ghost in the hills nearby? No. Only a ghost hunter like myself would venture near such a place.'

'Wouldn't the villagers be trapped?' asked Bryony. 'After all, this hungry ghost would eat them too, if they ventured out of their houses.'

'Ghosts hate the stink of dwellings, so it wouldn't go inside the village, and its potency, its strength, is reduced during the daylight hours. The inhabitants of the village would wait until noon to use the mountain paths over the passes. And if bandits are intent on raiding and plundering a village, they usually do it at night, when everyone's befuddled with sleep. During the day the villagers are on the alert and ready to repel any hostile groups. It all makes sense, when you think about it.'

'I can't see it,' said Scruff, looking into the sack. 'What's it look like?'

'Well, of course, it's not a *live* wolverine, but a wolverine's phantom. This one looks sort of white and misty, but with the usual slavering jaws and murderous eyes. So long as I don't open the sack more than a few centimetres, it can't get out. The heavens help us if it could! A live one has thick brown fur with cream or yellow markings on its face, sides and bushy tail. It's about eighty centimetres long and weighs about eighteen kilos.'

Maudlin's eyes started out of his head. Nearly a metre long and weighing that much! And this was one of his cousins, for the wolverine was a mustelid. 'What do they eat?' he asked.

'Anything,' said the mole-rat, turning the full force of his gaze onto Maudlin. 'Anything at all.'

Scruff cried, 'Oh yes, I see it now. Grey thing. Look at it struggle.'

The wolverine's ghost, on seeing a face peering down at it, leapt up at the opening and tried to force its way out, its spectral jaws snapping and snarling. The mole-rat had to fight to keep hold of the sack but Monty gave him a paw and soon the pair of them had tied the neck again and all was safe. Maudlin, who had been standing well back, now approached the flames again. He was not happy about sharing the rock overhang with this horrible supernatural creature that could tear things to bits. What if it got out in the night? But he dared not say anything to the others, in case they thought him a coward. So he chose to sleep well away from the sack, with several bodies between him and it, hoping that by the time it reached him it would have sated its hunger.

CHAPTER TWENTY-ONE

Maudlin lay awake with his mind spinning. Following their discussion about the wolverine's ghost he had had a long talk with Bryony about who and what he was. He was a 'least weasel' of the mustelid family, he knew that. But what he hadn't known was that there were many other species of weasel. There were mountain weasels, black-striped weasels, yellow-bellied weasels, tropical weasels, to name but a few. So, all over the world he had these cousins he never knew existed – cousins who, more importantly, didn't know *he* existed. Then there were all kinds of stoats, ferrets and polecats, a score or so of martens, nearly a dozen different kinds of otter – from the hairy-nosed otter to the spot-necked otter – something called a tayra and something else called a zorilla, all weasely creatures of the same family.

'It just goes to show,' he told himself, 'you have to keep up with your relations or they get out of paw.'

The fire had died to a dull red glow. One or two embers had spilled out and now flared up in the wind. Apart from these charcoal stars on the ground, Maudlin could see very little. There were noises though: the sound of the wind in the mountain crevices; the odd shift of scree on the slopes when a beetle dislodged a stone; the hollow sound of limewater dripping in caves, forming stalactites and stalagmites. Then Maudlin heard quite a different sound: a sort of low moan, carried within the louder noise of the wind, which seemed to speak his name.

'Hello?' he said, sitting up. 'Monty? Scruff? Bryony?'

He heard their returning snores, nothing more, but the sound of his name still kept coming, riding on the back of the wind. '*Maudlin!*' it said. '*Come to me.*'

'Who is that?' he said, clacking his teeth in mock humour. 'Is that you, Calabash?'

No answer, except his name again.

'Gordon? Gordon the mole-rat?'

'*Maudlin.*'

Despite his fear, Maudlin decided to investigate. After all, a name was a personal thing, not to be bandied about. He was annoyed that someone he did not know – for he knew no-one out here in the mountains except those friends who were with him – should call him by name. How had they got to know it? That was the thing. Had they been eavesdropping on private conversations? He felt violated.

Once on his feet he stumbled about in the glow of the firelight, the noise of the wind and loose stones confusing him. Occasionally there was a loud cracking sound which came from the mountain walls. He had been told this was ice getting into crevices and expanding.

'Hello? Who's there?'

He found a brass lamp and, with a little difficulty, lit it from the embers. Shielding the flame with his paw he closed the little glass window and held the lamp up high. Now he could see! And it was true that his friends, and Calabash and Gordon, were all still fast asleep.

'*Maudlin.*'

'Oh, shut up,' he grumbled, being very weary himself, 'I'm coming.'

He followed the sound. It led him to the rock overhang and eventually to the sack itself. It was the wolverine's ghost which had been calling him. A shiver of fear went through Maudlin. How had the ghost learned his name? Why, because they had been talking, of course, in the vicinity of the sack. Funny, he hadn't thought of ghosts as having the power of speech; not hungry ghosts of mammals that had been hungrier still in life. Gluttons in fact.

'What – what do you want?' Why was it, he was thinking to himself, that strange gods and ghosts always chose *him* to speak to? Why not one of the others this time? He had had his turn.

'Let me out.'

'No, I'll get into trouble.'

'My name is Enchanter.'

'Why are you telling me that?'

'Because,' said the wolverine's ghost, 'now you know me – and I know you. We are known to each other. In a moment we will be acquaintances. Shortly after that, friends. Would you let a friend fester in a prison of sackcloth, in a hessian jail? I think not. I think my friend Maudlin has more honour than that. Let me out, friend.'

'I'm not your friend, and in any case, you'll just rip me to bits and eat my real friends. I've heard about you hungry ghosts.'

'Lies. All lies. We are as gentle as dormice.'

'I don't like the way this conversation is going. I'm off back to bed.'

'You know you won't sleep. Your conscience won't let you. Come on, cousin, just loosen the knot a little. Just let a bit of air into the sack. It's stifling in here – I'm suffocating slowly and painfully. You wouldn't let even a stranger die through lack of air, would you?'

Maudlin reached out for the knot, then drew back quickly. 'Wait a minute. You're already dead.'

There was a significant silence, then the voice

195

came back with a pathetic edge to it. 'Ah, you caught me out. True. True. I am but a captured soul, a phantom, a spectre, a thing that goes bump in the night.' The tone now changed and became laden with grievance. 'But do you think I have no rights? Do think you are morally justified in keeping me prisoner? What about the law of ghostly freedom? The right to roam, to ramble where I choose, over these mountains? Would you flout the law of mountain mustelids, of the Creator himself? Shame on you. Shame.'

'I'm going back to bed now,' said Maudlin. 'I'm not listening to you any more.'

He did indeed get as far as three paces towards his sleeping bag before the creature in the sack halted him with a deep sigh.

'What?' said Maudlin. 'What is it?'

'If I could just see the stars for a few moments. Tomorrow I shall be sold to a village and put out in a forest. One cannot see the stars through a forest canopy. Darkness. Darkness is mine inheritance. I cannot complain, I suppose –' another sigh – 'I have lived my life and now I must take what death has to offer. Yet – yet to see the stars one more time . . .'

'I bet you're not even worried about the stars.'

'Look up,' said the voice. 'Look beyond the mountain peak that lies directly above your path. What do you see? I'll tell you what you see. A bright star that seems to change colour with every moment. I know that star. It used to be my guiding light in life.'

Maudlin looked and there was indeed a shining brightness to that particular celestial light. 'Oh, all right then,' he grumbled, going back to the sack, 'but I'm only going to let you have a three-centimetre hole to look through. I don't want you slipping out.'

Maudlin tried to undo the knot, but like the mole-rat he found it an impossible task. So again like the mole-rat, he cut the cord. However, unlike the mole-rat he did not keep a tight hold of the neck of the sack as he did so. The wolverine's hessian prison jerked from his paws and fell open. A greyish white thing with claws and teeth leapt out. Luckily for Maudlin the ghost hunter woke just at that moment and let out a yell of anguish. Enchanter had no desire to be captured again and he streaked away like the wind.

'What have you done?' cried the mole-rat. 'Is this how you repay my kindness?'

'I'm sorry. I didn't think. It talked me into letting it see the stars. I thought I could hold it tight while it looked. But—'

'All my profit gone,' moaned Gordon. 'I shall starve.'

By now Scruff, Monty and Bryony were awake. So was Calabash Brown. They all looked at Maudlin. He felt their censure of his actions.

'I couldn't help it. Look, we can catch it again.'

'I think we'll have to try at least,' said Monty. 'Can we talk about it in the morning?'

'No,' replied Gordon, 'this has to be done now. By morning my ghost will be hiding in some cave high up in the peaks. I shall have lost him. We need to trap him again now, while he's still a little stupefied from hunger. He hasn't been able to eat while he's been in the sack. We must catch him before he gobbles a few ptarmigan or mountain hares. I shall set the traps again. But we need some bait.'

Scruff said, 'I'll be the bait.'

'No you won't,' replied Maudlin in a low voice. 'This was my doing – I'll act as the bait.'

'Good, that's settled then,' Monty said. 'Tell us what to do, Gordon, and we'll do it.'

The mole-rat had with him a carrying frame made of timber rods tied together with leather thongs. He took from this back-carriage a flat square pack of lacquered black wood. This he began to unfold, section by section. As it opened up it slotted and clicked into what eventually became a hollow box with perfect dimensions: a metre cubed. On it there were designs in muted colours of foxes and wolves, and also some black-stroked characters from a picture writing unknown to the weasels. Finally, the mole-rat opened a small set of cupboard doors, which revealed the interior of the box. When Monty peered through a peephole, the space inside the box appeared to be infinite. It stretched away for ever and ever on all sides. Within this infinite space were mazes and labyrinths, the walls of which were covered in sliding drawers and alcoves, niches and compartments, shelves and hiding spaces.

'Mirrors,' explained the mole-rat. 'And magic, of course.'

The starlight seemed to twinkle more brightly at the sound of the word 'magic', while the wind rustled the alpine flowers.

'It belonged to a Kathayan conjurer, a pangolin of great chicanery with dextrous paws. He built the box himself. It is a marvel of engineering and carpentry. And the finish, you must admit, is something to be admired. I am very proud of what I call my ghost trap.'

'Right,' said a nervous Maudlin. 'Where do I stand?'

Gordon the mole-rat ghost hunter looked a little puzzled. 'Why, inside the conjurer's box, of course.'

CHAPTER TWENTY-TWO

Spindrick and Quikquik heard two stories. One
that Wm. Jott had taken the trail north to big-
white-bear tundra country – ay, the land of the
silver birch and beaver, ay. The other that he had
gone south, where a revolution had broken out.
Spindrick decided to take no notice of the first
tale. After all, Wm. Jott had a revolutionary
weapon to sell. It followed that he wanted buyers
and would go where those buyers were to be
found. He and Quikquik took the Wills Cargo
mouse-stage south, to the countries beyond the
borders of the northern New World. There, on
the southern trail, they met two new mammals: a
tayra and a black-footed ferret.

'This is my country,' said the ferret, using her

paw to sweep the scene north of the border. '*He* comes from down there.'

'This ees true,' replied the tayra. 'I yam from the south.'

The ferret, whose markings made her look as if she were wearing a black mask, was as slim and lithe as a large stoat. The tayra was much longer and heavier, with coarse hair and a yellow spot on his front. Their names, Spindrick learned, were the Lonely Stranger and Pronto. Between them they patrolled the western hills, saving mustelids from mammal bandits and humans gone bad. There was not a lot they could do about the latter, except attempt to rescue any mustelid caught by a rogue human, but mammal bandits were a different matter and were dealt with severely.

'A do-gooder,' said Spindrick. 'A Dudley Do-Right.'

'If you like,' said the black-footed ferret, glaring through her mask. 'I suppose you're a Diddly Do-Wrong.'

'If you like,' replied Spindrick. 'For the right reasons.'

Yet despite their opposing philosophies, their different views and principles, the two mammals took to each other. The Lonely Stranger taught Spindrick the words to 'Home, Home on the Range', and Spindrick showed her how to make a simple bomb using match heads and iron filings mixed with saltpetre. They shared an affection for the purple sage and the tumbleweed and a mutual dislike of the desert cactus. Both thought the world was too full of mammals, though each had his or her own idea about how to thin down the numbers.

Pronto, the tayra, was something else. He kept himself to himself and rarely offered an opinion on anything. One or twice he drew his seven-shooter and picked the flowers off a nearby cactus with some deadly shooting, but for the most part he simply stared dreamily into the middle distance and hummed an unrecognizable tune. He and Quikquik seemed of like mind: they only said something if it was important. Both disliked small talk and chit-chat.

In the middle of the night all four mammals were woken by the sound of an eerie wailing coming from the hills behind them.

'What's that?' cried the superstitious Quikquik, throwing more wood on the fire. 'Is that banshees?' He clutched his lucky barracuda tooth, the one carved in the shape of a northern sea god, and trembled. No physical danger could scare Quikquik, but the Other World was another matter.

'Have no fear,' replied Pronto. 'Thees is the Mad Fiddler of the Mountains. Up in the hills ees a lizard who play the fiddle in the middle of the night. Keep everyone awake. One day Pronto go looking for heem and shoot heem dead. Then, no more fiddle-faddle.'

They listened to the weird music, which seemed to be from an ancient source, a primitive sound that chilled the blood with its minor chords and sudden high, piercing notes.

'Only in the New World,' said Spindrick. 'It couldn't happen anywhere else.'

The following morning the four of them continued southwards together. At noon they came to a village full of tayras, where Pronto was known by name. 'I take you to the cantina,' he said to Spindrick. 'There we ask about thees Billy Jott.'

A belltower overshadowed the low, single-storey mud dwellings, one of which had a sign outside. The cantina was a sleazy-looking bar called El Miel-rocío Abrevadero, which, roughly translated, meant the Honey-dew Trough. It was full of tayras wearing big, wide hats and jangling with silver spurs, studded belts, bandoliers of bullets and shiny buckles. The place was gloomy and misshapen, with dark corners in more than four places. Spiders' webs decorated the ceiling and mangy cockroaches supped at the pools of honey dew that had spilled on the bar and dripped to the floor. Mammals were gambling at hollyhockers, playing for high stakes.

They asked about Wm. Jott. Among the tayras there was a sprinkling of opossums. One of them told them that Billy Jott, the Welkin stoat, had gone north to beaver country.

'I seen him,' said the opossum. 'We was in Kaliphornya together, Billy and me. Billy went north to the gold mines of the Meekon. Me an' my partner, Moondance, came south to rob banks, and to create mayhem and myth.'

'And who are you, sir?' asked Spindrick, nettled that he had come so far south for nothing at all. 'Your name, if you please?'

'They call me Batch Cussidy, on account of I'm always using swear words in bunches.'

'Well, good luck on your bank-robbing ventures,' replied Spindrick, taking his leave. 'I'm always pleased to meet ambitious mammals, anxious to further their careers in foreign lands. And I hope there will be many myths created around your death, once you've been gunned down.'

'Mighty nice of you to say so. Give Billy Jott my love.'

The next day the Lonely Stranger and Pronto moved on, saying they had souls to save somewhere out on the range. Spindrick and Quikquik started out north again, cursing their initial choice of direction. Once more they had to endure a night of the Mad Fiddler of the Mountain's eerie violin playing, before finding the trail.

Back in San Ferryanne they took a fishing boat north along the western shore, until they reached the Clondike. As this was snow country, they hired a mouse-sleigh pulled by muskies. Being a native of the region, Quikquik knew how to drive this vehicle and get the best out of the muskies. On their very first night they were pursued by wolves. The polecat and the weasel built a fire to keep the ravenous canines at bay, but Quikquik assured Spindrick that there were 'few attacks by wolves on healthy creatures. Usually go after sick and lame. Humans like shooting wolves. Seem to have unreasonable hatred for wolves – very strange when they like dogs so much – dogs same family. Most strange. We all right, with huge fire you built.'

It was indeed a great blaze, which lit the snow for some way around. Indeed, it attracted two humans, who came and asked to warm their hands by it. Spindrick, like most of his kind, distrusted humans who carried rifles. They were often too trigger-happy for safety. However, there was not a lot he and Quikquik could do. They couldn't turn the men away, not on a cold night. The two strangers almost immediately hogged the flames, blocking out the warmth which should have reached the other two mammals.

'Where you from?' asked one of the men, a great bearded creature with size fifty boots. 'San Ferryanne?'

'That's right,' said Spindrick. 'What about you?'

'We're from over there.' He waved a hand out into the darkness. 'From the north-west. Bin looking for gold.'

'Find any?'

'A little,' said the other man, staring nervously out into the night, where the wolves were still at choir practice. 'Not much, though.' He felt for a little leather bag on his belt.

Spindrick noticed that the fur coats and mittens the humans were wearing were made of mink, a cousin of the weasel and polecat. 'And – er – you've been hunting?' he asked.

The man looked down at himself, then said, 'Yes, moose. You wear mouse, we wear moose.' He laughed, showing his teeth, the sound booming out into the night. Immediately the wolves went silent. Spindrick's blood chilled in his veins. There is nothing like the laugh of a man to put the fear of death into a four-footed beast. Certainly the muskies stampeded at the sound. Spindrick and Quikquik had to go out with torches and round them up again. They persuaded the creatures to return to the camp only with great difficulty.

Then the two mustelids spent the whole night awake worrying about those two huge animals with glinting eyes who hogged their fire.

In the morning, much to the relief of Spindrick, the two men moved on. The humans were concerned about the number of wolf pawprints which were peppered around the camp. For once Spindrick was glad of the company of wolves. They pressed on that day, in and out of pine forests, driving themselves through blizzards, until they reached a frozen lake. There was a cabin on the shore. They thought it might be owned by beavers and hammered on the door. Instead it was opened by a female mustelid the like of whom Spindrick had never seen before. Her fur looked so soft she could have descended from the couches of mustelid gods.

'Hello?' she said. 'Such a noise!'

'Sorry,' answered Spindrick. 'We – er – wondered if you'd put us up for the night.'

'We?'

'My seafaring polecat friend and myself. He's seeing to the muskies out back. He's a rough sort of fellow, but very gentle for all that. A heart of gold really. We mean you no harm, I assure you.'

She looked a little worried, but then said, 'I suppose so. Yes, come on in. Sorry I'm a little unwelcoming. There was the smell of humans around this morning.' She looked out and around, as if expecting to see them. 'It's always worrying to have humans nearby, out here in the lonely wastes of the Clondike. The law isn't as effective here as it is down south.'

'We met them last night,' replied Spindrick gravely, entering the cabin and knocking the snow from his snowshoes. 'They've moved on. I can see why you would be worried, with that beautiful fur. What . . . ?'

'What am I?' She clicked her teeth in amusement. 'I'm a sable, an immigrant, originally from Sableland. You appear by your accent to be an immigrant too. Are you here for the gold?'

He was about to say, No, for the guns, when he changed his mind. Somehow that wouldn't sound right to this divine creature standing before him, her pelt fluffed up in a most delightful way, her dark eyes moist with understanding. For some reason Spindrick wanted to impress this sable jill and so he answered, 'No, not the gold. I'm a naturalist. I've been commissioned by the Royal Society of Muggidrear to track down a rare beetle. I expect to do a paper on it in the spring.' He let his little pink tongue show between his teeth and flicked his tail. 'I say, is that stew?'

'Oh, yes,' she said, turning with a flash of her gorgeously silky fur. 'Would you like some?'

At that moment Quikquik, shaven tattoos and all, appeared in the doorway, his harpoon in paw. He brushed the snow from his head and stared at the female sable. Their eyes locked. Something magical passed between them. Spindrick was shocked; he knew he could have been whisked to Timbukthree and the pair of them wouldn't have noticed.

'I say,' he said through gritted fangs, 'are we going to eat some stew or just stand looking at each other?'

'Who's looking at you?' asked the sable, her eyes still on the tall, magnificent fish hunter in the doorway. 'I'm not.'

CHAPTER TWENTY-THREE

'I can't go in there!' cried Maudlin. 'The ghost will have me trapped in a small space.'

Monty said, 'I'm inclined to agree with Maudlin. Yes, he was responsible for letting the wolverine's ghost go free, but I hardly think the recapture of the spectre is worth the risk of a mammal life.'

Gordon the mole-rat made an expansive gesture. 'There's no risk – no *real* risk. Ghosts have very little memory – the wolverine won't remember being trapped by the box the first time. Ghosts are easily confused, especially by things like mazes and labyrinths. You see how vast the space within the box looks to the naked eye?'

'Infinite to my eye,' replied Monty.

'Exactly. But it's all a trick, all a matter of illusion. All done with smoke and mirrors. So long as Maudlin keeps his head, doesn't run wild so to speak, he will be able to keep the exit in view. As soon as the wolverine's ghost enters by the trapping-flap, Maudlin simply jumps out and I will be ready to close the lid behind him.'

'So the space isn't real?'

Gordon looked cagey. 'Well, it is and it isn't. I mean, the space is there because it *looks* as if it's there. What a mammal believes becomes real for the time he believes it. You can defy the laws of physics, *if you let yourself*. The brain is a very strange organ. It can make straight things look curved and near things appear far away. When one walks towards a distant mountain, that mountain seems to move not nearer, but further away. Looking along a hot roadway in the sunlight, it often appears that pools of water lie on the surface. These are illusions, mirages, *fata Morganas*. The area within this box *seems* to be vast, and *is* vast so long as one looks at it in a particular way. The idea is to remember that, despite appearances, it really is only a box. If you do this, there is no danger. Danger only occurs when you forget that it is a box. In other words, do not panic, keep your reason, and all will be well.'

'Gobbledegook,' muttered Scruff. 'It don't make sense. Here, Maud, I'll go in the box.'

'No, no,' replied Maudlin seriously. 'It was my

fault. I must put things right. I don't understand what it's about, but I'll do my best.'

Bryony said, 'Are you *sure*, Maudlin? You are given to flights of fancy, you know. You have been known to be poetical. Why not let someone more down to earth like Scruff or myself go in the box?'

'No.'

'All right then,' said Monty. 'Let's get on with it.'

Gordon opened the lid to the box and without any hesitation Maudlin leapt in an agile weasely manner into the void. The lid was closed.

Immediately Maudlin found himself in a series of mazes with shiny black walls that glinted in the light that came through the peephole in the front of the box. When he looked about him, the place seemed vast. There were smoky mirrors everywhere, reflecting the fuzzy images of a weasel. When Maudlin turned quickly, shadowy weasels danced around him. There were handles within reach – dozens of them. He turned one, opened a door, and found himself looking down a long, endless corridor into silky blackness. He closed it. Pulling on another, a drawer opened. It was large enough to climb into. When he felt around inside, it appeared to have no bottom or sides. The same with a cabinet, which could apparently have held all the cloaks and dresses, all the hats and accessories – not to mention the shoes – that Princess Sybil of Muggidrear had ever owned. Sybil was a classy dresser, a fickle owner of shoes and hats, and the size of her wardrobe was legendary.

'Think box!' he told himself. 'Think small!'

He managed, with difficulty, to force his mind to remember that he was in a small space. Reaching up with his paw he touched the lid of the box. It gave a little under pressure. It was loose, not locked or shut tight. Yes, he could jump at that lid and be out in the open air within a second. Maudlin quashed a sudden desire to do so, as he poked his claw through the peephole, just to make sure fresh air was behind it. Like many mammals, he disliked confined spaces. It was probably the result of his ancestors being caught in traps set by humans. However, despite his resolve to remain reasoning and objective he began to stare about him with an imaginative eye. Almost immediately he was in a huge space, a great hall – a set of great halls, the linked interiors of many mansions. He was in a place with no beginning and no end. He was in a vast universe with but a single star, which shone brightly high above him, providing the only light.

'Brave little star,' he murmured. 'Lone giver of light.'

At that moment something came hurtling into this universe with its solitary source of light. It was like a whirlwind of snow, a small blizzard with fangs of ice that had the shape of a wolverine. Maudlin stayed just long enough to see those terrible white eyes and slavering jaws before wrenching open a door and slamming it behind him. He fled with all possible speed through half-lit tunnels, along a corridor beyond, through another door, down a shaft, into a wardrobe without a back, out into a forest of dark columns, down a hole which led to a maze – only then remembering that he should have kept his head and jumped for the lid of the box.

'Well?' cried Monty, rushing out from where the waiting mammals had been hiding. 'Where is he? You saw it. The wolverine's ghost went inside. *Hurtled* inside like the deranged beast it appears to be. The instant that creature entered by the side flap, Maudlin should have leapt through the lid. Where is he? Gordon?'

The mole-rat sighed. 'I fear he panicked.'

'You said that wouldn't happen,' Bryony pointed out.

'It *shouldn't* have happened. It's not difficult to keep one's head, even over the course of an hour or two. Your friend appears to have lost his almost immediately. He was only in there for five minutes. We were so lucky to recapture the hungry ghost within such a short period. Maudlin didn't have *time* to become beguiled by the illusion of the box.'

'You don't know Maudlin,' sniffed Scruff. 'Well, there's only one thing for it. I'll 'ave to go in after him.'

'Impossible. You now believe your friend is lost in infinite space. Once you enter the box, you'll never be able to find him. Who can search a whole universe, an area without a beginning or an end? No-one. It's a Catch Twenty-two. You can't begin to look until you believe in what you think you see, just like your friend. Once you do that it will be impossible for you to find him. It will be like looking for a snowflake on the South Pole.'

'Then how do we get him out?' asked Monty. 'Surely, if we open the box, he will be there inside?'

'True,' replied the mole-rat. 'But so will the wolverine. They will suddenly be sharing a small box, not a vast universe. The wolverine might pounce on him immediately and devour him. We may be unable to prevent it.'

'So please to tell me,' said Calabash Brown, coming into the conversation for the first time, 'what will be happening now, inside?'

'The wolverine's ghost will be relentlessly hunting down its prey.'

'But,' Bryony pointed out, 'he won't catch him, will he? You said yourself the space inside is too vast. There are too many mazes and labyrinths. The hungry ghost won't be able to find Maudlin any more than we could.'

'As to that,' said Gordon apologetically, 'why, the ghost has its supernatural sense of smell to guide it to its quarry.'

'So Maud's done for,' said Scruff, 'unless a miracle 'appens?'

'You have hit the nail on the head.'

'How do I get inside without disturbing the beliefs of those already in there?' asked Monty. 'Quickly now.'

'The same way as the wolverine. Through the trapping-flap on the side of the box.'

Without any further ado, Monty snatched up the ghost hunter's sack and entered the box.

For a while he was disoriented. Happily the other occupants of the box were engaged in their own pursuits. Gradually he adjusted to his surroundings. He told himself he was not in a place without boundaries, but in a large box. There were two other creatures in there with him, Maudlin and a white wolverine. The wolverine was hurrying round the box, chasing its weasel prey. The pair of them, the hunter and the hunted, seemed to be going in a circle, the wolverine gradually gaining on the weasel. Monty picked his moment and then pounced, throwing the sack over the wolverine's ghost. Once he had the creature inside, he choked off the neck of the sack. Whipping off his belt with his free paw, he secured it. The wolverine screamed and struggled, but to no avail. It was firmly imprisoned.

Maud was still hurrying along, chasing his own tail, running around the interior of the box in circles. Every so often he looked over his shoulder with wild eyes, as if he thought a frightful fiend did close behind him tread. Maudlin was still in a huge immeasurable space inside his own head.

Monty tapped his friend on the shoulder. Maudlin jumped, as if someone had pricked him. He stared at Monty with swimmy eyes.

'Monty? You too? We're both trapped in here now.' Maudlin looked around, his eyes full of endless darkness. 'We'll never get out, you know. It's too big. Too big. I've been running for hours and getting nowhere.'

Monty jumped up and threw back the lid of the box. Light flooded the interior. Maudlin blinked. Gordon did something with a secret catch and the walls of the box fell away. Monty grabbed the sack and gave it to the mole-rat before gently urging Maudlin to step away from the now flattened box. The other weasel, still bemused and stupefied by his experience, did so. Gordon folded the box and clipped it to its carrying frame.

'So,' the mole-rat said to Monty, 'you are a ghost hunter too!'

'Not really,' replied Monty modestly. 'I just didn't believe my own eyes. I'm a very practical mammal. I use logic in such circumstances. Illusion, phantasmagoria, tricks of the light and mind are no match for cold logic.'

'Being a hunter of ghosts, a dealer in magic and thimblerig, I could argue, but not today. Today I am all admiration. But now I must be on my way. Good luck to you, weasels. You have a fine leader there. A fine leader and—' he nodded towards Calabash – 'a good guide. I hope you reach your destination safely. And you, brave weasel—' he was speaking to Maudlin – 'you have the imagination of a god. You should be a teller of tales, a writer of stories. I have never known a creature so easily lost in his own mind. You have the creative genius of a dreamer. Go forth and make words which will astound the world and its wife, young weasel.'

With that, the mole-rat left them to ponder on *his* words.

CHAPTER TWENTY-FOUR

The day finally came when Calabash Brown led the four friends down a long sloping hill to the Yingtong river. It was this mighty, swirling grey waterway that would carry them to the capital of Far Kathay, Siungsuong, to the Great Pangolin's Forbidden Palace. Siungsuong was so named because it was the city of a million crickets, which sang from its thousand parks. Every public and private garden had its patch of grass or bamboo where the cricket choirs gathered of an evening. The citizens of Siungsuong carried little cages with a single cricket inside. They hung these cages in the trees so that the tame crickets could learn the songs of the wild crickets.

'Look at all the boats,' cried Maudlin excitedly.

'Hundreds and hundreds of them, all different.'

Well, they were not all different. There were many that were similar – there were quite a few sampans, for instance, and a great many junks – but Maudlin had every reason to be amazed, for the river was simply teeming with craft. Back and forth, over and across, up and down. It was quite amazing that there were not more collisions. These river vessels were manned by a variety of creatures, ranging from the numerous pangolins to otters, civets and mongooses. The waterfront itself seemed to be managed in the main by spiky porcupines, who looked rather unapproachable. A pangolin passed them with a sideways glance.

Bryony stared after the creature. 'That's the first pangolin I've ever seen,' she said, breathing in the life and activity of the river as if it were air. 'Such strange but wonderful-looking mammals, aren't they? How lucky we are to be able to experience such a sight. Not many Welkin mammals have seen this.' She looked around, then asked, 'Where are the humans?'

Calabash replied, 'They live beyond the southern plains of this vast country, on the far side of the Opal river. It is there they have their own city and its port to the sea. We shall meet with no humans here, Jis Bludd.' He called everyone except Bryony by their first names now. She had insisted – in vain – that he do the same with her, but he was overawed by her qualifications. Calabash knew nothing of Right Honourables like Monty, but he was immensely impressed by surgeons and healers. To him they were the magicians of the Age of Steam and were to be revered; he could not be familiar with them.

Bryony studied a pangolin sitting on the deck of its boat. It had a long, tapering body – extending, with the tail, to around seventy centimetres in length – which seemed to be covered in scales. There were five large claws on each of its feet. With its tail and pointed face it looked rather like a very large lizard, but without the sheen of a reptile's skin. It was eating what appeared to be a pancake with lots of black and yellow bits in it.

'What's he having for dinner?' Bryony asked, pointing to the pangolin without making it a rude and obvious gesture. 'Do you know?'

'*She,*' corrected Calabash. 'What is she devouring? It has the appearance of a wasp or hornet pancake, Jis Bludd. This is a very common dish here in Far Kathay. Pangolins are very partial to the wasps, the ants and the termites. Of course, modern pangolins eat other foods, but traditionally they are quite liking these insects for their suppers.'

Monty, ever practical, was scanning the river craft for a suitable one to take them up to the capital of the country. 'What is that craft there?' he asked Calabash. 'The one just mooring up at the third jetty?'

'That, Monty, is a Foochow pole-junk. I see you like it, but we shall have to choose the boat that goes with the sailor. I am having thoughts that we shall choose a captain with command of Welkin language, to make the passage up the river easier for you. For in truth, I must leave you here and travel home. I am missing my deserts, with their horizons in a straight line. Here all the horizons curve upwards to the sky.'

Calabash Brown, that dashing adventurer-guide, found them the captain of a junk known as a Ma-yang-tzu. He then bid them goodbye. 'Farewell, my new friends,' he said, as he drew away on a sampan making for the sea-going vessel which would take him home. He waved his broad-brimmed hat. 'Come to tea any time you are passing through Eggyok.'

Monty paid the guide, adding a generous bonus.

'Goodbye,' they chorused. 'Safe voyage.'

'He was a good 'un,' sighed Scruff.

'The best,' said Maudlin. 'I've never met a jerboa like him.'

'Which isn't surprising,' said Bryony, 'since he's the *only* one you've met.'

The four weasels were shown on board the Ma-yang-tzu junk, which was moored next to one of the river police boats known as Fast Crabs. The junk was made to withstand the strong currents and dangerous rapids of the Upper Yingtong. It had a single sail like a patchwork quilt, a flat covered deck and shallow draught. There were cabin houses aft, standing proud of the deck. On the other side of the police boat, with its cannon on the bows, was a bull-headed sand boat, a huge craft with several sails. Porcupines were unloading its cargo, sacks of something which they carried up to the warehouses on the slope above the harbour.

The captain of the Ma-yang-tzu junk, a pangolin, welcomed them on his vessel. 'Please to rest your paws,' he said, clicking and bowing. 'There is warm water in china bowls for to wash them, scented with lemongrass. In one moment my crewmammal will bring to you some food. Is it your liking to eat termite stew?'

'That would be most satisfactory,' said Monty before Maudlin could protest. 'We are very much looking forward to trying your local dishes.'

'Good. Good. In which case, I must take heed of the sails, if we are to get under way. By the way, I learned my Welkin from polecat and marten sailors, who come to these shores to trade. I hope I am not making too many mistakes.'

'You put us to shame,' said Bryony. 'I wish I could speak another language half so well.'

Clearly the pangolin, whose name was Hi Lo, was pleased with this reply for he gave them another clicking. Once his attention was on his work, however, his expression changed. He barked orders to his crew, obviously expecting them to be carried out instantly. He himself jumped to the rigging and his expert claws did expert things with sheets and halyards and stays. In the meantime the four weasels rested as instructed, sitting on the warm deck while being served with termite stew.

Bryony washed her paws and the others followed suit, before tasting the steaming dish before them.

'Very nice,' said Scruff, spooning up the stew with great relish. 'Very appetizin'. Luverly.'

Captain Hi Lo turned and clicked his appreciation at this compliment.

Monty tried it. Yes, a light pleasant flavour, mostly cardamoms and bay leaves at first, with an underlying taste of insect. There were grass seeds in there too, which gave it body. Certainly nothing to get anxious about, as Maudlin seemed to be. Monty watched him put his spoon to his mouth and tentatively sip at the edge. Maudlin's expression remained suspicious, but he continued to sip the liquid without actually eating any of the stew itself. Finally there was nothing but sludge in the bottom of his bowl.

'It's all sludgy,' he complained, turning it over with his spoon. 'I don't like sludgy food much.'

'You ain't tasted it,' said Scruff. 'Go on, take a spoonful. Be a weasel. Get some grub inside yer.'

With all eyes on him Maudlin scooped up half a spoonful and put it in his mouth, his expression already turning sour before he had even swallowed. 'I don't like it,' he said, putting down his bowl and screwing up his face. 'I don't like the bits. Look, you can see ant things in it.'

Monty and Bryony sighed, looking at each other and raising their eyes. It was like dealing with a kitten. Maudlin had made up his mind long ago not to like the food.

'Isn't there any egg and chips?' asked Maudlin. 'I could really do with some egg and chips.'

'I'm sure we'll get some egg, if not the chips,' replied Bryony, 'but you'll have to wait. This stew is quite substantial. I don't think we'll be getting anything else to eat for quite a while, since the river sailors on this boat will be taken up with managing the craft. The river looks quite dangerous. See how the currents and eddies swirl around us? I'm sure they're not going to be able to cook again for ages.'

'Oh, in that case . . .' said Maudlin, and he spooned down the rest of the stew without another murmur. Bryony had said the right thing. Maudlin might be fussy about his food, but he had to have some. He would rather eat cockroaches than starve.

Unfortunately there was a head wind that evening and they had to tack back and forth across the river to make any progress. This kept their captain busy until some time after darkness had fallen. Finally, when the evening star was high above their craft he took the tiller from his helmsmammal to steer the junk towards the bank and moored there.

'We will stay here the night,' he said. 'Tomorrow perhaps the wind will have turned and the sailing will be easier.'

All along the river other sailors were continuing with their voyage, using lamps which swayed in the wind to avoid running into one another. But Hi Lo was aware that his passengers needed to settle in gradually. If the junk sailed all night they would have no time to get used to the motion. One or two nights moored to the bank could do no harm.

The four weasels slept on deck. It was a night of fireflies and glow-worms and contentment. Bryony wondered if she had spent a better one, ever. Fish plashed on the surface of the river. Crickets chirruped on its banks. The welcome boards of the junk accepted the weary weasels to its bosom, and they drifted, drifted, drifted, off into a sweet world of sleep.

Chapter Twenty-five

They came to a stretch of river where the boats grew fewer and fewer, until theirs was the only craft sailing between two high banks. Beyond the shores were steep-sided mountains with sharp peaks. Rugged little pines clung to cracks halfway up the rock faces. Storks' nests littered the ledges. Mist drifted between these mountains, and down over the river surface, to shroud the whole scene with a sense of mystery.

There were shallow islands in this stretch of the waterway, where long-legged birds stood and glared at the foreign weasels as they passed by. Here too were shallow waters where pike lurked in manes of long, flowing tethered weed. Their glittering eyes looked up at the boat as if hoping that someone might accidentally fall overboard. Pike were to weasels as sharks were to humans.

'Don't lean out too far,' said Maudlin to Scruff. 'They'll strip you to the bone within seconds!'

'Nah, that's piranha, that is. Pike swallow yer whole.'

Monty was speaking with Hi Lo, whose darting eyes told a story on their own.

'You seem worried, Captain. Are these dangerous waters?'

'Bandit and pirate,' muttered Hi Lo. 'Many such bandit can walk out into shallows, wait for us, and pounce like civet cat. And pirate – well – they of course on boat like this one, only faster. Both must swarm over us, if they get chance. They escape up backwater, or hide in mountain place, and I think there is no finding them once that happen.'

'I see you have a long-barrelled brass cannon on the bows?'

'Yes, but no gunpowder and no ammunition. Too poor to buy any this trip. Maybe next time, if next time come.'

Monty said, 'I might be able to help you there. My cousin Spindrick taught me a few tricks when we were kittens in the nursery together. Do you have any boxes of matches? A rasp or a coarse file on board? Saltpetre?'

Captain Hi Lo nodded. 'We have plenty of match in galley. We use to light the stove. And as for rasp, you find one in tool box, in third hold. But this saltpetre . . . ?' He shrugged.

There were many holds in the ship, all sealed off from one another. It meant that if the boat ever hit anything and was holed, it would not sink. There were other airtight compartments to keep it afloat. Monty found the matches and scraped the heads into a piece of newspaper. Then he took an old iron boat hook and used the rasp on it until he had some fine ferrous filings. Mixing the two together, he told Hi Lo, 'Saltpetre would improve the mixture, but it's not essential. There's enough sulphur in the match heads to serve our purpose – to make an explosive compound. Now all we need are some old nuts and bolts for ammunition . . .'

There were no nuts and bolts. What Hi Lo did have was a cargo of spices in small ceramic containers the size of salt and pepper pots. Monty stuffed about half a dozen of these down the barrel of the long brass cannon and rammed them home.

'They won't be as deadly as nuts and bolts of course,' he explained to the others, 'but they might do to frighten off marauders.'

'How many shots will we have?' asked Maudlin. 'More than one?'

'There were only enough matches to make three charges,' replied Monty. 'I'm hoping that will be enough to deter the pirates. For the rest of it, we shall arm ourselves with these stout bamboo poles and ward off any attempt to board us.'

Thus they continued to sail down the Yingtong, their keen eyes on the banks, their paws on the bamboo poles. Storks, herons and egrets watched them go by. Towards the next evening the junk rounded a bend in the river to find two sleek-looking craft waiting in the middle of the current. Sinister black flags were flying from their prows. Monty spotted a lookout up on a hill, who had no doubt warned his pirate comrades that a merchant boat was coming. A battle could not be avoided.

'Kwai-tu boat,' murmured Hi Lo, on being informed of the blockade. 'That means Quick-leaping war-junk. Very swift vessel. Come one either side and squash us between. Then many pangolin pirate jump on board, stab us with sword, take my cargo. They leave us for dead and sell my junk down-river. Bad mammal. Very bad mammal.'

'How have you got by them in the past?' asked Bryony.

'I pay them tribute. But have no more money. They take everything now. Strip us clean.'

'Not if we have anything to say about it,' said Scruff. 'Eh, Maud?'

'That's right, Scruff.' For once, Maudlin was ready to fight. The fact was, he had little choice. There was nowhere to run, so why make a big fuss? Why not show a little bravado for once? A little mammal spirit.

Hi Lo seemed very pleased. He had long since wanted to give the pirates a thrashing. Well, they might not be able to do that, but they could put up a good fight. There were good pangolins and bad pangolins. Those who faced him now were definitely the second sort of pangolins. Somewhere up and down the river were police boats, but whether they could reach them in time, once the fighting started, was a matter of guesswork.

As the Ma-yang-tzu junk got closer to the Kwai-tu war-junks the weasels could see that the pangolins on board the latter were bristling with weapons. They stood all along the sides of the vessels and hung from the rigging. Wielding sharp swords they yelled savagely, swishing the air with their blades, and were no doubt uttering threats of violence. Maudlin stared at the vicious, snarling creatures and wondered if he would ever see another morning on this earth. One or two were already shooting with muskets, but these weapons were old flintlocks, so worn their barrels rattled when they were fired, and the balls fell uselessly into the water in front of the merchant boat. Maudlin realized they were more for show than any serious attempt at wounding weasels.

Now Hi Lo's crew gathered on the deck. Most had colourful bandanas on their heads and in truth it was difficult to tell the difference between them and the pirates. Maudlin immediately wanted a bandana and was given one by the junk's boatswain. It was red – his favourite colour. There were some picture characters on the front of it. No doubt they said something like IMMORTAL WARRIOR or UNDEFEATABLE ONE. Magical without a doubt. He tied it around his furry head and waved his bamboo pole and yelled back at the pirates. Who did they think they were, these miserable river-raiders? Maudlin was suddenly filled with battle fury, with blood passion, with confidence. No-one could be vanquished, wearing a bandana like the one he had around his head. It protected its wearer from harm, imparting strength and vigour. It warded off blows from clubs and parried sword thrusts. It was better than wearing a suit of armour.

'Come on!' yelled Maudlin, jumping up into the rigging and waving his pole at the pirates, the tails of his red bandana flapping in the breeze. 'Think you can kill me? Not a chance.'

'Get down from there,' said a more rational and sober Bryony. 'You'll get hit by a bullet if you're not careful, Maudlin.'

'Just let 'em try, eh, Scruff? Eh? Just let 'em try. Not with these magical characters on my bandana. A sorcerer wrote them. A brave Welkin mammal now wears them with pride.'

'What do those characters on Maudlin's bandana say?' asked Bryony quietly of Hi Lo.

'They say, NUMBER ONE STIR-FRY CHEF. Bandana belong head galley cook.'

'Well, don't let Maudlin in on the secret.'

Monty was in the process of laying the gun: that is, aiming it at the first war-junk, the one on the right. In his paw was a lit taper. Once the gun was levelled and set, he applied the taper to the hole in the breech. The gun fired, recoiling. Maudlin and Scruff let out cheers. The air above the first war-junk was suddenly full of yellow, red, black and brown powder. Nutmeg, paprika, chilli, cayenne, turmeric, cinnamon and ginger floated down and enveloped the pirates' craft. There was a lot of yelling and sneezing. Pirates began leaping into the water, their eyes sore and streaming, their noses running, their fur full of multi-coloured spices. They splashed about in the water, as the currents took the spices downstream.

Monty shouted above the din, 'The pots hit each other in mid-air and burst. I meant them to rip into the sails of the war-junk and perhaps shatter the hull.'

'Never mind,' Bryony told him. 'This is working fine!'

Monty quickly re-laid the gun, pointing it at the second craft, whose crew was now furious with the merchant junk. Scruff and Maudlin sponged out the barrel of the cannon, rammed down another charge, then loaded it again with more spices, this time adding mace and caraway seeds for good measure. Again the gun was fired.

Small pots smashed together in mid-air, burst like shells, and sent their coloured hail down on the enemy. Again the ochre hues: dark red pieces of cinnamon bark, yellow turmeric, some dried green *herbes de Provence* floating like shattered autumn leaves on the breeze, a shower of hard, stinging cardamoms, a dash of salt, a spray of black peppercorns.

The second war-junk was enveloped in flavourful clouds. Pangolins fell from the rigging, choking, into the shallow waters of the river. Pangolins jumped for the middle sand bars, hoping to escape being spiced. Pangolins dangled from the rigging, their claws caught in the ropes, wailing and crying that their throats were on fire, or their eyes were burning, or their noses were about to explode. It was, for the merchant junk sailors, a wonderful spectacle. For too long these pirates had humiliated them. Now they were getting their own back and they clicked their teeth in glee.

The Ma-yang-tzu junk sailed gently between the two war-junks, still lost within many-coloured mists. Pangolin pirates tried to climb aboard the merchant craft, but they were warded off by weasels and pangolin crewmammals using bamboo poles. On, on went the merchant junk, leaving the enemy to fend for themselves in the murky waters.

The pirates struggled to the banks, watched by a gathering crowd of amazed river wading birds, who shook their heads in wonderment.

'What fools these mammals be,' said a purple heron, the spices and herbs streaming round her legs. 'It's like watching a circus.'

'But have you tasted the water?' said a small white egret excitedly. 'I've not drunk anything like it since the great gravy flood of 'seventy-two, when that junk went down with its tasty brown cargo . . .'

'Deliciously savoury,' said another. 'Did anyone think to ask for the recipe?'

But the Ma-yang-tzu junk was gone around the next bend, and the birds could only shake their heads and curse. They were born to wade, not fly after evening junks. If they left now, they would miss their share of the soup. They had to be content with what was to beak and claw. They spent the rest of the evening until the sun went down drinking, comparing the tastes of backwaters and pools, and clacking their beaks noisily at the sorry, sodden pangolin pirates, drying on the banks of the Yingtong river and shouting oaths at their captains.

CHAPTER TWENTY-SIX

After spending several more nights in jail Zacharias Falshed and Princess Sybil were thoroughly fed up. Even when they were released they were followed through the streets by murmuring stoats and were in danger of being re-arrested. Pictures of Queen Neferhapen were beginning to appear everywhere, on walls and doors, and the government of Eggyok was starting to worry about revolution. Sybil had no intention of leading a revolution against anyone, but convincing the authorities of that was difficult.

'I think we should get right away from here for a few days,' said Sybil. 'Let's take a steamboat south, down into the heart of the Hot Continent, and see what adventures we can have down there.'

'Good idea, Sib,' said Falshed. 'Er, I mean, Princess Sybil.'

'I should think so, Chief Falshed,' she said, tight-lipped. 'I'm not prepared to become too familiar with my brother's employees, even though I know you're here to assist me in any way I should desire, even to the point of sacrificing your freedom or your life.'

'Actually, I'm employed by the city,' he said stiffly.

'By the city council, which is run by my brother.'

'Well, yes, he's the mayor . . .'

'So, your point is?'

Falshed shut up. He knew he was not going to win with Sybil. Not when she was in one of these moods. Sometimes she could be almost friendly, offering him chocolates and tweaking his whiskers when he became pompous about something. At other times she was cold and distant and treated him like a servant. He never really knew where he was with her and could not work out whether it was the female in her which was responsible for these changes of mood, or the royal blood. He tended to believe it was the latter, because so far as he had observed, Bryony Bludd did not behave like this with Montegu Sylver. Sybil was like the weather. She could be sunny and bright, or stormy and bleak, or any combination of a dozen different climates.

'Does my tail look big in this?' she was asking him now, as she stood before a dusty full-length mirror outside a stall in the souk. She was trying on a sort of dust coat which a lot of the locals wore to keep the sand out of their fur. 'Does it look too stubby?'

He saw his chance to get his own back, but being Falshed he sighed and said, 'It looks fine.'

Her furry brow furrowed. 'Fine?'

'It looks adorable. Slim and attractive.'

'Well, no need to go overboard, Chief Falshed, it's only a dust coat, not a ball gown. I'll take it. Be a pet and pay the little weasel, will you, Chief?'

'Little weasel,' growled the little weasel stall owner under his breath. 'Patronizing jill!'

'Let's have less of that tone and more respect for customers,' warned Falshed, as he put some coins into the weasel's paw. 'Where are you from, anyway?'

This particular type of weasel had a yellow belly and, though clearly a cousin of the least weasel, which was what Welkin weasels were, came from a region where weasels were different. There were other strange-looking weasels around. One had a stripe down its back. Another, Falshed knew, called itself a mountain weasel. Yet another sported a very long tail. There was not, as he had always imagined, just *one* sort of weasel in the world, but a great many varieties, who fetched up in places like this, an international crossroads. The same could be said of badgers. In his travels through Eggyok the chief had met stink badgers, ferret badgers, hog badgers and honey badgers, all slightly different. When it came to martens there were over a dozen, from stone martens to fisher martens to yellow-throated martens. There were even thirteen species of otter!

Yet, so far as he knew, there was only one type of stoat. What did that tell him? That stoats were special? Or that stoats were inferior? It was all very difficult. He wanted to feel special. All species wanted to feel special. Yet was he in any way superior to all these other creatures? No, he told himself truthfully, he was not. They were all of them equally important to the richness of the natural world and its wonderful inhabitants.

'Sorry,' said Falshed, coming out of his reverie. 'What did you say?'

'I said I'm a weasel of Far Kathay – at least, my grandfather was; I was actually born here in Eggyok.'

'Good for you!' said Falshed, suddenly in high spirits. He went down on all fours and ran after Sybil, who was now looking through purses and wallets made of tree bark. 'Let's do what you said,' he told her. 'Let's take a steamboat south and see what we can find. Look at all the rich varieties of creature we've met so far! We might meet more and more. I wonder your brother doesn't take a trip like this. Stuck in that office of his, he knows nothing of the wider world, does he? A certain narrowness of mind, your brother.'

'Are you criticizing Jeremy?'

'No – yes, yes I am. He's a bigot, your brother is. I've come to see that recently. His mind is so narrow it's a wonder his brain doesn't fall off it.' Falshed gripped her by her slender shoulders. 'Sibyl, look at us, in this colourful land, *learning* things. Then look at him, stuck in that poky office in smog-ridden Muggidrear, scheming, dreaming only about money. Filthy lucre. Oh, I know many mammals *can't* travel like this, but we're so lucky, we should make the most of our good fortune. Up-river it is then, eh? Let's get out there and see the world. We should have gone with Sylver.'

'Well,' said Sybil, taken aback. 'Well, I don't know. I'm very fond of Jeremy and I won't have you talking about him like that, but . . .'

'But?'

'But, yes, he has a certain tight schedule he sticks to, which can be inhibiting to someone like myself, who seeks to enjoy other cultures, wider interests.'

They went straight to the steamboat company, followed by a trail of local stoats, and booked their tickets. It was an expensive business, going a long way by river boat, so they did not get hordes of locals following them on board. Soon they were cruising between sand banks, then through cultivated fields, and finally the rainforests and jungle. Before long the foliage tumbled over into the river, hiding the banks. They witnessed many strange and marvellous sights, found hidden cities, climbed volcanic hills and inhaled the fragrance of aromatic flowers and blossoms. They absorbed all the exotic sights, sounds and smells of a new continent.

'How wonderful this all is, Zacharias,' said Sybil, leaning on the rail of the steamboat as it left the main river to travel down a spur to the great ocean. 'You were so right to bring me here.' She adjusted her shawl, worn mainly to keep the mosquitoes out of her fur, rather than to ward off the cool humours of the evening. 'Listen to those crickets! And the noises of the jungle. Yet I feel quite safe on board, don't you? Shall we go to the front of the craft?'

'Why not?'

Falshed was feeling warm and squishy inside. He had discovered a romantic part of his soul that he hadn't known was there – the romance of foreign skies and nights, the romance of travel in exotic lands, the romance of drifting along a river.

They stood together in the bows, watching the darkness of the jungle slide by. Then they emerged into the wide river mouth, a delta with a huge sea port. Lights sparkled around them. The boat let out a low, mooning note from its horn. Sybil suddenly had the urge to stand on the prow, to get a better view.

'Be careful,' warned Falshed. 'It looks a bit unsafe.'

'Oh, you scaredy kitten—' Sybil had begun to say. At that moment the steamboat struck a huge floating log and the boat lurched violently to the left. Sybil let out a faint cry and then disappeared overboard. She hit the water with a splash and was luckily washed aside by the bow wave. She was swept alongside the craft, while Falshed ran along the deck, looking down to keep her in view, and shouting, 'Stoat overboard! Stoat overboard!' He finally managed to grab a cork float and throw it down to her. 'Hold on, Sybil, I'm coming!' he cried.

Falshed snatched another cork float and jumped into the cool waters. The river boat went on, steaming towards a berth in the harbour. Falshed's cries had gone unheard and unheeded in the confusion following the collision with the log. Plates and glasses had crashed down from shelves in the dining room. The mammal at the wheel had been flung aside and navigation instruments had crashed to the deck around him. There had been screams and shouts and no-one had noticed the couple had gone; what was more, no-one would be likely to notice they were missing for several hours yet.

'Sib? Sib?' Falshed called in the darkness.

'Here!' she cried only a few metres from him. 'This way.'

Falshed followed the sound of the splashing until at last he grabbed a wet, furry forelimb. 'Is that you?' he gulped, his mouth full of river water. 'Is that you, Sib?'

'Who else would be messing about in the river at this time of night?' came the answering growl.

'Chief Falshed, what are we going to do? It looks as if we're drifting towards the open sea.'

Oh, yes, *now* her mood had changed again. It only took a little thing like falling overboard to cause that to happen. Yet she was right, they were heading towards the ocean. He thought about trying to swim to shore, but the currents were very strong and the shore was a long way off: too far to risk letting go of the cork floats and swimming for it. Sybil was thrashing about now, attempting the impossible.

'I'd – I'd keep a bit more still if I were you, Sybil,' Falshed advised.

'Why?'

'Crocodiles.'

Sybil immediately went quiet. Then she whispered, 'Are there really crocodiles here?'

'Yes,' he replied, 'and possibly sharks hanging around beyond the harbour mouth. We must remain very calm, very quiet.'

He didn't *feel* like remaining calm. He felt like screaming his head off. It was horrible to think of his body dangling down amongst some awful creatures – creatures with razor-sharp teeth and very little brain.

'What are we going to do?' asked Sybil.

'Go with the flow,' replied Falshed. 'That's all we can do.'

And that's what they did. They were swept by the currents out of the river mouth and into the open ocean. Very soon the lights of the land dwindled away behind them. Very soon there was nothing but waves of salt water all around them. Things looked very dismal for the stoats indeed. It was cold, it was miserable. Drowning seemed a likely prospect.

CHAPTER TWENTY-SEVEN

There were seven seven-banded civets guarding the doors to the Forbidden Palace, with spears in their paws.

'Nice touch,' murmured Monty. 'Seven sevens.'

'Forty-nine,' said Maudlin automatically. Then, when everyone looked at him in surprise, he added, 'You know, times tables?'

'Very good, Maudlin,' Bryony replied, 'but Monty was referring to the civet guards. They're called that because they have seven black-and-white bands on their pelts.'

Maudlin the mathematician counted. 'There's only five,' he said.

'That's a different one you're looking at,' said

Bryony patiently as a five-banded civet – a completely different species – passed by with a bowl of rosewater in its claws.

'Oh, right.'

It looked very superior, this civet, as if carrying rose petals in fresh water were the most important job in the world.

As the weasels entered the outer courtyard, with its high tiled wall and spiked corners, there were more exotic beasts to behold. Here there were leopard cats with savage bandicoot rats on long leashes. The leopard cats strolled this way and that, along the marvellous marble paths that crisscrossed the palace gardens. You knew that it would only take a moment for them to slip the leash on the bandicoot rat and urge it to attack a hostile intruder.

The gardeners, busy-busy with rakes and hoes all over the grounds, were, surprisingly, shrews. These often violent and war-like rodents did not as a rule choose tranquil occupations like gardening. However, thought Monty as he passed one quietly scraping leaves from the path, who could tell what shrews were like in Far Kathay? Perhaps they had a different disposition, a more peaceful nature, than those in Welkin?

And there were of course pangolins, mostly courtiers, walking hurriedly from one place to another, carrying rolled scrolls or trays of tea or pots of black ink from which quills stuck up like flags. They wore beautiful robes decorated with red dragons and golden horses. Some of them went bare-headed, others had little four-cornered hats of dark blue silk.

River pirating aside, pangolins were not in general known for their fighting prowess, but for their administrative abilities. They were good at paperwork and organizing things. Sybil Poynt had probably been a pangolin in a past life. Pangolins loved to be busy-busy. The invention of the clipboard was, to a pangolin, the most significant stride forward in the nineteenth century. The paperclip, the staple machine – these extraordinary devices were at the hub of their universe. The world only continued to revolve because there were pencils with rubbers, blotting paper, string and sealing wax. Cabbages and kings would come and go; bureaucracy was there for ever.

Monty felt that no-one in the palace stood still for very long. There was work to be done. Art, it seemed, was work too, for painters sat at easels in various parts of the outer courtyard, recording the flowers and blossoms in full bloom, or the patterned fish in the ornamental ponds, or the gilded sparrows decorating the grass lawns.

'Amazing!' whispered Bryony. 'How tranquil it all is.'

They had left Hi Lo's junk that morning, at the Siungsuong quay, and were now being escorted by the grand vizier, a porcupine, through the palace to meet the emperor. Maudlin was over-excited and kept touching the tips of the porcupine's quills. The porcupine was mildly annoyed by this display of bad manners, but said nothing for the moment. His job was not to give lessons on protocol, but to make sure these weasels didn't run amok in the palace. He was a guide but not a mentor.

They passed into the inner courtyard, where some squirrels tended the flowerbeds and made sure the fountains worked.

'Belly-banded squirrels,' whispered Bryony to Monty. 'How fascinating.'

Suddenly, goaded beyond endurance by Maudlin, the porcupine turned round and rattled its quills very noisily. All work stopped in the inner courtyard. The squirrels looked on with round eyes. The grand vizier said stiffly, 'You do that once more and I'll roll on you!'

'What?' asked Maudlin nervously.

'You know what I mean,' said the vizier. 'Just once more.'

When the vizier turned and motioned for the weasels to follow him once more, Scruff whispered into Maudlin's ear, 'They've been known to kill cats with them spines, Maud. You don't want to get punctured, do you?'

Maudlin definitely did *not* want to get punctured. He was a very pneumatic weasel and would surely deflate instantly if the vizier carried out his threat.

Finally the group came to a beautiful blue-stone building in the centre of the inner courtyard. This was the inner sanctum of the palace, where the Great Pangolin held court. All around it were statues of free-tailed bats. Underneath the statues were names, presumably of the bats themselves. On request, the vizier translated the names – Wally the Magnificent, Maddy the Terrific and suchlike. Monty asked the porcupine why there were so many statues to these nocturnal creatures, thinking they were perhaps soldiers – generals, no doubt – who had defended the kingdom for the emperors.

'They were clerks,' came the answer. 'All of them brilliant at taking things down and later copying them into their best paw-writing. Let me tell you, weasels, that the paw-writing here is the best in the world. No-one can do a character as perfectly as a clerk of Far Kathay. I have heard that there are badgers in your country who work in the banks and are good at copying figures, but they cannot be a patch on our bats.'

'I believe you,' said Monty. 'But why bats?'

'The Great Pangolin does not want his secrets read by any old mammal looking over the shoulders of the clerks. They are able to fold their wings around their work as they do it, to keep it shielded from other eyes.'

'You used to do that at school,' said Maudlin to Scruff, 'with your forelimbs. To stop me copying your homework.'

'Also,' continued the porcupine with a glare at Maudlin, 'the bats are very jealous of their talents. They do not want others to imitate their skills with the pen and brush. Thus they use their wings to cloak their fine script.'

'But,' said Bryony. 'But – aren't bats supposed to be blind?'

The porcupine stared at Bryony for a few moments before replying, 'Not *totally* blind, but they are very poor-sighted. They work by *feel* rather than sight. That's what makes them so valuable to our ruler. They can't read what they've written; they have poor memories too . . .'

'That's because they hang upside down and their brains dribble out of their ears,' Maudlin told Scruff confidentially. 'That's what I heard anyway. I heard—' He stopped short when the porcupine gently pricked him with his spines. 'Ow – that hurt.'

The vizier continued, 'As I was saying, they can't read their work and can never recall what they've written down by feel. Thus the Great Pangolin's secrets remain secret. It would not do for an emperor's beautiful thoughts and wonderfully embroidered ideas to be known to the ordinary mammals in the street.' The porcupine gave a shudder and poked Maudlin with his claw. 'Common pick-yer-nose Herberts like this one here. How ghastly that would be.'

'I don't pick my nose!'

Bryony nodded, as if to say, Yes you do, I've seen you.

'So,' said Monty, as they proceeded towards the inner sanctum, where the Great Pangolin was presumably having beautiful thoughts, 'who does the fighting around here?'

'We have mercenaries who guard the borders and the walls around our kingdom. Wild boars. We keep them permanently wild by not paying them every month. Oh, they get their money eventually, but we keep it from them as long as we can, making excuses, delaying things, giving them cheques that bounce, all that sort of thing. They get in such a temper! They're always angry. Wild isn't the word for it. Ah, here we are.'

By the entrance to the building sat a life-sized greenstone carving of a winged tree-shrew, with ruby eyes and a collar of pure gold. Its whiskers were made of silver and its claws were fashioned from pale opal. There was a purple sash around its waist with a mother-of-pearl clasp. Only its feet looked shockingly exposed. The sacred toes were bare of any footwear. This, of course, was the Green Idol of Ommm. The vizier explained that the idol had been moved from its usual place in a courtyard of its own to be on show for the weasels. There was a fierce-looking civet guard at each corner of the relic, to protect the rest of its adornments.

'How very gratifying,' said Monty. 'Please thank the emperor.'

The group entered a magnificent hall. There were no windows, but it was lit by a thousand candle-flames. In the centre of this vast room a pangolin sat on a high throne; he was swathed in gold robes, and had a tall, spiky gold crown on his head. A marbled polecat, clearly the emperor's jester, was frolicking around the throne, amusing a little princess pangolin at least, if not his great lord. Circling them was a ring of bats, all cloaked by their own wings, scratching noises coming from within. Everywhere there were busy-busy courtiers with clipboards and pencils behind their ears. The porcupine, now only one of several, advanced bowing and scraping the floor with his nose. The weasels followed suit, as instructed by the grand vizier.

There was a bird perched on a silver rafter close to the emperor's throne.

'The Great Pangolin,' whispered the vizier, 'has a nightingale to translate his words into Welkin.'

A mutter came from the emperor's mouth and the nightingale sang, 'Welcome to my country, weasels from afar.'

All the other creatures in the room suddenly stopped what they were doing and clapped. Maudlin was about to say something, but Scruff anticipated a terrible breach of protocol and nudged him. He wisely remained silent. Instead it was Monty who replied.

'Emperor of Far Kathay,' he said, 'we are honoured to be here in your kingdom, indeed in your house. I and my companions, my assistants, are here at your request to try to solve your mystery. May I say how impressed we are with your wonderful palace; we have been treated with nothing but kindness by the citizens of your great land.'

'We are gratified,' sang the nightingale, after

translating Monty's speech for the emperor, 'and hope that you will be able to solve our problem as soon as possible. My grand vizier will give you all the help you need. Simply ask and it shall be done. You will do me the kindness of staying here in the palace as my guests. On the successful completion of your investigations, you may request such rewards as you desire.'

'Thank you, my lord.'

Then the Great Pangolin turned his eyes on one of the civet cat guards, who visibly wilted under the royal gaze. 'We suspect,' said the emperor, 'these civet cats. We are sure they are responsible for the theft and will order a mass execution if we prove to be correct. Already we have banished several of them to the far corners of the globe.'

'We must not prejudge the situation,' Monty said. 'The civet cats may turn out to be perfectly innocent.'

The nightingale decided not to translate this, fearing that Montegu Sylver would be executed on the spot for arguing with the emperor. Instead she said to the Great Pangolin, 'Have a nice day!'

Then came a shock. The emperor turned slowly, hampered by his heavy golden robes, to point with a delicate claw to a shadowy corner of the hall. He spoke again, and again the nightingale translated his words with silken voice.

'Another has arrived, from Slattland, unbidden. This mammal claims that she is better

252

at solving mysteries than you are, Montegu Sylver, and that your fame is overrated. She claims she can find the jade shoes of the Green Idol of Ommm before you do. We are inclined to test her bragging words and let the two of you strive against each other. We do not care who discovers the truth, only that the shoes are restored to the idol. You will therefore have a rival, Jal Sylver. Do you accept the challenge?'

Monty could not see the creature in the corner, but he had not come all this way along the Silk Road for nothing. 'If you wish it, Great Pangolin.'

'Good,' trilled the nightingale. 'May the best mammal win.'

Monty took a candle from a holder and advanced towards this mysterious stranger. 'You!' he said.

'Me,' she replied. 'What a surprise. I beat you here, even though you started out from Eggyok before me. Amazing, these hot-air balloons.'

'You came over three massive mountain ranges in a hot-air balloon? You must be crazy,' said Monty.

'Crazy, but *fast*. I'm here, aren't I?'

Bryony let out a little cry of anger. Monty regarded the creature quizzically, not even his whiskers revealing his true feelings. They were mixed and various, those feelings, born of several encounters with this female lemming. There was distaste there, but deep, deep down there was also a small fire often called by the name of passion.

There she was, those flashing dark eyes, that sleek fur. Beautiful, dark, exotic creature. The Countess Bogginski of Slattland, better known to Monty and the others as Sveltlana.

CHAPTER TWENTY-EIGHT

The presence of Sveltlana in Far Kathay was disturbing. She had at various times tried to kill Monty for interfering with her plans to become dictator of Slattland. Now, here she was, following him halfway around the globe. What was her game? Bryony trusted this female lemming about as far as she could throw an oriental temple.

'What's she doing here?' she asked Monty after a set of six civets had arrived to carry off the Great Pangolin in a sedan chair. 'Time for elevenses!' the nightingale had trilled. 'Biscuits and tea.'

They were now outside, in the inner courtyard, where the many fountains fell with sparkling waters and the sun glinted on the hundreds of statues to magnificent clerks. They walked under oriental maples, through gardens of sweet-smelling shrubs, by fruit trees whose blossoms were so flouncy it was difficult to believe they were real. Caged crickets hanging in the trees were sawing away with their back legs, producing at least half a dozen tunes between them. Leopard cats and banded civets strolled the many marbled paths. Shrew gardeners worked in the flowerbeds.

'How could she have known you were coming here?' Bryony questioned, clearly very upset and puzzled. 'Where did she get her information from?'

'Oh, she has her ways. I'm not surprised she left Slattland. President Miska has been trying to get rid of her for ages. She's been a pain in the presidential neck ever since the ex-prince took office. Anyway, it's time for a showdown. We're on neutral ground here. It's time this thing between us was settled.'

'What thing?' snapped Bryony.

'Why,' replied Monty, turning to her, 'this animosity, this hostility. I want to find out what makes her tick. Why does a beautiful creature like her feel the need to subject the rest of the planet to her cold command?'

'A *beautiful* creature like her,' repeated Bryony, in acid tones. 'Why, I could tell you that and save you all the trouble. This is very dangerous, Monty. She's a self-seeking, conceited, ambitious megalomaniac.'

'I'm sure it's a little more complex than that, Bryony.'

'That *is* complex.'

'Well, I'd like to talk to her, get behind the front of hostility.'

'It's not a front, it goes all the way through to her heart.'

'If you say so,' replied Monty, refusing to be goaded into an argument. 'In which case, I'll find that out for sure, won't I? You need have no part in this, Bryony, if you don't want to. In the meantime –' he became brisk and business-like – 'we need to start questioning mammals about the missing shoes. We'll need some translators. The grand vizier promised us one each, when I last spoke to him. They'll be birds.'

Maudlin looked alarmed but Monty continued, 'Oh, I know we're not used to birds. I'm not at all comfortable with sharp beaks and talons either, but I expect they feel the same way about us, with our fangs and claws. Fact is, I'm told the birds learn languages in the egg, while they're forming. It's much easier to teach an egg. An egg sits still for you – doesn't keep looking out of the window at the sunshine. It's a captive audience. An egg doesn't play the piano or slip away to go fishing. An egg learns quickly.'

'Thank you for that,' said Bryony stiffly, still annoyed about Sveltlana. 'So, when do we get these birds?'

'We're supposed to meet them in the Muskrat

Courtyard at noon.' Monty looked up at the sun, then took out his pocket watch. 'Which is right about now.'

They made their way to the Muskrat Courtyard, using a little map the vizier had given them. The birds turned out not to be exotic like the nightingale the emperor used, but common drongos. One of them looked as scruffy as Scruff and she immediately attached herself to him as his soulmate. Another, a cock drongo, offered his services to Bryony. The other female went to Maudlin and Monty was allocated the youngest of the translators, a cock drongo named Xixes. 'I'm all at Xixes and Xevens,' the drongo said, before adding, 'That's a joke.'

'Very good,' said Monty discouragingly. He studied the dark feathers of the large, forbidding-looking drongo. Some of the birds in Far Kathay seemed to have evolved into a higher form of creature than those in Welkin, which simply provided eggs and graced the Sunday lunch table. Not surprisingly, there was a good deal of malice at home, especially amongst rogue robins and gangs of starlings. But this chap seemed to be quite friendly.

'I've always wanted to fly to Muggidrear,' confided Xixes, when the two were alone and interviewing the palace guards about the theft. 'You hear so much about the cockney sparrows there. Are they really that chirpy?'

Monty was wary. 'I'm afraid I don't have a lot to do with them.'

'You don't number them among your best friends?'

Monty shook his head. 'We don't mix a great deal. The sparrows tend to stick to the rooftops and garden walls, while weasels like myself remain close to the ground. You couldn't get much closer to the ground than a weasel. Our bellies brush it. Whereas birds tend to like human washing lines and high hedges.'

'So it's the environment that keeps you apart, rather than choice.'

'You could say that.'

'Well,' said Xixes, 'I hope that at the end of all this we are able to call each other friends.'

'I hope so too.'

They questioned several guards. Some of these civets and leopard cats had been on duty the night the jade shoes went missing. They said they had not heard or seen anything. One thought he caught a sound like the whisper of a paw on the roof tiles of the temple, but on looking up had seen nothing but the moon beaming back at him. The moon hadn't stolen the shoes, had it? No, well then, it might have been a shrew. Why? Well, shrews would steal anything that wasn't nailed down, wouldn't they? What more proof could you need? No, it wasn't the brush of a branch in the breeze, dusting the tiles of the roof with its blossoms. It sounded like a shrew.

'They don't like shrews, do they?' said Monty. 'Is this an old antipathy? Are they ancient enemies, shrews and civets?'

Xixes explained, 'Shrews, though small, are extremely good at fighting. The civets regard themselves as the best soldiers in the world. Consequently there is jealousy between them. When you consider that these civets are guarding the graven image of a winged tree-shrew, you must realize how mixed-up they feel. And to be accused of stealing the very object they are supposed to be guarding, well . . . Excuse me a minute, I feel a bit dusty . . .'

In the middle of his explanation, Xixes suddenly left Monty's side and went for a bath in a nearby fountain. His wings fluttered, his feathers fluffed up. He took mouthfuls of water and gargled with it, before spitting it out into a flowerbed. Then, after a great deal of shaking, he returned with droplets still clinging to his feathers.

'Now, where were we . . . ?'

'It doesn't matter. Look, Xixes, you are aware that there's a female lemming here in the court by the name of Sveltlana?'

'I've seen the creature. Soft and warm looking.'

'Don't let that fool you. However, what I would like you to do, if you wouldn't mind, is to set up a meeting between us. Could you do that? Some neutral place, preferably where no knives are available. Somewhere quiet . . .'

'And romantic?'

'No, no, you've got it all wrong. This lemming is trying to kill me. I want to find out if that can be avoided without bloodshed on my part. I do not want to have to defend myself against a mad assassin, you understand.'

'There are many of those here,' chortled Xixes. 'Shrews in black bodysocks, doing the old one-two. Shrews with claws that are lethal weapons. Martial arts. It's a favourite sport here, you know. You can pick up assassins at the local market like you can buy onions. Two a penny. They'll climb up walls without ropes, jump from high buildings, swing through windows and onto balconies, chop bricks in two with their elbows, break logs with their noses. You have to see them to believe it. They've even got these little spiky discs that they throw at you. If you hear a humming in the air, duck, because it's probably a metal bee with deadly razor-sharp edges.'

'Thank you for the information. Will you arrange this meeting for me?'

'With pleasure. In the meantime, I could teach you a few phrases in the local dialect.'

Monty said, 'I would like that very much – if you have the time.'

'Time enough, and worlds,' came the enigmatic reply.

While Monty was sifting through the interviews with the guards, a message came back to him. Sveltlana had accepted his invitation. Could he call at her room in the palace an hour before midnight? It would give her great pleasure to see him again and they could talk over old times. She especially remembered the mayor's garden party in the city of Muggidrear, where they had had such a jolly evening together.

That had been the time she had thrown a knife at his heart, missing only because of a timely warning from a watcher.

Oh, and the masked ball in Slattland.

That had been the ball where she had tried to stab him with a carving knife taken from the buffet table.

'Thank you, Xixes,' said Monty. 'You may take the rest of the day off. I'm going to go looking for clues during what's left of the afternoon.'

'What are *clues*?'

'They are evidence of some sort or another. A button from a coat. A hair from a pelt. A stain of something or other. Clues are what detectives like myself collect and study and try to deduce past events from.'

'Sort of like reading a book?'

'More like doing a crossword puzzle.'

'Well, good luck,' said the drongo, hopping up onto a perch. 'See you tomorrow early. Say, six?'

'Xix would be fine,' joked Monty.

CHAPTER TWENTY-NINE

Mayor Poynt was sitting at his desk, looking at two postcards. The first was of two jolly, pink-faced, fat, bristling porcupines in undersized bathing suits, lying on a towel on a beach. The caption read: 'No-one comes between me and my jill.' It was a typical seaside postcard, but it was the message scrawled on the back which irked Jeremy Poynt. This read: *Having a lovely time, glad you aren't here.* Underneath was Falshed's signature, *Zachary F., Chief of Muggidrear's Coppers.*

'Not for much longer,' growled the mayor. 'Not if I have anything to do with it. I suppose since he decided not to follow my orders and tail the weasels into Far Kathay, he thought he would throw all caution to the winds.

Well, he's made a mistake this time.'

Mayor Poynt scratched at his chest. A previous surgery wound was beginning to irritate him. He had recently had a piece of mountain hare's fur grafted onto his permanently white ermine pelt. At first it had influenced his mind and for a time he had thought he was turning *all* hare. But he had recovered from that breakdown. Now it was rearing its tall ears and scut again, darkening his mind with supernatural fears. New dreams were appearing on the Poynt dreamscape – of running from hounds, of being caught by the neck in snares, of being blasted by guns.

At the moment the mayor had more worries than he could rationally deal with (which was why he was becoming irrational), for his ex-assistant, sacked just two weeks ago, the weasely Pontifract Pilote, was now making a bid for the mayorship. The traitor had been out canvassing votes and now seemed likely to supplant the mayor in office. Jeremy Poynt had been mayor of Muggidrear for as long as anyone could remember, and his father before him, and his grandfather before *him*. It was no wonder he had felt secure. Yet then he had had Sybil by his side. Now she was off gallivanting with that twit Falshed, while Poynt was undergoing all sorts of attacks – from weasels, from the infant queen, even from his own stoats.

'There's never been a weasel mayor of Muggidrear,' grumbled the mayor to himself, 'and there never should be.'

He studied the other postcard, which was from his sister, written in a tight, neat paw-writing, perfect copperplate.

It said: *My dearest brother Jeremy. I would be having a wonderful time if it were not for the fact that I have become a queen.* She's gone potty, thought the mayor. She's been a princess for so long she's taken a mental leap to the top and last step on the royal ladder. He read on: *I know you will think I've gone potty and have been a princess for so long I've taken a mental leap.* Blast her, he thought, she always could read me like a book. *But the fact is, there are stoats here who believe me to be the re-incarnated Queen Neferhapen, a warrior-queen who led her mammals to freedom some 3,000 years ago.* So what's wrong with that? Take advantage of it. Wring 'em dry, sis. Take the money and run. *I don't want to take advantage of this in any way, so Zachary and I* – Flipping stub-tailed upstart that he is! – *are going to go on a cruise to get away from the glare of publicity. Zachary can be very kind, but he is also very irritating. He thinks himself to be in love with me. Quite flattering in its way, but I couldn't fancy him, even if we were cast away on a desert island together.* I should think not. He's ugly for a start. He's not from a high-born family either. And finally, he's a flatpaw. Size twelves! *In fact, the more I'm away from Muggidrear, the more I think of Lord Hannover Haukin. He's never shown the slightest interest in me, but that may be shyness. He's such a gentlestoat, so longright and so handsome. But very, very reserved, like all aristocrats of our kith and kin. I shall not pursue him, dear brother, but I wonder if you could test the waters for me? Please, in a very discreet way which will not compromise your sister or cause her to lose any dignity or humiliate her in any way, try to discover if Hannover has any feelings for me whatsoever.*

The card was signed: *Your affectionate sister, Sybil.*

There was a disturbing PS scrawled at the bottom of the card: *I had a bad dream last night, that we would never see each other again, dear brother.*

So, it seemed Sib was besotted with Hannover Haukin. Well, that was all right with Jeremy. He would welcome Haukin into the family, even though the Haukins had always been at odds with the Poynts in the past.

'We can't apologize for our ancestors,' muttered the mayor. 'The sins of the fathers are not the responsibility of the sons.'

He picked up the telephone and arranged a meeting with Hannover.

They met at Jumping Jacks the same day.

'What ho, Poynt!' cried Lord Haukin, throwing himself into a forelimbchair and fitting his monocle to his left eye. 'What's the mouse-meat then? You wanted to see me?'

'Yes, yes I did. Have you still got that butler-weasel, whatshisname?'

'That's *my* line. You mean Culver?'

'Yes, that's him,' said Poynt, scratching his chest. 'Intelligent sort of mustelid, ain't he? The

266

sort that would know how to win elections. I'd like him to be my campaign manager.'

'Are you in trouble?'

Poynt screwed up his mouth and bent his whiskers. 'It's this blasted weasel, Pontifract Pilote. He's going against me in the mayoral elections. Thinks he can win.'

'And can he?'

All the wind went out of the mayor incumbent. 'Yes. He's bright too, blast his eyes and liver. *And* popular. And I taught him all there is to know about mayoring and running a city. I was his mentor, for heaven's sake. He came to me a poor weasel and I gave him a job out of the goodness of my heart. Now he's biting the paw that fed him. Treacherous snake. Betrayals. I am surrounded by betrayers.'

'One betrayer.'

'It's enough. I *feel* surrounded.'

'I'll ask Culver. See what he says.'

'Can you spare him?'

'Culver? It'll do me good to get shot of him for a while. He can be a real pain in the tail. Oh, don't get me wrong, he's good at his job – any job – too good. But he's also insufferable. Makes me read his books of poems. Tries to instil culture in me. Don't like that at all. Once—' Hannover paused and shuddered – 'once he tried to get me married off. Said all aristocrat stoats should have mates, for purposes of offspring and heirs, that sort of thing. I told him he'd gone too far. Confirmed bachelor, me. Can't be doing with females in the house. Bad enough when Aunt Hortense comes to stay.'

'You – you wouldn't even consider taking a mate?'

'Not in a million years. Stars would fall from the heavens before that happened. Sun would drop into the sea. Moon would go flying off into space. Never happen. No, not ever. Adamant. Steadfast.'

'Not even if she was ever-so, ever-so attractive?'

'Not a chance.'

'And very intelligent.'

'*Especially* that. Imagine talking about arts and crafts at breakfast! Carving bowls from applewood. Painting boaty pictures. Embroidering pictures of windmills. Impossible situation.'

'That's not intelligence, that's arty-crafty.'

'Well, same thing, ain't it?' growled Hannover.

'What about if she was very rich, had her own money, and a title as well? What about royalty?'

Hannover stared at the mayor and swapped his monocle over. 'See here, Poynt, what *is* all this?'

'Oh, I don't know,' said the mayor airily. 'One day your princess might come. There, I've said too much already.'

'Sybil?' gasped Hannover.

'I promised her I would be discreet.'

Hannover sat there and contemplated things for a moment, taking a dried worm out of his pocket and chewing on it. 'Sybil! Who'd have thought it? Handsome jill, I grant you that. Good strong whiskers. Sturdy tail. But . . .' Hannover sighed. 'Not for me, I'm afraid. Very flattered. Very. But I'm a bachelor jack and that's the way I'll stay until my dying day.' He paused before adding, 'I keep thinking about Sybil's idea of decorating a place. I mean, all those vases! What were they? Mole Dynasty? Couldn't bear them, meself.'

'Nor could I, Hannover. Nor could I. But they've all been smashed, thank goodness, with no possibility of them ever returning. Look, if Sybil ever considered buying any more of those dreadfully gloomy vases, I would leave home too. But she won't. She can't afford them. They're gone for good.'

'Still and all – I couldn't.'

'She'll be *very* disappointed. You wouldn't have to do much, you know. You don't have to entertain Sybil. You could do all the things you do now – watch cricket matches, play with steam engines, go dragonfly shooting, fish for stickle-backs. She wouldn't mind. She's so busy herself, arranging and organizing things – garden parties, balls, writing *billets-doux*, tying things up with pink ribbon, arranging flowers, organizing talks to jill groups. You'd just get in the way of all that. You could be off, doing jackly things.'

'Wouldn't work, old chap. Just wouldn't work.'

The mayor sighed. 'But you will speak to Culver?'

'Soon as he gets back from his holiday in the unnamed marshes. He's gone to take pictures of the war against the rats, you know. Fancies himself a bit of a war chronicler, does Culver. I don't hold with this new thingy – what's it called? – *photogoly*. Not very fond of ologies meself.'

'Photo*graphy*, it's called. One takes photographs with a device called a camera. Pontifract told me about it.'

'Well, that's where Culver is, taking photographs. Says it's the art form of the nineteenth century. Cheatin', if you ask me. You just point and press a button and there it is, scene copied, shade for shade. Nothin' artistic in that, is there?'

'When's he get back? From the war?'

Hannover shrugged. 'Oh, in a few weeks.'

The mayor groaned. 'A few *weeks*. The election will be over by then. There'll be a new mayor in office.'

'In that case, can't help you, Poynt. Tell you what, though, once you finish with all that business, you can come on a boat trip with me. Great sport, messing about on the river. Get you out of that stuffy office and into the fresh air. You can join a friend and me. Jarome's his name. Badger, does something in the city. Falls asleep in a bank vault or something. You know him. We're going to take a row boat along the Bronn. You'd love it. You get to open and close lock gates without asking permission. Camping. The great outdoors. Three mustelids in a boat. Think about it.'

Poynt went home, thinking about it. He couldn't imagine a worse fate than having to share a boat, or a tent, with a bloated badger who worked in the city. Those bank badgers did nothing but bore you with talk about figures in ledgers. They were also very windy creatures, from all the pickled sparrows' eggs they ate for their hasty lunches in the park. No, Hannover was a confirmed bachelor and Poynt was a confirmed mayor. Nothing else would do.

Yet . . . yet . . . he was going to lose. He could feel it in his bones. How depressing. And he had the feeling that he would never see his sister again. How *very* depressing. He was going to end up a lonely old ermine in a nasty little basement flat in Cheepside. How very, very depressing. What a waste of a brilliant life in office. To be reduced to making cups of tea and hoping the paperjack called for his money so there would be someone to talk to. Shuffling about in an old pair of slippers and dreaming of the past. How very awful. How very, very awful.

Jeremy Poynt went to bed that night with a glass of honey dew and wept salt tears on his silk pillow. His dreams were of big pointy ears and running along the furrows of ploughed fields. He was just beginning to enjoy himself when the dark part came, where an enormous harvesting machine came thundering over the skyline, filling the air with straw dust, its rows of blades blocking every retreat along the whole line of the horizon.

CHAPTER THIRTY

Monty made his way through the fabulous gardens of the palace to Sveltlana's room at the west corner. He had considered wearing one of the new bullet-proof vests made of spider's-web thread (the strongest natural material known to mammal) but in the end had decided against it. He did, however, go armed with a pistol. It would be foolish in the extreme to assume that Sveltlana was now a peaceful lemming.

She was sitting on her veranda in the company of her drongo interpreter. She was brushing her fine fur, but put down the hairbrush when she saw Monty coming. As he approached she dismissed the bird.

'We need no translators,' she said. 'Besides,

don't you find the closeness of these feathered creatures a little disconcerting?'

'How so?'

'You eat birds in Welkin.'

'They are a different order of birds,' replied Monty, defensive and unconvincing. 'A domestic variety. Humans keep dogs and cats, treat them like royalty, yet they eat cows, sheep and pigs. Some breeds of pig are considered to be pets, while others go to make ham and bacon. Humans find the sight of lambs playing in the fields quite delightful, yet roast them for dinner. Horses are ridden and work in the traces, while there would be no thought of harnessing an eagle. The world is a strange place, Sveltlana, with strange creatures in it. If I were not a carnivore I am sure I would find the eating of flesh very distasteful, but I am and there's no help for it. You, on the other paw, are basically a herbivore, and therefore can't know what strange needs exist in the blood of a weasel. In truth, there are many rodents in your country who now partake of cooked meat. It's all a great contradiction. I am as confused as any human must be by the conflicting ideas and emotions which inhabit me.'

'You try to rationalize the unthinkable.'

'Sveltlana, I am not at all comfortable with this conversation. If this is all we are to talk about, then I shall leave now.'

She sighed. 'It amuses me to see you squirm, but I shall stop now. There are more important issues to discuss.' She suddenly sniffed the air. 'What lovely scents of honeysuckle and jasmine in these gardens! And the mimosa hangs its fragrance on the breeze. I wonder I never came to Far Kathay before now. It's a land I could learn to love.'

'Is this what you call an important issue?'

She turned her dark eyes onto him. 'No, but we need to settle down. Please, sit here beside me.' She patted the seat next to her. When he was in his place, she asked him, 'Would you like a drink of something? I have tea, or lemon juice.'

'A glass of arsenic, please,' he said simply.

'You think I would poison you?'

'Yes.'

She clicked her teeth. 'Well then, you must do without.' Her fur seemed to ruffle in the breeze as she suddenly stood up. Monty's paw automatically went to the pocket with the pistol in it. She saw the gesture and her eyes flashed for a moment. Then she was calm again.

'I brought you here to ask you whether it might not be in both our interests to work together on this case.'

'You tell me what you know and then I'll tell you what I know.'

'But if I go first, you might not follow.'

'You'll have to trust me, won't you?'

Sveltlana shook her head. 'This won't work, will it? We have lost all trust for one another.'

'Now, I wonder why?' said Monty, stroking his

whiskers. 'Could it be because you've tried to kill me on numerous occasions?'

'And you've not tried to harm me?'

'I do not go in for assassination, Sveltlana, as well you know. We good mammals are always at a disadvantage, since we have to wait for you bad mammals to make the first move. Only then can we call on the mighty forces of law and order, and let justice take its course. You can't be arrested for murdering me until you've actually murdered me, no matter how certain we both are that you will try to do it. This is something good mammals have to live with.'

'Surely, here in Far Kathay, the rules can be bent? We are no longer under our own laws. Here, you could be like me.'

'They have laws against murder here too. And if they didn't, there is always honour to prevent me from becoming like you. I'm an honourable mammal, Sveltlana. You, on the other paw, are not concerned with honour. All you want is power and your own way, and you'll break every rule in the book to get them.'

She clicked her teeth again. 'How well you know me.'

He moved closer to her and secretly snatched at something on the floor with his hind-leg claws, hiding it in the turn-up of his left trouser leg. She saw nothing since her eyes were on his forelimbs, wondering whether he was going to draw his pistol.

'And you know me not at all.'

'I know one thing about you. You're fond of your female companion. You wouldn't like anything to happen to her, would you?'

Monty said coldly, 'Are you threatening me with harm to Bryony?'

Sveltlana shrugged. 'Is that how it sounds? Well, then I suppose I must be.' She leaned closer to him – so close he could smell the musky perfume on her fur. 'I think you should go home, Montegu Sylver. I think you should leave me to find the Green Idol of Ommm's shoes.'

Monty stood up. 'And I think I should warn you that Bryony Bludd is as formidable an opponent as I am. Perhaps even more dangerous, since she is a female of the species – they're always more deadly, you know. What I'm saying is, I don't need to protect her. She's quite capable of protecting herself. In fact, if you had had this meeting with *her*, instead of me, and threatened to harm *me*, it might have worked. You've got it all the wrong way round, Sveltlana. As usual, you have no idea who you're dealing with and how we think. Goodnight.'

With that, Monty left her seething, and went back across the fragrant courts towards his own quarters.

Suddenly he was aware of a shadowy figure in the myrtle bushes which skirted the fish pond. An agent of Sveltlana? Monty drew his pistol and called, 'Come out, whoever you are!'

'Put that gun away,' said a gruff Bryony, emerging from the myrtle with twigs and leaves in her fur. She began to pick them out. 'It's only me.'

'And what's only me doing, sneaking around at midnight?' said Monty.

She didn't answer this question; instead she said, 'If it hadn't been for the bright moonlight I would have got away with it.'

'I heard you, as well as saw you.'

Bryony sniffed. There were a few moments of silence before she said, 'You've been to see *her*, haven't you?'

'The Countess Bogginski? Yes. She sent me a message earlier.'

'And what have you agreed between the pair of you?'

'Well, she wanted to pool resources. Or said she did – but we both know what that means. She wants us to tell her everything, while she tells us nothing in return. When I wouldn't play, she threatened to harm you, in order to make me play.'

'You didn't go along with it?' cried Bryony.

'I told her that you were a far more worthy opponent than I was and to leave me out of it.'

Bryony was pleased, as well as amused by this reply. She considered herself the equal of any jill or jack. She was just about to tell Monty that he was a wonderful weasel, when there was a rustling in the myrtle bushes. After being challenged, first Scruff appeared, then Maudlin. On seeing that it was Bryony and Monty, the two weasels let out sighs.

'I just heard voices,' said Scruff. 'Thought I'd come and investigate.'

'Me too,' added Maudlin.

'I'm glad we're all alert,' said Monty, 'and while we're here, all together, perhaps we could see what we've got so far.'

'Footprints,' muttered Maudlin darkly. 'Me and Scruff found them, going away from the back of the altar where the Green Idol sits. Footprints of a ferret badger. It's a good job the ground is clay and it hasn't rained hard since the robbery, otherwise the prints might have been washed away. Looks like we know what type of beast stole the jade shoes, if nothing else.'

'I saw the same prints,' murmured Monty. 'And I have no doubt they were made by the thief.'

Maudlin found this statement a bit hard to swallow. He felt that Monty was trying to steal his glory and said as much.

'No, no, I can understand why you're saying that, Maudlin,' continued Monty, 'but I *did* find the same prints. What I also found were traces of plaster of paris *in* the prints.'

Maudlin was confused. 'Meaning what?'

'Meaning that the thief had plaster feet.'

Maudlin was incredulous. 'A ferret badger with plaster feet?'

'Of course not,' replied Monty. 'But what if the real thief wore the plaster feet of another creature to disguise his own species?'

'That'd make sense,' Scruff said. 'You mean

some geezer's gone and made some plaster feet, put 'em on to do the robbery, then chucked 'em away afterwards. That way tryin' to put us off the scent? Tryin' to make us look for a ferret badger when all the time he's a . . . What is he?'

'We don't know that yet, but he's a creature smaller than a ferret badger, that's certain. An elephant couldn't wear the feet of a badger, nor a tiger or anything larger than the badger itself. Only something smaller could pull the plaster feet over its own.'

Bryony said, 'That leaves quite a lot of creatures.'

'Yes it does, but the field has already narrowed and we've only been collecting clues for a few hours. Other clues will emerge over the course of time. You've all done very well, so far, especially Maudlin, who normally can't see the nose in front of his face. Oh, don't look like that, Maudlin – I'm only joking. Your contributions are *always* valuable.'

Maudlin was mollified. They all said good-night to one another before retiring. Weasels tend to fall asleep quickly after a wearying day. Drongo birds, on the other paw and claw, are nappers, who tend to doze for a few moments, then wake again. This makes them good watchers-over. They watched over their weasels dutifully, as instructed by the Great Pangolin. No assassin would pass by *their* beaks in the night.

CHAPTER THIRTY-ONE

'So what do we do now, guv'nor?' asked Scruff.

'Well, what I would like you to do, my friend, is to go through the palace's rubbish. Find out where the rubbish tip is and search for those plaster feet. Do you think you could do that?'

'Do I? Why, it's right up my street, guv'nor. Muckin' about in the garbage? My fav'rite hobby. Used to do it all the time as a young kitten. Me and my mates used to live on the rubbish dump. You comin', Maud?'

Maudlin did not like the sound of sorting through other mammals' leftover dinners and stuff, but he hated being parted from his best friend. 'Oh, all right.'

The two weasels left Monty and Bryony alone

on the veranda of Bryony's bungalow. They were at the breakfast table, where a variety of fruit had been laid out for them. Bryony almost said she fancied a soft-boiled egg, then her drongo walked by, patrolling the gardens in front. The word 'egg' stuck in her throat. All her life Bryony had been toying with the idea of becoming a vegetarian, but it was terribly difficult for weasels, who unlike humans were not actually omnivores, but died-in-the-wool carnivores. When thoughts of food drifted into their minds, or were driven there by hunger, the first picture that came up was always of meat.

Weasels had learned to eat fruit and vegetables – they'd always had small amounts, even when they were wild creatures without the power of human speech – but they had never quite thrown off their urgent desire for flesh. Beans on toast was fine in its way, but it did not compare with rabbit stew.

One of Bryony's ancestors had become a vegetarian, but that was in the days when weasels lived in poverty and there was little to tempt her. Bryony was always being tempted: by sparrow livers, by lean cuts of mouse-bacon, by fish and – sorry, drongos – by fowl too. Definitely by fowl. She let out a huge sigh.

'Oh, dear, what's all that about?' asked Monty. 'Not because I met with the jill lemming, is it?'

Out in the garden the pink and purple fuchsia bells were trembling in the breeze. The bamboo grasses swayed in a kind of slow, rhythmic dance.

Emerald-green grasshoppers leapt from leaf-tip to leaf-tip, playing their back legs like violins for unseen audiences. Bryony tried to concentrate on these wonders of nature to get rid of the bitter feelings in her breast, but she was unsuccessful.

'What makes you think I'm interested in your liaisons with Sveltlana?' she said. 'They're of no interest to me whatsoever.'

Monty realized he had made a huge mistake. 'Oh, no, of course not. I – I don't know what made me say that.'

'Neither do I.'

Bryony was silent for some while, during which all that could be heard was the creaking of her swing seat. Then, finally, she said, 'You realize she will try to kill you again.'

'Of course. I'm constantly on my guard.'

'Good.'

The two of them passed the rest of the day in forensic detection. The afternoon came and went and it was evening when Scruff, with Maudlin in tow, returned triumphantly carrying a plaster of paris ferret badger's foot.

'Found one!' he cried.

Maudlin said, 'He had to burrow deep down into the rubbish. You should see Scruff burrow. He's a tunnelling genius, he is.' Maudlin picked a fish-bone off his friend's shoulder and then found some paperclips attached to his fur. 'Course,' he grumbled, 'he could've had a quick shower before bringing the plaster cast to you, but he wouldn't.'

'Water's not good for you,' said Scruff.

The others ignored the musty smell which surrounded Scruff like an aura.

'I knew if anyone could do it, it would be you,' said Monty, 'but even so I wasn't expecting you to do it so quickly! What a fellow you are, Scruff. I've never known a mammal root things out quite so efficiently.'

Monty took the plaster foot and reached inside his jacket pocket for a magnifying glass. With this tool of his trade, rarely seen by the rest of his crew, he studied the object. After a while he found what he was looking for. 'Here it is,' he murmured, peering hard through the magnifying glass. 'A trade name. It's in Pangolin, of course. I'll ask Xixes to translate.'

The drongo was summoned and gave his verdict. 'It's a little workshop on the west side of the Great Square, not far from the Great Wall and close to the Great Park.'

'Great,' said Maudlin, and Bryony gave him a severe look.

'What sort of workshop?' asked Monty.

'The marks don't say.'

The following morning Monty set off at a brisk pace for the palace gates. Bryony, Scruff and Maudlin scurried after him, determined not to be left behind. Xixes, who hated walking, said he would fly ahead and meet them at the workshop. The weasels walked through streets filled with pangolins – sometimes accosted by the shop-keepers, who of course wished to sell their wares, at other times followed by pangolin kittens, who chanted things, then ran away clicking their teeth when Monty or one of the others turned to shoo them off. They had to accept they were strangers in a strange land. So few foreigners were permitted to enter the kingdom of Far Kathay they were an unusual sight and were bound to attract attention.

'What I like about this country,' said Bryony, as they skipped around goods in the street, 'is the way the shops spill out onto the pavements and into the roads. Look at all those pots and pans! And brass kitchen scales – I could do with some of those. And there's a shop where you can buy paper models of things that are important to you in life. They burn them at funerals, you know, so that the smoke will accompany the spirit-mammal on its way to the Other World.'

Eventually they found the shop they were looking for. Xixes was waiting outside, looking a little bored, but he brightened on seeing the weasels. They all trooped into the small shop together, rather worrying the pangolin proprietor, who felt as if he were under invasion. Not only had he never had more than two customers in his shop, he had never seen a Welkin weasel in his life before now. Monty immediately saw the problem and ordered the three other weasels out. Only he and Xixes remained.

The shopkeeper became a little calmer.

'I wonder,' said Monty, banging the plaster foot down on the counter and making the shopkeeper jump again, 'whether you could identify this?'

Xixes translated this for the shopkeeper.

'Yes,' he replied in his own language, 'I made it.'

'Could you then tell us who you made it for?'

'That's rather a private matter. I must keep confidence with my customers.'

'I have to tell you,' said Monty through Xixes, 'that I am on the business of the emperor! I am charged with finding the thief of the jade shoes of the Green Idol of Ommm, and I have been told by the grand vizier that I am entitled to receive the full co-operation of all citizens of Far Kathay.'

'That's what the other one said,' replied the shopkeeper, less than impressed. 'That's what she said.'

'She?' Alarm bells rang in Monty's head. 'What *she*?'

'The lemming-thing. First time I've seen one of those, too. All these strange mammals, coming out of nowhere. It's quite a shock to a creature, it is. I was three years of age before I realized there were others in the world beside pangolins. Lemmings and weasels? Very odd.'

'Ah!' Sveltlana had obviously been there before him. 'And this lemming had another of the plaster feet?'

'Yes, she did.'

'And did you also *not* tell her about the customer who ordered these feet?'

'No, I didn't not tell her,' said the shopkeeper. 'That is, I told her.'

'Then why won't you tell *me*?'

The shopkeeper merely stared back at Monty with a blank expression. Clearly his principles had been cast to the wind when it came to Sveltlana. A customer's confidences were only good for what they were worth. Xixes immediately saw this and intervened.

'She bribed him,' he said to Monty. 'Then paid him not to tell anyone else.'

'Ah!' Distasteful as he found it, Monty could see no other course to take than the one already taken. He took out a bag full of gold coins and laid three on the counter. The pangolin's expression did not change. A fourth was added. Still that same stony look. Finally a fifth brought animation and words to that face.

'A shrew,' said the shopkeeper.

'Thank you.'

When he was outside the shop he told the others what he and Xixes had learned. 'I knew it of course,' he added.

Maudlin, as usual, was sceptical. 'How did you know, Monty?'

'Well, to say I *knew* is overstating it. I *guessed*. You don't believe me, do you, Maudlin? Well, I'm not going to bother convincing you, for that would take valuable time, but let me ask you a question I asked myself last night. How would you smuggle a pair of priceless shoes out of the country? A simple yet effective method, when all luggage, all pockets, are thoroughly searched before the traveller is allowed to proceed?'

Maudlin thought very hard, but could not come up with an answer.

'Say then, it was a vest? Or a belt that was missing?'

Bryony cried, 'I've got it! Basic, my dear Monty, basic. You would *wear* the item.'

'Thank you, Bryony, I knew I could rely on you. Of course, you would wear them, after disguising their value. You would turn them into an ordinary-looking pair of shoes, either by painting them, or covering them with some sort of material. And what is the nature of the idol which normally wears the shoes? It is a tree-shrew. Therefore the jade shoes would best be worn by a member of the shrew family. As you say, Bryony, very basic. I'm surprised you didn't all follow the same train of thought.'

'That isn't fair,' said Maudlin. 'You're brainier than us.'

'Not so, not so. I simply break things down, bit by bit, then look at all the pieces, fit them together again, and see what's what.'

'So a shrew has stolen the jade shoes,' said Bryony, 'and has smuggled them out of the kingdom by wearing them on its feet?'

'Or perhaps it is still here?' Monty said. 'Perhaps that very shrew is wearing the shoes now, while it rakes the palace gardens.'

'Of course!' cried Scruff. 'The gardeners!'

'Now,' said Monty, 'you three go back to the palace. I have to do something. I want the shop-keeper to make me something.'

With that, Monty left them and re-entered the little shop.

CHAPTER THIRTY-TWO

The splendour of the Great Pangolin's court, with its many silver- and gold-robed mammals, its fantastic gardens, its fountains and buildings, its decorative walls and wonderful paths, held the weasels enthralled. After the dull, foggy streets of Muggidrear, the palace and its surrounds seemed full of sunshine and flowers. Butterflies, dragonflies and damselflies flitted amongst the plants like flying jewels. Fish made silvery circles on the ponds as they surfaced to snatch insects. Leaves shone like coins on exotic shrubs and ornamental trees. The weasels loved it.

Yet Monty reminded them they had work to do. They were getting closer to the thief of the

Green Idol's shoes, but then so was Sveltlana. In fact she seemed to be always a step ahead of them.

Bryony asked, 'Why didn't the emperor's detectives discover what we have? Pangolins seem just as bright as we are.'

'Perhaps the mammal sent out to do the job was in league with the thief?' said Monty. 'I've a feeling Sveltlana knows more about this than is apparent on the surface. I think I should have another word with her.'

Before Monty could do so, he and the others were summoned by the Great Pangolin. There was to be a festival, combined with a feast, which no-one was allowed to miss.

'Not that we'd want to stay away,' said Maudlin, 'and let all that food go to waste.'

As they passed through the gardens on the way to the court, Maudlin stared hard at the shoes of the gardener shrews as he passed them. One of the gardeners glared back with great ferocity. The other weasels could see that Maudlin was going to get a rake wrapped around his head. These Far Kathay shrews might *seem* placid creatures, but they were shrews after all, and Maudlin was taking a chance.

'Please,' murmured Monty, 'not so obvious, Maudlin.'

'I want to be the one to find them.'

'Of course you do, but this has to be done with subtlety, or our thief will skip the nest and head up into the mountains.'

'Oh. Didn't think of that.'

When they reached the court they found it full of entertainers of all kinds: jugglers, acrobats, dancers, poets, storytellers, musicians. Things were already in full and colourful swing. There were huge wooden tables covered with all kinds of food. The grand vizier had taken the time to have the food labelled for the guests. There were jellyfish pancakes, seaslug sausages, snail-lips, caterpillars' feet dipped in sugar, puffball soup, and a thousand other dishes. The group went from plate to plate, picking and choosing at will, while the emperor beamed at them from a lofty throne set up high on a platform.

The Great Pangolin's favourite kitten was there, his own dear daughter, the Princess Poppychu. The court jester, the marbled polecat, was helping her select some toys to play with. She sat on a palanquin raised on the shoulders of four strong civets. On this mammal-carried platform she had her doll's house. The court jester glanced across at the visitors and then passed the princess a weasel-doll. She took it and began reprimanding the doll in a high voice, for being a 'bad, bad, weasel', or so it seemed to the visitors, who stared with horror as she suddenly raised the stuffed toy by its tail and beat its head on the floor of the palanquin.

''Ere,' whispered Scruff, 'I think someone's bin givin' us a bad name. A kitten her age wouldn't do that unless someone told her we was a nasty species and deserved to get our heads bashed.'

'Sveltlana, no doubt,' growled Bryony.

'Never mind,' Monty said, 'we're here to enjoy ourselves. Where is she? I wonder.'

The Great Pangolin said something and his nightingale trilled, 'I hope my guests are comfortable.'

'Most comfortable, o Sun of the High Heavens,' replied Monty, having learned from Xixes a number of grand titles with which to address the eastern emperor. 'We have never been so comfortable in our lives before.'

'And progress?' chirruped the nightingale. 'The case progresses?'

'It does indeed, o Moon of the Wide Night, o Bright White Star Lighting the Tall Darkness. We believe we know the type of creature that has stolen the shoes, but whether that creature still has them is not certain, nor whether he or she remains within the palace walls.'

The Great Pangolin sat bolt upright. He shrieked something.

The nightingale used the same high screeching tones, but managed somehow to look bored while she was doing so. 'What is this creature? I shall have him and his kind annihilated. I shall remove the species from the face of the earth. Give me a name! Who has the jade shoes of the Green Idol of Ommm? I must have your answer, now!'

Bryony looked panicky. She put a claw on Monty's forelimb. Monty knew what she was thinking: the Great Pangolin would send in his

292

leopard cat guards with their bandicoot rats, accompanied by the civet soldiers, and the shrew gardeners would be massacred.

'My lord, first I must ask whether the Slattlander, the Countess Bogginski, is still here in the palace?'

The furious despot told Monty that Sveltlana had left the country that morning, heading towards the mountains of the north.

At that moment a civet came running into the room, threw himself forward and prostrated himself before his emperor. He gabbled. The emperor shrieked again. The nightingale kindly translated it all for the benefit of the weasels.

Civet: 'A gardener has been found knocked on the head in the mulberry bushes.'

Great Pangolin: 'What, one of my faithful shrews?'

Civet: 'Just so, o Wind of the South on a Warm Afternoon.'

Great Pangolin, sarcastically: 'Well, do we know *why* he was attacked and left unconscious? Was his purse missing? Had he upset someone? Did he leave the toilet seat up in the gardeners' loos? What?'

(Monty was not sure how much the nightingale was inventing here and how much was the literal truth.)

Civet: 'His boots were gone.'

Great Pangolin: 'What, his good gardening boots, the ones I issue to all my faithful shrew gardeners?'

Civet: 'Just so, o Flower of the Early Morning, o Dewdrop from a Heaven Paved with Crushed Diamonds.'

Monty felt it was time to intervene.

'I think I can explain, o Shining One. It is the Slattland lemming who struck the gardener and took his paw-wear. I had some replica jade shoes fashioned yesterday in order to trap her. They were not made of the precious mineral, of course, but out of a fake jade that would fool a foreigner in a great hurry. I believe the Countess Bogginski was responsible for hitting the gardener and taking those shoes, which I gave to the poor shrew yesterday evening. I thought she would steal them quietly, without fuss, and I'm very sorry she decided to harm the gardener. She is a vicious and self-serving creature and now on her way back to her homeland. It may only be a short while before she discovers the shoes are fake. I apologize for putting the shrew gardener in danger and hope he recovers quickly.'

While Monty was speaking the emperor was turning this way and that on his throne as if trying to wind himself up like clockwork. Monty guessed it was just pent-up frustration which was responsible for this extraordinary behaviour, for he noticed the Great Pangolin's eyes were rolling with the rhythm too. The emperor was a creature who sat in a chair all day and slept in a bed all night. He rarely got any exercise. Thus, when he was excited he did not jump up and run around the room six times, as Maudlin did, but rolled around on his seat, gripping the edge with white claws.

'I don't care about the Countess Bogginski. Nor do I care much about the gardener. I simply want my jade shoes back.'

'We are getting there, o Merciless One with Thieves and Vagabonds,' replied Monty. 'I would ask you to preserve patience and understanding, while I take this case to its conclusion.'

The feast was not a success. The emperor was in such a bad temper everyone was wary. At any second, it was felt, he might order the removal of a dozen heads from their parent bodies. Indeed, one courtier sneezed during a particularly deep silence, and the Great Pangolin commanded that he be roasted immediately over a blazing charcoal fire. As the unfortunate pangolin was being dragged away, his face bloodless with fear, the vizier intervened and suggested that since it was summer, and they had no fires lit, why not throw the creature into the nearest pond and leave him to drown? The emperor seemed to accept this suggestion, without stopping to think that the ponds were only three centimetres deep. The courtier's life had been spared by the quick-thinking vizier, whose eyes caught those of Monty.

Shortly afterwards, Monty and the others slipped out through a side door, happy to be out from under the emperor's furious gaze.

'Well,' said Bryony, 'what do we do now? Your idea that the jade shoes had been stolen by a shrew was obviously wrong, Monty.'

'Not necessarily. But I have another idea. I'll tell you about it later. In the meantime, I must go after Sveltlana. My plan did not work all that well. I expected her to take the shoes and hide them, then make an excuse to leave, in which case we could have exposed her for what she is. Now she is still on the loose. I must get to her before she descends on the barbaric side of the mountain where the savage tribes hold sway.'

'Why?' asked the other three weasels, almost in unison.

'Because she will stir up trouble amongst them,' said Monty. 'When we leave here, she'll be waiting in some mountain pass with several thousand warriors of some species or another. She won't be fooled by the fake shoes for very long and when she learns we've tricked her she'll want immediate revenge. We won't stand a chance if she manages to get barbarous hordes of hill creatures to rally to her cause.'

Bryony said, 'What cause is that?'

'Oh, she'll find one,' Monty replied, 'and if she doesn't, she'll invent one. She's very resourceful when it comes to revenge.'

'We'll come wiv you, guv'nor,' Scruff said.

'No. You must all remain here. This is between me and Sveltlana. What I will do is take a pair of palace guards with me – a brace of trustworthy civets. I'll ask the grand vizier to give me two of his best mammals. I'm sure he'll oblige. We'll pursue the lemming, overtake her, take her in custody, and then come back to turn her over.'

'Sounds simple enough,' said Bryony gloomily, 'but is it?'

'We'll see,' replied Monty.

CHAPTER THIRTY-THREE

In the event, Monty did not ask for the two civet guards. When he was sure the other weasels were engaged elsewhere, he set out alone. He passed through the city, out into the villages beyond, and before nightfall he was in a territory where no mammals dwelt. It was not exactly a wasteland – there were forests and rivers, but there were no villages and precious few lone travellers in this wilderness.

Monty entered a wood and soon encountered a ground squirrel. 'The route to the northern mountains?' he asked in the local language. 'This way?'

His pronunciation of the words was not good, but he hoped it would be understood. To illustrate it further, he drew a picture and an arrow pointing north in the dust and repeated his phrases.

'*Xi ji lo xen,*' replied the local mammal. '*Cho xik hok yen ho.*' Then he ran off, his teeth chattering.

Monty sighed. So far as he knew, the squirrel had told him that he could not build anything, let alone a huge hill in the middle of nowhere, due to the strict planning laws and building regulations in this part of the world. Nor, so he understood, could he do any archery practice in the emperor's forest, or he might damage the trees. It seemed Monty's language skills were wanting.

Having consulted his compass and the very rough map he had, Monty was convinced he was going in the right direction. He continued and was rewarded eventually by the sight of a magnificent wall, which meandered around the ridges of some impressive-looking foothills. He had taken the precaution of obtaining a travel document from the grand vizier before he left, and this he showed to the sentries patrolling the wall. A grand-looking captain of the guard eventually opened a gate for him and he was able to step out into the forbidding territories of the northern lands.

Here the mountains swept upwards far more steeply than those he had previously encountered on the Silk Road. Somewhere up there was the formidable Sveltlana, whose courage and resourcefulness were to be admired. She might be a bad lot, thought Monty, but she did not lack grit.

Nightfall came, and with it a deep darkness blacker than Monty had ever seen. It seemed a weighty thing, this darkness, as if it were made of something more than air. It pressed down on him, and it was all he could do not to fall into a gloom. Once he had his fire lit and had made himself a bivouac, he felt a little better. He then took out some dry rations of hard biscuit and dried meat, and with a little stream water fashioned himself a crude meal. Finally he rolled up in his thick cloak and went to sleep under his bivouac, hoping there would not be a frost the next morning.

There was. He woke with white crystals clinging to his fur. Shivering, he rose, stirred the embers of his fire, and made himself a hot drink. 'Got to keep warm,' he told himself. 'Mustn't get into that dull state of mind that extreme cold brings.'

He congratulated himself on not being eaten in the night by strange beasts. His knowledge of natural history told him there were not only tigers in this part of the world, but other members of the cat family too. To a tiger a weasel like Monty was but a mouthful. A tiger would not waste his time with a least weasel. But a wildcat might be hungry enough to make three or four mouthfuls of him, and there were other carnivores who were not too fussy about eating carnivores themselves. He would have to watch his back in these uncharted regions.

All that day he tramped up goat tracks, gazelle trails, deer paths, hoping to come across some sign that Sveltlana had been there before him. He found nothing conclusive and became a little dispirited. The only thing that kept him going was the certainty that Sveltlana was in these mountains somewhere. He knew that she had gone before him and this kept him on the case. What she could, he could do.

A night on the bare mountain. This one less pleasant than the first. Morning did not break too soon for him. It pierced the passes, filled the chasms with its light, and brought with it some sunshine. His heart lifted a little. On with the backpack, and then walk, walk, walk. At noon he came across the ashes of a fire, still warm.

'Was this *her* fire, though?' he mused. 'Let's have a look around before I get too excited.'

He searched the immediate area, coming up with nothing at first, then finally he found three hairs from a mammal's coat, caught on some thorns. Had she been careless at last? He took out of his backpack a small envelope. In it were some hairs from a Slattlander lemming – from Sveltlana's coat, in fact. He had secretly taken these from her hairbrush while talking with her on the veranda. He compared these stolen hairs with those he had found on the bramble.

His delight at the discovery proved justified. The three hairs were indeed Slattlander lemming hairs, identical to those he already carried.

'Yes,' he murmured to himself. 'She has been careless. No doubt in the cold night she rose to find herself some more wood for this fire, stumbled around in the darkness and got caught by the thorns. I'm sure in the morning she would have checked the bush, and taken some fur from it, but missed these three hairs.'

Monty continued onwards, now knowing he was on the right trail. Once past the snowline he would be able to follow her prints. Even if she tried to trick him by dragging a branch behind her, he would know the marks had been made by her.

Indeed, this proved to be the case. What was more he could now smell her musky perfume on the breeze. She would have washed herself thoroughly in streams and rivers on the way, but a countess like Sveltlana would have a lifetime's fragrance on her pelt. It would take more than cold water and a few days to get rid of that scent altogether.

However, as he studied his map by the fire-light, while he camped for yet another night on the mountain, he realized he had been careless himself too. The charts might be poorly drawn, the scale awry, but they showed that though there was really only one path *up* the mountains, due to the nature of the pass through which it climbed, there were *several* down. She might have time before he got there to lay false trails, thus delaying his pursuit. He knew he had to catch up with her before she reached the valleys on the other side, or she would have a thousand places to hide and a thousand bandits to assist her.

Monty decided to complete the climb that night. It was extremely dangerous – he could easily step off the edge and plummet to his death in some mighty gorge; or tread on some loose scree and slide over, hitting ledges and over-hangs on the way down, a ragged corpse before he even hit the bottom.

'But I have no choice,' he told the wind, which was wailing at him from amongst the crags. 'I must catch her now!'

To add to his troubles the wind had not been joking. A blizzard rose in the night and battered his poor body with hailstones the size of almonds. Then more snow came, hampering his progress. It was bitterly cold in those high regions and he knew he was in danger of losing his extremities. His tail stood the most chance of getting frostbitten, because it stuck out from under his cloak. Even before his watch told him it was midnight his whiskers had frozen solid. Without thinking, he wiped his face with his paw and broke them all off on one side.

Wonderful, he thought. Now even if I live I shall be ridiculed wherever I go.

Having half his whiskers was like a man having only half a moustache, only worse, since weasels *used* their whiskers for various tasks, especially in the kind of darkness he was experiencing at that moment. Until now he had used them to brush lightly against the wall of rock on the inside of the path, but that guide was now denied him. His precious whiskers, shattered like needle-thin icicles, had been scattered by the wind.

Before the dawn came, Monty's fur had frozen too. It began to get heavy – a sheet of ice on his body. Icicles formed and hung from his furry cheeks. His tail he simply dragged behind him. Still he forged on, the one thought in his mind to reach that female lemming before she eluded him yet again. Sveltlana, in leaving the palace, had taken herself beyond the protection of the Great Pangolin, and was now legitimate prey.

But could he kill her in cold blood?

'I have never yet killed a mammal, good or bad, without using the due processes of the law,' he told himself, 'but this time – this time . . .'

The trouble was, Sveltlana could wriggle out from under the law a dozen times, and yet still come back to murder him. He knew he would never again be safe in his bed while she lived. There was too much hate between them now. One or the other of them had to walk down from these mountains alone. Monty was determined it would be him.

Onward and upward he struggled through the mighty blizzard, knowing she was probably safe in some cave or under a rock overhang, waiting out the storm. When he arrived at the top of the pass, she would be fresh and ready for him. In fact she was in a perfect position to ambush him as he slogged ever upward. At any second a boulder could hurtle down on his head and squash him flat, or a bullet come out of the night's whirlwind ice, to strike him in the heart. He was as vulnerable as a kitten and, at that moment, almost as weak.

Towards dawn he heard the sound of thunder, which he knew almost immediately was *not* thunder. It was indeed an avalanche somewhere in the mountains. He prayed that Sveltlana had caused that avalanche and was now lying under the snow. It would save him the trouble, salve his conscience, if such an act of Nature took away the necessity for him to destroy her.

'I do not want to do this thing,' he told himself. 'Yet I must make sure she does not return to destroy *me*.'

When dawn broke he saw that the avalanche was a long way off – too far away to have interfered with Sveltlana's progress. It was going to have to be by his paw that she left the world. It grieved him not for her sake, but for his own. How would he live with himself after such a deed? Perhaps it would be better if he never descended from the mountain?

CHAPTER THIRTY-FOUR

Spindrick and Quikquik were trapped in the cabin. The night they had slept there it had snowed prodigiously and by morning the doors and windows were locked tight by white stuff. Quikquik managed to dig a tunnel out from the window, but it was clear that they could not travel far. Huge snow drifts were visible as far as the eye could see. The mountains had disappeared under white armour and looked even more formidable than before. Ice hung from the fir and pine trees like the fangs of some terrible frozen beast and bitter winds blew down from the heights.

After an initial show of temper, which was not appreciated by the sable jill, Spindrick became resigned to remaining at the cabin for the rest of the season, until the winter broke.

'How do we live?' he asked the sable, whose name was Nicknack. 'How do we spend our time?'

'For food, we cut holes in the ice and catch fish,' she replied. 'For fuel, we have plenty of logs. If we run out we'll use fallen pine branches. A lot of them drop down under the weight of the snow. What do we do? Well, when my mate Highwater was alive, we used to spend the winter making a canoe, and a couple of pairs of moccasins on the side. It's useful work. You'll need a canoe to cross the lake, once the thaw comes.'

'A canoe?' groaned Spindrick, adding sarcastically, 'That sounds like fun.'

'Yes, it does,' said Quikquik enthusiastically. 'It's a long time since Quikquik made a canoe. And moccasins! How exciting.'

Spindrick rolled his eyes. 'So, let's start with the fishing. I see I'm going to *love* fish. How did Highwater die?' he asked Nicknack conversationally. 'Did he choke on a fish-bone?'

'No, no.' The sable looked very sad. 'No, he was out one day and a human hunter saw him.'

The hairs on the back of Spindrick's neck rose. 'And?'

'And of course, he was shot. He's probably a scarf now, around the neck of some human. Or part of the coat on their back. We sables are very prized, you know, for our soft fur. Humans are not supposed to kill us any more, but there's always bad ones amongst them. They'd risk anything to get this pelt.' She plucked at her fur and sighed. 'It's a curse.'

'What about weasel fur?' asked Spindrick.

She wrinkled her nose. 'What about it? You think anyone would actually *want* to wear that coarse stuff unless they had to? You have to, I know, but no-one is going to take it from you, believe me. It's bad enough to have to look at it, without having to touch it.'

'Well, thank you,' replied Spindrick indignantly. 'How very polite of you to tell me that you hold my coat in contempt.'

'You're welcome,' she said sweetly.

That morning they went out and cut a hole in the ice on the lake. Quikquik did most of the hard work. Then Nicknack showed Spindrick how to make a fishing hook from a paperclip and tie it to some cord. Once they had the equipment ready, they sat around the hole with their lines dangling, waiting for a bite. Nicknack and Quikquik began pulling out fish straight away, but Spindrick's bait remained untouched. He became indignant and frustrated.

'How come you get all the fish?' he cried.

'There's a knack to it,' said Nicknack.

'You have to be quick,' said Quikquik.

They told him it was timing, picking the right moment for the swift snatch. When the line so much as twitched, he was to jerk it quickly. The hook would then take hold in the nibbling fish's mouth, and he could haul it up. He tried this simple technique, and behold, a shining silver fish was landed.

'I like the way the line zigzags in the water,' he cried excitedly. 'They're quite strong, aren't they? They'd pull you in if you didn't have a good grip. I think I'm a natural, really. Hey! Hey! There's another one. What a jack I am. What a natural . . .' And so on.

All winter he fished for fish. All winter he ate them. They made a canoe out of branches and bark, and two pairs of bark moccasins each. When the logs ran out he went with the others to collect firewood by the forest fence and lost two of his toes to frostbite. All winter he drank cocoa, the only drink in the cabin, until he was sick of it, even though Nicknack could make it with froth on the top. By the time spring came round he had cabin fever. He raved, he ranted, he swore at the other two, who had long since ceased speaking to him, being lost in each other.

With the first touch of the sun, the melting of the snows, he left them sleeping one morning, and headed out on his own towards the mountains.

Spindrick had left a note for Quikquik, apologizing for his unannounced departure and saying that the harpoonist had done him a great service, but it was sadly time for them to part. Spindrick had come to loathe his companions. He knew everything about them – every single little detail of their lives, from the way they brushed their teeth in the mornings, to the way they filed their claws in the evening. He shuddered every time he thought of bath nights and de-fleaing. Snoring. Breaking wind. Sneezing. Snuffling. Coughing. Spindrick had heard the lot, a thousand times over, and it had driven him mad. He knew every hair on their pelts, every spot on their noses, every twitch, every gesture, every breath they took, and his life had not improved with the knowledge.

No-one should live in such intimacy, he told himself, as he trudged on his snow shoes over the thawing wastelands. No-one should reveal all their common ugly secrets to another. Walls, that's the answer. Walls everywhere, to keep us from seeing our neighbours. When I get home I shall start a wall-building programme. I'll do the Muggidrear marathon to raise money. I'll do a sponsored swim across the river Bronn. I'll bike from Jack O'Giblets to Land's Edge and back again. High walls is the answer. High walls with barbed wire on top. Each mammal to his own space. Once a month, perhaps even once a fort-night, we shall be permitted to knock on our neighbour's wall and ask him, 'How-d'ye-do?' but apart from that we shall keep to our own patch and be happy in our own company.

Spindrick crossed the mountains on his own. He fought off bandits, cut his way through impassable country, repelled wild beasts. He became a mountain weasel, a frontiersmammal, a trapper and hunter (he was already, as you know, a fisher), a self-reliant mammal who could live on two beans a day and five minutes of snatched sleep. There was a hunting knife glued to his right paw, his eyes had narrowed to slits through looking into sharp winds, and his pelt was raw with the great outdoors. Spindrick's cousin, the Right Honourable Montegu Sylver, would not have known him.

Finally, he came to the gold fields. There was a town of sorts – more of an encampment of tents, with one or two large wooden shacks. The mushy snow had turned to mud and the mud had been churned to a quagmire. It splattered the citizens of the gold town, from head to foot and back again. There was not a clean spot in the territory.

Spindrick accosted the first creature he met, an opossum. 'Where can I find Wm. Jott?' he croaked.

The opossum looked him up and down, knew a rough mountain weasel when he saw one and nodded at one of the large shacks. 'Up yonder,' he said. 'Chawin' the fat.'

Spindrick made his way up yonder and entered the shack. There, around the pot-bellied stove, sat a group of mammals warming their paws and chawin' the fat. Good Old Jacks, drinking honey dew and rye. One of these he recognized as the stoat, Wm. Jott.

'Billy,' he called across the room. 'I've come for you.'

Wm. Jott's paw went immediately to the pistol at his belt, but Spindrick said, 'No, not that. I've come to buy guns. Your guns.'

'Guns?' said the stoat inventor, looking mystified. 'What guns? I've only this pistol at my belt. No others.'

Spindrick looked at him in disbelief. 'But – but you invented the steam-driven pistol. A gun that would shoot a thousand rounds a minute. I heard tell it would blast anyone to bits. I need it to start a civil war in Far Kathay. The civet cats depend upon me and I want to thwart that rotten cousin of mine, Monty Sylver. I want him to eat his pith helmet.'

Jott's face screwed up in thought, then a light seemed to appear behind his eyes. He clicked his teeth in merriment. 'How far have you come?' he asked. 'Have you come from Welkin?'

'All the way,' groaned Spindrick. 'Every centimetre of water and ground. Look at me. I've been through hell. I was once soft and gentle. Now I'm as hard as a bear and as vicious as a mountain lion. I can wrestle ten wolves before breakfast. I eat my eggs with the shells on, raw. I sleep in the fork of a tree and call darkness my friend. All these changes have been wrought in me because I sought you out, here in the wilderness.'

'Wow,' said one of the Good Old Jacks. 'He's tougher'n Dangerous Dan McGlue.'

Spindrick spat on his paw and smoothed the fur on his face with it. 'You better believe it. Now, these guns . . .'

'No guns,' replied Wm. Jott. 'At least, not the kind of guns you're talking about. Blasting guns with steam-driven *pistons* – not pistols – that drive a wheel a thousand *revolutions* – not rounds – a minute. It's an invention that helps miners blast away the earth and rock from the mine face, so that they can get at the gold ore more quickly. At least it was supposed to, but the government has banned its use.' Wm. Jott's expression became grim. 'They said it was ruining the environment, that it was scarring the landscape. Who cares? Out here, who cares? But there it is. They said they would send the mounties in to arrest me, unless my machines were broken up.' He nodded towards the rear of the building. 'They're all out back, in pieces. Junk. You can have the whole pile for a hundred dollars. That's the price of my ticket back to Welkin. Take it or leave it.'

Spindrick didn't know whether to burst into tears or collapse in a heap on the floor. All this way! All those experiences! For nothing? He trudged across the floor and looked out of the back window. There it was, a pile of scrap metal, pistons sticking up at all angles. Who would want junk like that, even for a mere one hundred dollars? Then, as he stared at the scrapyard, an idea came to him. It wasn't brilliant, but it would do.

'I'll take it,' he said. 'Here's your hundred.' He took out his wallet and paid the grateful stoat. 'I'm going to load up sledges with those pistons and take them to San Ferryanne, to sell in the markets there. Recycling. That's the thing of the future. Making old junk useful again.'

'You're mad,' said Jott, taking the money. 'I've never heard of such a thing. Junk is junk, and evermore shall be so.'

But Jott was wrong. Spindrick became a stall owner in one of San Ferryanne's open markets. He was modest in his business ambitions, happy to make a small living. A thousand pistons he had to sell in a country which was growing fast, building clocktowers and belltowers by the score. His street cry became famous for years afterwards and eventually an opera was written around it which took the New and the Old World by storm.

'Come and buy! Come and get your bell clappers 'ere. Your nice shiny clappers. Ding-dong, ding-dong. Set the tone. All you need's an empty bell and here's the clapper! Break the sound of silence. Wake up the world. Come buy your clappers 'ere. Your nice shiny clappers . . .'

Spindrick Sylver built a house without windows and never ate fish or drank cocoa again.

CHAPTER THIRTY-FIVE

They were in a vast ocean, a blue world of water.
Sybil was still clinging – just – to her cork float.
Falshed's claws were firmly embedded in his lump
of cork. They were drifting, drifting, the sun beating down on their furry heads. No crocodiles had
snatched them up at the mouth of the river. No
sharks had so far appeared to swallow them
whole. Fearsome creatures of the deep had stayed
away. The only fish trying to eat them were tiny
multi-coloured ones which nibbled their paws.

'I can't believe you jumped in after me,' said
Sybil, realizing they were close to death. 'You
could have saved yourself, yet without a thought
you leapt overboard to try to save me. Foolish
stoat.'

'Stupid, that's what it was,' replied Falshed, unable to raise any real anger at himself. 'If I'd stayed I could have alerted the rescue authorities and we might have found you. Now there's no-one who knows we're missing . . . Is that a boat?' His voice was raised slightly, but they'd had so many false alarms he did not want to lift her hopes unduly.

Sybil stared at the horizon. There did indeed seem to be a black speck there. A flicker of hope entered her heart. 'I – I don't know. It could be, Zacharias. It could be. Oh, I do hope it is.'

The pair of them, soggy as they were, summoned their last vestiges of strength to paddle towards that distant black speck. For a while it did not get any bigger. This didn't strike either of them as odd at first, but then after a while Falshed said, 'If that's a boat, why isn't it moving away from us or towards us? It just seems to be sitting there.'

'Perhaps it's at anchor?'

'In the middle of the ocean? Unlikely.'

Still, it was *something*. The closer they came to it, the more obvious was the explanation. It was an island. Quite a small island by the look of it, but dry land nevertheless. Falshed would have preferred a ship, but in the circumstances an island was better than nothing.

'A mother-in-law gift,' he said.

'What?'

'You know, not quite what you wanted, but it'll do.'

316

Despite her agony, Sybil chuckled. 'Oh, you.'

As they got closer they could see the island was ringed by a coral reef. Huge breakers crashed on this outer barrier, throwing up clouds of spume and spray and Falshed soon began to wonder how they were going to cross the reef without being torn to pieces on the jagged, sharp coral beneath. He searched anxiously for any gaps in the reef, but could see none. Just as they were approaching, a pelican flew over their heads. Falshed called up to it.

'Hey!'

The pelican wheeled round and looked down. 'Hey yerself.'

Falshed gulped down seawater as he tried to speak. 'Could you – could you give us a lift over that coral?'

The pelican wheeled again. 'You've got to be joking.'

'No, no, we're not,' said Sybil. 'We're in dire straits.'

'No you're not, you're in open waters.'

'I mean we're in trouble. We can't get over that reef without being hurt. I know birds and mammals aren't all that friendly with one another, but we could break the mould.'

'Egg-eaters,' said the pelican.

'Yes, true,' groaned Falshed, 'but never again, I promise.'

The pelican said nothing to this, but didn't fly away. Nearer and nearer they came to the crashing surf. There was no getting away from the reef now. If they weren't plucked from the water the currents and tides would drag them in. Falshed had heard that creatures and objects caught on a coral reef often ended up trapped beneath the shelf, to rot and be picked at by fishes. It was not an end he had envisaged for himself. There had been moments when he saw himself being shot by some criminal, or struck by a passing pawsome cab, or even strangled by Jeremy Poynt during one of the mayor's frequent bouts of rage. But to be drowned in tropical waters and chomped on by nasty angel fish had not been one of the scenarios.

'Oh, all right then,' sighed the pelican, swooping down, 'let go of those bits of cork.'

The two stoats did as they were told. The next instant Falshed felt himself being scooped up in the pelican's beak, along with Sybil. They sloshed in some seawater for a moment, until the pelican squirted it out of the side of his beak, then they were lumped rather embarrassingly together. Sybil tried to draw away, but there wasn't a lot of room in the soft-lined pouch. It was a strange feeling to be *inside* another creature, juices and all. Not an experience one would want to recall too often, once the ride was over.

Then over it was. They were dumped on a soft coral-sand beach. The pelican waddled away from them. Agile and graceful as it was in the air, the bird was quite awkward on land. It ran along, trying to get up enough speed to take to the skies. When it was aloft Falshed called out to it.

'Hey, first of all, thanks. Next, couldn't you take us to the mainland? I'd make sure you were amply rewarded.'

'Don't live on the mainland,' said the pelican. 'Live on a rocky island with some turtles and lizards with fleshy beards. You wouldn't like it. Stark, barren, bleak. Plenty of fish in the sea, but no trees and stuff. You wouldn't like it at all. Better here, with coconut palms and greenery.'

Then he wheeled away into the sun. Finally, he turned south and was gone.

The two stoats lay on the hot beach and dried their fur. At last a salt-encrusted Falshed got up and began collecting driftwood from the shore line.

'What are you doing?' asked Sybil.

'Got to make a signal fire, in case a ship comes.'

'How are you going to light it?'

Falshed looked down at himself. His clothes were in shreds. He looked at Sybil. She too was in rags. She could have come straight from a Muggidrear workhouse. If there had been anything in their pockets, that anything would be of no use, since their pockets had now gone. They didn't even own a pocket, let alone what might be in it.

Falshed peered closely at the princess. 'You – er – you don't happen to have a glass eye, do you?'

'Of course I don't,' snapped Sybil indignantly.

'Pity,' he said. 'We could have used it like a magnifying glass and started a fire that way.' He stared at her intently again. 'You could pop it out and pop it back again, just like that. I wouldn't look.'

'I – don't – have – a – glass – eye,' she said emphatically.

Falshed sighed. 'Oh, well. Maybe we can find some flints or something. Knock them together and make sparks? In the meantime would you mind shinning up one of those palms and slinging down a few coconuts?'

'You want me to climb trees?'

'Look,' he replied with some grit in his tone, his paws on his hips, 'we're in this together, madam. We both need to pull our weight, otherwise we starve. Yesterday you were a princess. Today you're a castaway. They're two different members of society. One gets everything done for her, the other does everything for herself. Get it? Now move your furry—'

Sybil drew herself up haughtily. 'No need to be rude.'

'I'm just telling it like it is. I'm going to look for roots and things.'

She stood up now and folded her forelimbs, thinking that of all the dunderheads to be shipwrecked on a desert island with, she had to choose a bumbling police chief who probably knew nothing except how to blow on a silver whistle and clap pawcuffs on the wrists of weasels. 'What sort of roots and *things*?' she

320

enquired, one eyebrow lifted condescendingly. She fully expected the next few minutes would expose his ignorance.

'Oh—' he seemed to sniff the wind – 'in this region I'm sure we can come across some arums, sweet potatoes and taros. As for the trees, perhaps we'll be lucky and find breadfruit or even plantains? Or both? There's probably some pandanus and yams too, if we look hard enough. And already I can smell "buds of the vine". I don't think we'll starve, even though we've promised not to eat birds' eggs – a promise I intend to keep, by the way, even though there's probably fulmars here, and frigate birds, and perhaps some boobies up on the heights. Maybe even a tropic bird. They're quite beautiful, by the way. They're as white and delicate as a bride's veil and they fly backwards when they're doing their courting ritual dance.'

She looked at this flatpaw, this city copper, in awe. 'How do you know all that?'

He shuffled. 'Oh, you know.'

'No, I don't. I'm *very* impressed.'

'Well, it's all rather pathetic really. I'm a lonely soul, back in Muggidrear. Don't go out much. Nowhere to go, no-one to see. So I stay in at nights, do a lot of reading. I know how to make pandanus flour and turn it into bread – or could do, if we had a fire. I could do you a plantain fishcake like you've never tasted before. And baked yams are easy. I've never tried to make an earth oven, but I expect I could. I know *how*.'

321

She was amazed and enthralled. What a stoat! To think that all her life she had considered him to be a bit of a bore. 'Could you – could you make us a shelter?'

'Easy-peasy,' he replied.

Before nightfall he had gathered everything on his list, including some wild almonds. He had built them a lean-to of pandanus leaves, which he said he would convert into a hut within the next few days. He cut her and himself a staff, carved a point with a sharp-edged clam shell, and nicked a barb in it, so they could spear fish in the lagoon. Shellfish? They were his special study, back in his dreary flat in the city. He had learned everything there was to know about molluscs under a sickly lamplight – which ones to eat and which ones to avoid. Anemones, sea cucumbers, seaweed – all very tasty given the right conditions. Since the island was hilly there was fresh water to be found if one dug above the high tide mark, which had flowed down under the ground from the heights. It was all very simple, really, he said. You just needed the knowledge, that was all.

'I think you're a marvel,' Sybil told him. 'I wish I did have a glass eye now, so we could make a fire.'

'Not necessary,' Falshed said, producing a piece of mineral he had found on a rocky place above the trees. 'I've got a crystal here, probably formed during the volcanic disturbance that first caused this island to rise up from the sea bed.

We'll use the sun's rays tomorrow to make a fire with it.'

'My hero!'

'Oh, I don't know. You said you wouldn't have anything to do with me, ever, even if I were the last stoat on earth. That's what you said.'

'I was a stupid princess then. Now I'm a castaway. They're two different mammals, you know. Quite different. I'm wondering, would it be very irresponsible of us to start a family on a desert island? We could make a colony. Our very own tribe. Tree houses, vines to swing between them, proper picnic tables. What do you think, Zacharias, my dear?' Her eyes were shining.

Falshed's heart swelled with pleasure. 'Don't see why not. Don't see why not at all.'

Suddenly, Sybil jumped up and pointed out to sea. 'A ship!' she cried. 'A ship!'

Falshed's swollen heart suddenly flattened faster than it had inflated. Always the same with his luck, he thought miserably. Just as bold heart had won fair jill, reality struck with a vengeance. One moment he had a bride, the next he had been jilted. Same old story. Back to that sordid old flat with its jaundiced lamplight. Why? Why? Why?

'Oh,' he said dully, forcing a note of optimism into his voice, so as not to spoil it for her. 'Jolly good. You'll soon be back with your lot again, drinking coffee, swapping gossip, showing each other your latest shopping. Nice life, really. Wish I had the same, but there it is. I have to go back to being your brother's minion again.'

He could not turn round and look. He did not want to see their rescue craft. He actually wanted it to go away and never come near the island again.

Sybil had been studying his expression with a little frown on her furry brow. Then she suddenly leapt in front of him, grasping his paw. She tugged him away from the beach. 'Just kidding,' she shouted in glee. 'No ship at all.'

He couldn't believe his ears. The light flooded into his soul again. 'You rotter,' he said, his heart swelling, full enough to burst. 'You little rotter. You deserve a ducking for that.'

She ran off into the forest, squealing. He ran after her, caught her and carried her to a seawater inlet circled by trees. There they splashed each other's fur and tumbled in the warm waters, blissful and carefree in their new lives.

Out in the night the ship that Sybil had seen coming slipped silently past the island, well within hearing of a mammal's shout.

CHAPTER THIRTY-SIX

As Monty continued to climb, the blizzard abated a little. Soon he could see a patch of clear blue sky through the white haze, like a broken piece of china. The flat-topped summit was very close now. He could see no sign of Sveltlana, but that was because the fresh snow had wiped out her tracks.

How wearisome was this climbing! There were so-called 'mountain weasels' in these parts. He wondered how they coped with the rock climbing. It was one thing to struggle up there and call it an achievement, then return to flatter land. It would be quite another to have to cope with it on a daily basis.

'I'm glad I was born a least weasel,' he said.

'Mountain weasels must have leg muscles of steel.'

As he neared the peak of the mountain, Monty drew his pistol. He hoped the thin, cold air would not affect its mechanism. The metal of the butt froze his paw. He only wished it would freeze his heart.

To his utter astonishment, as he rounded the crest, he saw Sveltlana waiting patiently for him. She was bare-headed but enveloped in a hooded cloak. Beside her was a sled. Had she hauled that up the mountain, or had it been left there for her by accomplices? Monty was, as ever, impressed by her ingenuity.

'You've lost half your whiskers,' she said. 'It makes you look lopsided.'

He reached up and touched that side of his face. 'One of the hazards of the chase,' he replied.

'I had hoped you'd freeze to death and save us both the trouble.'

'Sorry to disappoint you. I had hoped the same of you.'

'We're not very good at satisfying each other's wishes, are we, Montegu Sylver? What a shame you were born good. We would have made such a great couple of evil geniuses.'

'What a shame you were born bad.'

She said, 'If I had not been, we would never have met. I'm glad we met, Monty, for all that. It has been an interesting few years. The world would have been a greyer place without you.' She paused, then continued, 'So, here we are, the angels by your side, the demons by mine. I suppose you came to kill me?'

Monty remained wary. What sort of trick did she have up her sleeve? He could see no visible weapon. There was no gun in her paw. But he could not imagine that she would simply give herself up. He quickly glanced this way and that, wondering if there were others of her kind hiding there, waiting for the appropriate moment to spring out and attack him.

'I'm alone,' she said, in an amused tone of voice. 'Did you think I had hordes of mountain creatures to assist me?'

'I thought you might have one or two.'

'Are you going to use that pistol? I'm willing to come quietly. I am, as of this moment, your prisoner. Can you shoot a prisoner, Monty? It's against all your own rules, you know. It would be murder.'

'I can't believe you're giving up, just like that.'

She raised her forelimbs. 'Believe it.'

Monty groaned inwardly. Now that it had come to it, could he pull the trigger? If she had put up some sort of fight, had run away even, he might have been able to shoot her. But a submissive creature with its paws in the air? She was right. It would be murder. He might call it an execution, but it would be murder. But it had to be done. It had to. He must quell these sentimental feelings just for once in his life, and do what was sensible and expedient. If he did not, he would have to watch his back for the rest of his days. He would never be able to rest. She would, in the end, kill him. It was better to get it over with now than drag out their feud until he himself faced death.

'Step away from the sled,' he ordered, in a croaky voice.

Sveltlana took two steps to her right, looking alarmed. 'No, Montegu . . .'

He raised the pistol. 'Shut up. This is hard enough as it is.' He took aim.

'Why should I make it any easier?' she cried. 'I expect you want me to jump off this mountain, don't you, and kill myself on those rocks far below? Well, I won't. You'll have to pull the trigger. You'll have to shoot me in cold blood.'

'A weasel's blood is hot when he's threatened.'

'Am I a threat to you, like this, with my claws raised?'

Her eyes were large, dark and moist. He stared into those soft eyes, trying to reject their pleading message.

'You will *always* be a threat to me.' His throat was dry and in that moment he knew he could not do it. He was no executioner. He was the Right Honourable Montegu Sylver. *Right* and *Honourable*. To kill her, helpless as she was now, would be wrong and *dis*honourable. Difficult as it would be, he was going to have to try to take her down the mountain. He knew she would try to kill him on the way, try to escape, but there was no other way he could handle it.

He stepped towards her. 'I'm going to have to

tie you—' There was a loud *clack!* and a terrible pain went shooting up his left hind leg. Bright lights flashed before his eyes and his brain felt as if it had exploded with a blinding white shock-wave. He fell full length in the snow. Even before his body had hit the ground Sveltlana had stepped forward and kicked the pistol from his paw. It went spinning away, over the edge, and fell clattering to the valley below.

At first he could not think straight, the pain was so awful. He lay there in his agony, knowing she had done something – but what? Finally, with a great effort, he pulled himself up. When he saw what it was that had slammed onto his leg, had broken it yet still held it fast, he was utterly horrified. How could she use such a barbaric instrument? This was the kind of device that all animals swore would never again be employed to capture any creature on the face of the earth. It was the ugliest, most foul invention that man had ever devised and if there was still hatred in mammals for humankind, it was this thing that held his leg which was responsible.

'A gin trap!' he said, feeling the cold ironwork of its jaws. 'A gin trap hidden under the snow. I – I can't believe . . .' The pain washed over him again and he fell back in the snow, weak and giddy. There was terror in his heart, too. If she left him to die with this metal monster gripping his leg, he would die very slowly, very painfully. It was the worst death imaginable. When men had used these on the animals, beasts had gnawed through their own legs to escape the traps rather than lie there and let the life drain from them. Worse than the gun. Worse even than the snare.

'I can't believe even you – you would stoop to such depths.'

'Well, there's the difference between us, isn't it?'

'Even—' he gasped for breath as a new wave of pain swept through him – 'even the gerbil Gangly Kan, despicable barbarian that he was, forbade the use of this terrible device on his enemies.'

'I know,' she said, stepping forward and looking down at Monty. 'He was such a softie, wasn't he? Slaughtered thousands by the sword, too. I think I'm badder than him, don't you?'

'You're a foul succubus,' he spat at her, some fire coming into his veins to fuel his contempt for her actions. 'To think that . . .'

'To think that you once found me attractive? I remember the way you looked at me, when we first met in your Muggidrear flat. How you stared into my eyes!' She clicked her teeth. 'These big eyes have always been useful. Poor Montegu. You have finally drowned in these eyes, haven't you?'

He turned his face away from her. Then a thought occurred to him, as she adjusted her cloak, pulling up the hood to cover her head. He had one last bolt for his bow. 'They're fake, you know. You've gained nothing.'

'What?' she said, her voice half-amused, half-concerned. 'What are you talking about?'

'The jade shoes. They're not jade – nothing like.'

'You're just saying that to goad me. You're dying, Monty. It won't help you to lie to me.'

'I'm not lying. You – you know me better than that,' he gasped. 'My name isn't Sveltlana. I never lie to my enemies, only to my friends.'

She reached inside her coat and pulled out the shoes. Opening her mouth, she bit into one of the shoes with her sharp teeth. A piece cracked and split from the heel of the shoe. She spat it out and stared at the broken edge. A cheap jade? Obsidian perhaps? Or malachite? But not the jade shoes from the feet of the Green Idol of Ommm.

She dangled the shoes in front of her, the laces tied, inspecting them carefully. It was true. The shoes were fake. The realization swept across her features like a dark storm over a mountain. Letting out a cry of fury she flung them at Monty's head with great force. The shoes flew like bolas through the air, and wrapped themselves several times around Monty's neck. The laces began choking the life out of him.

Sveltlana's eyes blazed with terrible ferocity. Her anger was such that when she flung the shoes, she lost her balance. Her feet slipped on the ice and she fell backwards onto her sled. It was not a hard fall, but it was enough to jolt the sled forwards. As she struggled to get up in her heavy cloak, the sled glided downwards, towards the edge of the mountain. Even through his dimming sight, Monty recognized a look of horror on her features. She reached up just as the sled went over the edge, as if feeling for ropes or handles in the thin air.

Then she was gone, out into the space beyond.

He listened to the thin scream until it stopped, abruptly, two or three seconds later.

Despite his failing strength, Monty managed to unwind the shoes from round his neck. He lay back, gasping in the cold snow. There was still the gin trap. The mechanism required strength to free a trapped victim from its iron jaws. One had to stand with one's whole weight on the releasing pad, while at the same time prising the jaws open with one's forelimbs. Impossible for a trapped creature, even if all energy had not already ebbed from its body. Even if the shock of the snapping jaws had not robbed it of all will to live. Monty knew that he would lie there until the night came and then would – hopefully – freeze to death.

'To come to such an end,' he said bitterly. 'To die in a *gin trap*. I had imagined many deaths for myself, but not one as ignominious as this! Oh, the devil in that lemming! She has had the last click on me. She died too quickly, too suddenly. Hers was a death I would have given my life for . . .'

The irony in this remark penetrated the pain

and he might have clicked his teeth in amusement if he hadn't passed out at that moment.

CHAPTER THIRTY-SEVEN

Some time later Monty came to and knew he was
close to death. The weather was closing in
around him. There was nothing he could do. He
was as weak as a new-born kitten. He stared
bleakly up at the sky, filled as it was with huge,
fluffy flakes of snow. Suddenly a face appeared
between him and the heavens.

'What a state to get into!'

He opened his eyes wider. 'Bryony,' he
whispered, with joy in his heart. 'You followed
me against my orders.'

'Of course I did. Who are you to give me
orders anyway? I'm my own weasel, I'll have
you know, Jal Sylver. Oh dear, oh dear. You've

334

lost some of your whiskers! Iced up and broke off, I suppose.'

She was muffled up to the eyeballs with scarves, gloves and coats, some of which she took off. 'Now, let's see if we can get you out of those terrible iron jaws.' She stood on the pawplate of the trap and used her claws to try to prise the trap open. It was almost impossible to move. The spring was strong and the low temperatures had frozen the mechanism solid. 'I'm going to have to breathe on this for a while, to try to thaw it out a bit,' she said. 'How's your leg?'

'Numb now. Frozen, I think. No pain, anyway.'

'Oh, good.'

Despite her words Bryony didn't think this was good. As a vet she was aware that pain had a function – to tell a creature that the leg was still connected to his nervous system and could send messages to his brain. A numb leg might mean it would have to come off. Would she be up to amputating her friend's hind leg? She didn't think so. Probably have to leave it to the pangolin vets, who were very good at their profession, so she had heard.

She breathed on the mechanism of the gin trap for a good ten minutes, then stamped down hard on the pawplate. There was a *creak*. Something had given. Bryony applied more pressure, this time evenly, and gradually she managed to get the jaws of the trap to open a fraction.

'Can – you – pull – it – out?' she gasped.

'Not yet. The teeth seem to be . . . Wait, yes.'

Gathering his strength Monty managed to pull at his own leg with his forepaws. The skin tore under the fur. Bryony pressed down with all her might and heaved on the iron jaws. They opened just a little more. He wrenched again, and suddenly the leg was free. The pain had come back now. Monty crawled away from the trap, irrationally wanting to put distance between himself and the monstrous contraption. He found himself at the edge of the precipice, looking down. Far below he could see a bundle of rags. Or was it? Of course, it was Sveltlana's body, crumpled on the rocks.

'Well, she's not feeling any pain,' he said, gritting his teeth. 'She'll never feel pain again.'

Bryony was now by his side, trying to pull him back from the edge. She too stared down at the corpse. 'Is that her?'

'Yes.'

'Did you kill her?'

'She fell – it was an accident.'

'Pity, I would have preferred it if you'd killed her, and she knew you had killed her.'

'Bryony, revenge is *not* a dish that's best eaten cold – in truth, it's better left untasted altogether.'

'Somehow I wanted to see her suffer.'

'Oh, she had her moment of terror, I can vouch for that. Now who's this? Good lord, have I lost all authority? Does no-one obey the expedition leader's orders any more? Here's a fine how-d'ye-do.'

This speech was uttered as Maudlin and Scruff

came up to the peak, pulling a sled behind them. They shook their heads in disbelief when they saw the horrible state of Monty's leg. It was broken in two places and the bone stuck out at a nasty angle. They lifted him up and placed him carefully on the sled, then started to make their way down the mountain again. To keep him cheerful, Maudlin and Scruff sang mountain songs.

'I love to go a wanderin',' trilled Scruff, 'along the old goat track, and as I go I love to sing, a—'

'Shut up,' growled Monty. 'Please shut up. I can stand the pain of this leg, but my head can't bear that grating noise.'

'Well, there's gratitude for yer,' said Scruff. 'My auntie says I've got a nice voice.'

'Your auntie must be tone deaf. And I will be too, if you keep that up.'

The journey down to the Forbidden Palace was hard and long. This was due both to the cold and to the darkness which fell with a storm. Between them the three intrepid weasels struggled with their leader, as he dropped in and out of consciousness. It was a wonder that none of them got frostbite on that two-day journey, which Bryony swore she would remember for the rest of her life. Their efforts were rewarded when they finally saw the lights of the palace below them and, exhausted, they managed to crawl the last few metres dragging Monty behind them.

'Get him into bed,' gasped Bryony to those

who came running at her call. 'He must be warmed up quickly.'

The same went for her and the other two weasels. She staggered away and immediately sought the warmth of her bed. Scruff and Maudlin did likewise.

'I used to moan about being too hot,' Maudlin said, as he shivered beneath layers of blankets, 'but I'll never do that again.'

'Oh yes you will,' replied Scruff, who knew his friend only too well. 'That's one of them certainties in life.'

Chapter Thirty-eight

The pangolin vets proved to be expert at mending broken bones. Pangolins, they explained, were always falling off things and breaking their legs. They were not very agile when it came to climbing. Still, it was a nasty break with lots of bone splinters and torn flesh. It was touch and go whether gangrene would set in. After two weeks, having treated the wound with poultices, the pangolin vets declared it clean. Monty then took himself on crutches to see the emperor.

'We are glad to see you up and around,' sang the translating nightingale, 'and we are sorry you have suffered.'

The four weasels had been invited into the

Great Pangolin's own sitting room for this interview. It was a very domestic scene. The empress was sitting doing some embroidery on an enormous couch. In the corner of the room the Princess Poppychu was playing with one of her dolls. This time it was a free-tailed bat with wire spectacles and ink stains on its bib. Clearly the doll was of the oriental clerk who did the palace accounts.

'O Rapturous One, you are too kind,' said Monty. 'I suffered only in the hope of ending suffering.'

'And the evil one is dead?'

'She is as the dust beneath your paws, o Silver in a Sparkling Teaspoon.'

'Good. But we still have not solved the mystery of the Green Idol of Ommm's jade shoes. Do you know where they are?'

'I have a jolly good idea, o Sea of Tranquillity.' Monty turned and pointed at the little pangolin playing in the corner. 'Does your daughter, the Princess Poppychu, have a doll which represents one of the palace gardeners? A life-size treeshrew doll?'

The empress looked up from her work. 'She does indeed,' she said, through the nightingale. 'Why do you ask?'

'Could we see it? Now?'

'Certainly,' the Great Pangolin cried. 'Poppychu, bring forth your favourite doll, this instant.'

The princess screwed up her face and burst

into tears. Her mother rose in stately fashion, went to her toy box and rooted around. Eventually she came up with the shrew doll. Sure enough, on its feet were a pair of pretty jade shoes. They fitted the doll exactly.

'My own daughter stole the jade shoes?' cried the emperor. 'How did she do this?'

Monty saw the court jester trying to sneak out of the back door of the living room. 'Not your daughter, o Magnificent Worm of Sacred Soil, but your court jester, the marbled polecat. He had some plaster ferret badger's paws made and sent one of the shrew gardeners to collect them. With these on his own feet he went and stole the jade shoes, giving them to Princess Poppychu, on whom he dotes. No doubt she had constantly asked him to take them for her, so she could put the pretty shoes on her shrew-doll's feet. I think, o Shell of the Wide Oceans, if there has been a crime committed, it is one of affection. Your court jester—' for the polecat was standing with hanging head, expecting the worst – 'meant no harm. He simply could not bear to be asked for something that he could not give the princess. My enquiries led me to learn that the princess saved his life once, when he was about to be executed. She asked you to spare him?'

'This is true,' said the emperor.

'And he is eternally grateful to the young princess.'

The emperor turned and pointed at the marbled polecat. 'Off with his head!' he shrieked

– or rather trilled as the nightingale interpreted this terrible sentence. 'Bring it to me in a basket!'

Civet guards grasped the unfortunate polecat by the forelimbs and began to drag him trembling from the room. The Princess Poppychu burst into tears again and threw her tree-shrew doll at her father. The Great Pangolin looked shocked and said something to his wife. The empress snapped at her husband and clicked her claws as if to say, 'I don't give a tuppenny claw-clack for your bad temper.' For a while the whole room was full of shouting and yelling, mostly amongst the pangolin royal family. Guards rushed back and forth, not quite sure whether orders were final or not. The ferret badger cook came out of the kitchen wanting to know whether lunch could be served, or was it to be put on the hot plate? It was chaos.

When everything had finally calmed down, the emperor recalled the polecat to the living room. The creature was made to lie face-down at his feet. A three-way discussion took place between the empress, the emperor and the court jester, which the nightingale interpreter saw no reason to translate for his weasel charges. Finally the princess wiped away her tears, a humble marbled polecat crept across the room and began to play with her again, and the empress settled down to her embroidery once more. The emperor looked ruffled for a while, but soon calmed down.

'What's happened?' asked Monty of the nightingale.

'The court jester has been let off,' replied the nightingale. 'He promised he wouldn't do it again.'

'And that's it?' cried Monty. 'Well, I'm very glad he's been reprieved, but I don't really understand.'

The nightingale stared at him for a moment, then said, 'Between you and me, the empress has a lot of authority. If her daughter is upset, that upsets the empress. The polecat serves the princess with utter devotion. You see where all this is leading?'

'I think so,' said Monty. 'All's well that ends well, I suppose.'

The emperor said something and the nightingale trilled, 'The Great Pangolin thanks you for finding the jade shoes of the Green Idol of Ommm. He has issued an edict that all banished civet cats may return to Far Kathay. He is very grateful and asks what reward you require. It is in his unlimited power to give you anything you wish for. Please tell me and I will pass on the request to the emperor.'

'Money,' murmured Maudlin.

'Medicines,' muttered Bryony.

'Mooks,' whispered Scruff. 'I mean, *books*.'

'Vases,' said Monty. 'Two dozen Mole Dynasty vases. To be shipped to Muggidrear, care of Princess Sybil.'

The nightingale trilled in the direction of the Great Pangolin, who looked surprised, but nodded his head.

Bryony nodded. 'I see what you're doing. Sybil's priceless Mole Dynasty vases, the ones we smashed when we foiled Spindrick's plot to put the city to sleep that time. Very good, Monty. I wouldn't have thought of that. What a brilliant and honourable weasel you are. No wonder I think so much of you. No wonder you're – you're the light of my life.'

'Am I?' said Monty. 'I didn't know.'

'Of course you did,' replied Bryony. 'You've always known.'

Maudlin and Scruff clicked their teeth in amusement. The quartet of weasels then left the palace sitting room, one hobbling along on crutches. They had a long voyage ahead of them – by sea this time, for Monty was in no fit state to walk. They had had enough of adventures for a while. They were going back to their flats in Muggidrear, to sit quietly by a fire and drink hot chocolate. The wide world was a fascinating place, but it was also an exhausting one and they needed time. Time to rest. Time to take stock. Time to suck on long-stemmed pipes and dream quiet dreams.

The journey to Welkin took many months. On their arrival they heard that the mayor had lost his seat at last and was living in the country somewhere under an assumed name. Spindrick was in the New World somewhere, seemingly out of harm's way. Sybil and Chief Falshed were both missing. They had apparently gone for a jaunt, were lost overboard, and never seen again.

'I can't believe they're dead,' said Monty to Bryony one night as they were playing holly-hockers with Scruff and Maudlin. 'It just doesn't *feel* right.'

'Maybe they don't want to be found?' she suggested.

'Well, there is that, but you know, Sybil is not that sort, really. If she could get home, I'm sure she would. Falshed? Well, he just might make a wandering weasel, but not Sybil. Nope, one day I'm going to solve that mystery too. I'm going to go looking for the pair of them. Anyone want to come?' Monty looked expectantly round the table.

Scruff and Maudlin kept their heads down, pretending to study the seeds that Bryony had thrown from the cup. Bryony herself gave a wry click with her teeth. 'You'd better wait until we've all recovered from the last experience,' she said. 'Just at the moment we're happy to be fore-limbchair adventurers.' She warmed her paws in front of the roaring fire in the grate, remembering the trek down the icy mountain.

'Ah, you lot,' replied Monty, clamping his teeth around the stem of his chibouque. 'You won't be able to stop at home, once I've shown you my plans.'

THE END

hour were had overthrown and had a seat again.

"I can't believe they're dead," said Monty to
Bryony, as, much as ever, between phoning bells,
his arm with Sarah and . . . But . . . It just came,
at once.

"So you don't want to be found," she
murmured.

"Well, there's that but you know, but it's not
that sort well. If she could get home. I'd love
he would. Perhaps. Well, I must might make a
wandering sense. But not sort . . . I was one day
. . . I'm going to where that mystery. No, I'm going to
no matter the part of them. Anyone want to
recover," Monty looked expectantly round those
again.

Sarah and Matilda were drinking sit down,
according to shake the socks that bryony had
slipped from the tap. Do my best sell care a very
else . . . with her feel. "You'd better you should
was all recovered from the lost expect," she said.

"Time at the moment has it by far to bother
forming the collision." She was none but gave in
room of list, raising her, in the grasp, remembering
she was down their explanation.

"Are you but," replied Monty, drawing his head
around the spot of his at beginning. You won't let
little to get just home, only I've should can say,
matter . . .

AUTHOR'S NOTE

 The Welkin Weasels trilogy featuring Montegu Sylver is set in a quasi-Victorian time with Monty himself taking on a role very similar to that of Sherlock Holmes, the fictional detective immortalized in the books by Arthur Conan Doyle. Whereas Holmes has a doctor as his assistant (Dr Watson), Monty – as an animal – has a vet (Bryony Bludd). Holmes is often pictured smoking a pipe; Monty (much more healthily!) sucks on a chibouque – a type of pipe. Spindrick Sylver, Monty's cousin, has shades of Sherlock Holmes's arch enemy, Professor Moriarty.

Much of this book is set in different parts of the world, but the land of Welkin and its capital city, Muggidrear, are analagous to the United Kingdom and the capital, London – the setting for the Sherlock Holmes tales. For instance, Monty and Bryony live at 5a Breadoven Street, whereas Holmes's fictional London address was 221b Baker Street. There are quite a few other London references within the text and, of course, Monty's travels take him on a journey across the world – via Eggyok (Egypt) to Far Kathay (the Far East). Did you spot all the place names that are based on real places in today's world? And did you spot some of the references to other books, belief systems, myths and movies? Check out the following list!

Heastward Ho!
'Eastward ho!' is, of course, a famous sailor's cry when setting sail

CULVER'S DIARY
Nineteenth-century people often kept journals and diaries to record events

Count Flistagga (featured in *Vampire Voles*)
Count Dracula

Mole Dynasty vases
Arguably the world's best china was produced in China and is named after the great dynasties of the times. Ming is probably the best known

CHAPTER ONE
page 11: Ratgency
Regency

page 11: Far Kathay
The Far East, primarily China

page 12: Marko Poko
The famous explorer, Marco Polo

page 13: the Forbidden Palace in Far Kathay
In the centre of Beijing (China) is the Forbidden City – the home of the emperors in China's history

page 13: the Green Idol of Ommm
Eastern religions believe the sound *Om* represents the primal sound of the universe and the Creator

348

and it is part of many chants or *mantras* in Buddhism and Hinduism

page 14: Lord Hannover Haukin and his weasel butler Culver
Resemble P. G. Wodehouse's characters Bertie Wooster and Jeeves

page 17: Lady Hannover
Dame Freya (Madeline) Stark, explorer of Arabia

page 17: Outer Mongrelia
Outer Mongolia, part of the Republic of China

CHAPTER TWO
page 18: Thos. Tempus Fugit
Tempus fugit is Latin for 'time flies' – an appropriate name for a clockwork inventor who, among other things, produces clocks

page 19: Hide Park
Hyde Park is a big London park

page 19: Oldgate
A famous London prison of Victorian times was Newgate (mostly for people in debt)

page 19: Ringing Roger
Big Ben, the clock at Westminster in Central London

page 20: Ned Belly (see also pages 33 and 34)
A famous Australian outlaw was Ned Kelly

page 20: 'whingeing Pams'
'Whingeing Poms' was a rude term used by native Australians to describe British immigrants who often complained, on first arrival, about the heat etc.

page 21: 'down the Nail, to see the prismids'
The pyramids of Egypt, along the banks of the river Nile

CHAPTER THREE
page 31: 'crossed the Bogi'
One of the world's largest deserts is the Gobi

page 32: Waterstoat's Bookshop; and Ottercurs
Two large booksellers in the United Kingdom are Waterstone's and Ottakar's

page 34: first paragraph
This is a parody of the Australian song *Waltzing Matilda*

page 35: Starlingrad
Stalingrad is a famous city in Russia, now called Volgograd

page 35: Emedine Prankfirst
Emmeline Pankhurst was a Suffragette who fought for equal rights for women

CHAPTER FOUR

page 40: 'there will be a chance to build a better world, a brave new world with brave mammals in it'
A reference to lines in Shakespeare's *The Tempest*

page 43: Just William
The *Just William* stories by Richmal Crompton

page 43: Violent Elizabeth
Violet Elizabeth Bott is a character from the *Just William* stories

page 45: *'You dirty human...you killed my brother'*
James Cagney: a misquoted line from a gangster movie – 'You dirty rat...'

page 45: Humpty Boghard
Humphrey Bogart

page 46: *Confessions of a Knicker Nicker*
Alludes to the *Confessions* books and films of the 1970s

page 46: East Cheep
East Cheam is an area of South London

page 46: New Sealand
New Zealand

page 47: the New World
This was the term used in Victorian times to describe the United States of America

page 48: *Financial Chimes*
The *Financial Times* is a business newspaper

page 48: transcobaltian
Transatlantic

CHAPTER FIVE
page 51: Curdish Delight
Turkish Delight – a world-famous sweet treat

page 51: Fortfox and Macings
Fortnum and Mason is a famous London store

page 51: apricot parfaits
Apricot parfaits from Thortons are the favourite
sweets of my good friend, Andrew!

page 52: pawsome cab
Hansom cab

CHAPTER SIX
page 61: Bay of Biscuit
The Bay of Biscay, off the coasts of western France
and northern Spain, is well-known by sailors for
its stormy seas

page 61: Gibarbary Straits
Straits of Gibraltar – a narrow piece of sea
between North Africa and Southern Spain

page 61: Spangle
Spain

CHAPTER SEVEN

page 74: Icingland
Iceland

CHAPTER EIGHT
page 76: Naffrude Desert
Nafud Desert, Saudi Arabia

page 76: the ancient city of Petal
Petra in Jordan

page 77: 'A cream-hued city, twice as old as hope'
'A rose-red city, half as old as Time', from the
poem *Petra* by John Burgon

page 77: the Salt Sea
Dead Sea

**page 81: 'You will dine with the Shamelion at
Wadi Drumm'**
Alludes to the line from the film *Lawrence of
Arabia*: 'You will dine with me, at Wadi Rumm.'

page 82: 'Once, I remember, I was in this cave...'
Alludes to the film *Raiders of the Lost Ark*

CHAPTER NINE
**page 85: 'His name would undoubtedly be
carved in the da-da rail of the Royal
Geographical Society...'**
The names of famous British explorers really are
painted on the da-da rail in the lecture room of the
Royal Geographical Society in London.

page 88: the giant statue of a dog
This monument is based on a famous poem by
Shelley, *Ozymandias of Egypt*

CHAPTER TEN
page 93: New Lankaster
New York

page 94: Samuel Bolt
Samuel Colt, a famous American gunmaker,
inventor of the Colt .45

page 96: Specific Coast
Pacific Coast – the western side of the USA

page 96: 'Go West, young mustelids'
'Go West, young man' is a famous saying by
Horace Greeley, a nineteenth-century American
journalist

page 96: shoot-outs, gunfights and cactus dew
A feature of the American West in the late nineteenth century was the shoot-out between cow-
boys and sheriffs. A popular drink in the South is
tequila, made from cacti

page 97: first paragraph
This alludes to the films *Gunfight at the OK Corral*
and *High Noon*

**pages 100–101: Kaliphornya and the cross-
continental railroad**
California is on the West Coast of the USA and

early Americans crossed the interior in pioneer waggons until the route was opened up by railroads

CHAPTER ELEVEN
page 103: Welkin Bob
English Bob, a gunfighter played by Richard Harris in the film *Unforgiven*

page 105: a tremendous pawfight
Familiar to fans of Western movies, a typical saloon fight in the Wild West

page 105: Duke from the state of Plexus
The cowboy figure was immortalized in movies by the actor John Wayne, known as 'the Duke'. He came from Texas

page 105: 'I have a creed I live by...'
Refers to the speech given by John Wayne's character in the film *The Shootist*

page 106: 'Badgers? We don't need no stinkin' badgers!'
From the film *The Treasure of the Sierra Madre* with Humphrey Bogart: 'Badges, we don' need no stinkin' badges.'

page 106: 'Someone shot the new sheriff...and the deputy too'
A twist on the Bob Marley song *I Shot the Sheriff*

page 106: 'up to a hill which had something to do with cobblers'
Graveyards in Western films are always called Boot Hill

page 107: vule, a cross between a vole and a mouse
A mule is a cross between a horse and a donkey and would have been used as a pack animal

page 107: 'A mousejack rode into town...'
From the film *A Fistful of Dollars*

page 108: 'chasing after nuggets'
One of the reasons many Americans headed West was to find gold – the Gold Rush

page 108: San Ferryanne and Bo Jangeles
San Francisco and Los Angeles, two major cities in California

page 108: Capt Apeg and the fish Dhobi Mick
Captain Ahab and his hunt for the whale Moby Dick, in the book called *Moby Dick* by Herman Melville

page 109: Quikquik
Queequeg, a character from *Moby Dick*

page 110: 'They call him Fishpail'
'Call me Ishmael': the first line of *Moby Dick*

CHAPTER TWELVE
pages 116–17: the play *Fowst*, featuring Mefistofeles – and the god's demand to Maudlin to trade his soul
In the famous play *Faust* by Goethe, Faust sells his soul to Mephistopheles, an agent for the Devil

CHAPTER THIRTEEN
page 125: Lieutenant Lowfence
Lawrence of Arabia, a famous soldier and writer in the First World War

page 125: the Khalifrat Desert
The Kalahari Desert

page 125: 'gone meerkat'
A common phrase amongst British colonialists was to say that someone had 'gone native' – i.e.: stopped being a European and started to live and think like local people

CHAPTER FOURTEEN
page 131: Moxy Street
Oxford Street is a big London shopping street

page 132: Pontifract Pilote
Pontius Pilate, a Roman administrator of Judaea, who ordered the crucifixion of Jesus

page 133: Mikelambulo
The great Italian artist Michelangelo

page 138: 'as rich as Creases'
'As rich as Croesus' is a common saying to describe unimaginable wealth; Croesus was an ancient Lydian king

CHAPTER FIFTEEN
page 141: 'Veterinary surgeon, cure theyself'
'Physician, heal thyself' is a famous saying attributed to St Luke

CHAPTER SIXTEEN
page 156: 'Lowing herds of voles were winding over the lea'
Alludes to Thomas Gray's poem *Elegy in a Country Churchyard*

CHAPTER SEVENTEEN
page 163: Sumerkand
Samarkand in Uzbekistan

page 163: the rat barbarian, Timberbrain
Tamerlane, a fourteenth-century Mongol warrior king

page 164: Gangly Kan
Genghis Khan was a famous Mongol ruler

CHAPTER EIGHTEEN
page 168: Xanadoo
Xanadu – referred to in Coleridge's poem, *Kubla Khan*

page 168: Queen Neferhapen of Eggyok
Queen Nefertiti of ancient Egypt

page 169: 'There was a ship,' croaked he…'
Refers to the opening lines of *The Rime of the Ancient Mariner* by Samuel Taylor Coleridge

page 171: the Great Prismid of Chops
The Great Pyramid of Cheops. The Welkin version is made of glass; the real pyramid was originally covered with a polished casing of white limestone so would have been very, very dazzling to look at

CHAPTER NINETEEN
pages 176–7: *'White fonts falling…clicking as they run.'* From the poem *Lepanto* by G. K. Chesterton

page 177: the mummy
Ancient Egyptians preserved their dead by mummifying their bodies (preserving them and wrapping them in bandages). There have been numerous movies showing mummies as horror figures, coming back to life

tle star... **Lone giver of light'**
m *El Hombre* by William Carlos

ch **Twenty-two**
ng, meaning that there is no choice
you want you want, originating in
mous novel about the Korean War by
er

**...as if he thought a frightful fiend did
ind him tread.'**
to *The Rime of the Ancient Mariner* by
Taylor Coleridge

PTER TWENTY-FOUR
218: cricket cages
hina owners of tame birds hang their cages in
trees so their pets can learn songs from the
d birds

ge **220: Foochow pole-junk**
ge **221: Ma-yang-tzu**
ge **229: Kwai-tu boat**
hese are actual Chinese boats which ply their
rade along the rivers of China – there are many
nore, of course

page **221: Upper Yingtong river**
A major river in China is the Yangtze river

CHAPTER TWENTY-FIVE
page 226: They came to a stretch of river...
The description is of Guilin, an area of limestone mountains in China, the source of many Chinese paintings

page 233: 'What fools these mammals be'
Alludes to a line from Shakespeare's *A Midsummer Night's Dream*

page 237: 'Does my tail look big in this?'
A common contemporary joke is that women, wanting reassurance that they don't look overweight, are always asking their partners: 'Does my bum look big in this?'

CHAPTER TWENTY-SEVEN
page 245: the description of the court in the Forbidden Palace
There are many similarities here to the historical customs of the Chinese emperors in the nineteenth century and earlier

page 249: 'Common pick-yer-nose Herberts...'
A putdown phrase often used by a good friend of the author

CHAPTER TWENTY-EIGHT
page 261: 'Time enough, and worlds...'
Alludes to the poem *To His Coy Mistress* by Andrew Marvell

CHAPTER TWENTY-NINE
page 270: 'Three mustelids in a boat'
A classic funny book is Jerome K. Jerome's *Three Men in a Boat*, about a short trip that goes hilariously wrong

page 271: Cheepside
Cheapside is an area of East London

CHAPTER THIRTY
page 276: 'she is a female of the species – they're always more deadly, you know.'
'For the female of the species is more deadly than the male' from the poem *The Female of the Species* by Rudyard Kipling

CHAPTER THIRTY-ONE
page 287: 'Basic, my dear Monty, basic'
Sherlock Holmes would say, 'Elementary, my dear Watson, elementary.'

CHAPTER THIRTY-THREE
page 301: A night on the bare mountain
The Russian composer Mussorgsky composed *A Night on the Bare Mountain*

CHAPTER THIRTY-FOUR
page 307: Nicknack and Highwater
Nocomis and Hiawatha from Longfellow's poem, *Hiawatha*

page 310: the river Bronn
The river Thames, the main river that runs through the centre of London

page 310: Jack o'Giblets to Land's Edge
John o'Groats (Scotland) and Land's End (Cornwall, England) are traditionally the top and bottom of the United Kingdom

page 311: Good Old Jacks
In small midwestern towns of the USA some elderly male citizens are known as Good Old Boys

How many of the above did you spot? I have a great deal of fun coming up with inventive and imaginative names that have a link with the world we actually live in. I hope you enjoyed the result!

Garry Kilworth

Garry Kilworth

ABOUT THE AUTHOR

Garry Kilworth was born in York but, as the son of an Air Force family, was educated at more than twenty schools. He himself joined the RAF at the age of fifteen and was stationed all over the world, from Singapore to Cyprus, before leaving to continue his education and begin a career in business, which also enabled him to travel widely.

He became a full-time writer when his two children left home and has written many novels for both adults and younger readers – mostly on science fiction, fantasy and historical themes. He has won several awards for his work, including the World Fantasy Award in 1992, and the Lancashire Book Award in 1995 for *The Electric Kid*.

Garry Kilworth lives in a country cottage in Essex which has a large woodland garden teeming with wildlife, including foxes, doves, squirrels and grass snakes.

*Have you read Garry Kilworth's other Welkin Weasels
adventures featuring Montegu Sylver?*

GASLIGHT GEEZERS

Can Montegu Sylver ferret out the truth when he learns
that the anarchist Spindrick plans to blow everyone to
smithereens with a fiendish bomb? Or find a lemming
prince who vanishes almost as soon as he sets paw on
Welkin soil?

Aided and abetted by his trusty weasel companions,
Monty is soon on the trail, but time is running out –
especially when he becomes a fugitive from the law . . .

ISBN 0552 547042

VAMPIRE VOLES

Ghostly, unmammaled ships are arriving in Welkin
from Slattland, filled with coffins, and the vampire
voles are becoming a real pain in the neck. Montegu
Sylver, the famous weasel detective, suspects that someone is deliberately sending the vampires to destroy
Welkin for ever. Will Monty come whisker to whisker
with the evil master-vampire?

ISBN 0552 547050

About the Welkin Weasels:

'A quicker, slicker read than Brian Jacques' *T.E.S.*

'Thrilling and imaginative and reminiscent of Tolkien'
Carousel